MYS   NEB
                             C.2
Maling   Maling, Arthur
  Z
                A taste of trea-

A
TASTE OF
TREASON

Books by Arthur Maling

A TASTE OF TREASON

ARTHUR MALING

A Brock Potter novel

HARPER & ROW, PUBLISHERS, New York
Cambridge, Philadelphia, San Francisco,
London, Mexico City, São Paulo, Sydney
1817

FIRST EDITION

Designer: Jane Weinberger

Library of Congress Cataloging in Publication Data

Maling, Arthur.
A taste of treason.

    I. Title
PS3563.A4313T37   1983   813'.54   82-48580
ISBN 0-06-015128-5

83 84 85 86 87 10 9 8 7 6 5 4 3 2 1

For
Arnold Durham and
Marion and Bailey Markham,
who pointed the way

A
TASTE OF
TREASON

1

I SHOULD HAVE GUESSED that something was wrong, because everyone was so nice to me.

My partner Mark Price, who normally isn't effusive, told me not once but three times how well I looked, adding that I ought to take vacations more often.

Tom Petacque, my other partner, spent a quarter of an hour briefing me on what had been happening while I was away without mentioning a single problem, which wasn't like him at all.

And the five members of the research department, who work under my supervision, were too polite; not one of them, at that Monday morning's staff meeting, came down hard on any of the others, although our meetings are usually rough-and-tumble affairs. It was such a decorous session, in fact, that I finally said, "Come on, people, let's go at it." But even after that, the meeting proceeded quietly.

At lunch Irving Silvers, my assistant, ordered a martini. This surprised me, because he has an ulcer and rarely drinks anything alcoholic, but I didn't comment on it.

The two of us were lunching together so that he could bring me up to date on events in the department, and he did give me a quick rundown, but mostly we talked about my trip.

I'd gone to Switzerland ostensibly to attend an international conference of money managers. What I'd mainly done there, though, was goof off at Zürich's Dolder Grand Hotel, playing golf, swimming, taking long walks in the hilly suburb of Dolder, and in general trying to regain my mental balance—as everyone had been urging me to do. I hadn't been myself in quite a while, they'd said.

Toward the end of the meal, in an attempt to bring the conversation around to matters of immediate concern, I told Irving that I thought Brian should follow up on the Arden rumor. At the staff meeting, Brian Barth, the youngest member of the research team, had reported hearing that Bill Arden was under pressure to step down from his position as Chief Executive Officer of Arden Electronics.

Irving gave me a vague nod. His thoughts obviously were elsewhere. "Did you read any newspapers in Switzerland?" he asked.

I shook my head.

He'd barely tasted his martini, but now he took a swig. "So you were out of touch."

"Completely. That was the best part." People had been telling me to forget about everything, and I'd taken their advice. "The first few days it was tough. There'd be a dozen copies of the *Herald-Tribune* stacked up on the newsstand, and half a dozen copies of *Time,* and I'd be tempted to buy one, but I didn't give in. Not once."

Irving sighed unhappily.

"All of you were right," I conceded. "I needed to get away. I was in worse shape than I realized."

"You sure were."

There was a silence.

Irving began to look miserable. Finally he picked up his glass and gulped the rest of his drink. Then, in a heavy voice, he said, "Brock, someone has to tell you, and it might as well be me. Kevin Rand is dead. He was stabbed by another inmate."

The feeling I'd had before going to Switzerland came back. A feeling of confusion, of depression, almost of despair. I fought it off.

Irving took a newspaper clipping from his coat pocket, unfolded it and put it beside my plate.

I read the headline: CONVICTED SPY KEVIN RAND SLAIN IN PRISON.

Eyeing me anxiously, Irving said, "Perhaps it's for the best, Brock."

I forced myself to picture the Dolder Grand's golf course. The image helped. "Yes," I said, "for the best." I crumpled the clipping into a ball and dropped it into the ashtray. "Now the story's ended."

"I didn't know—none of us knew—how you'd react." Irving sounded vastly relieved.

I took a deep breath. "The story's ended—that's how. End of story, end of reaction. I made a bad mistake about a man. Everyone's entitled to an occasional bad mistake. Over and out."

Irving grinned. "You should take more vacations, boss."

I glanced at the wadded-up clipping in the ashtray. And resisted an impulse to retrieve it. Kevin Rand was dead. The details didn't matter.

After lunch, as I passed through Helen Doyle's office on the way to my own, she looked up worriedly. Helen was my secretary. She too had been anxious about me. She knew how deeply I'd been affected by the Rand case.

"Relax," I said. "Irving gave me the news."

She offered a wan smile.

"Let's start on the mail."

She brought her notebook into my office, and I dictated for almost an hour. Then, while Helen did the typing, I began to make notes for my Tuesday market letter.

The opinions I express in the Tuesday letter reflect the consensus arrived at by my staff and me at our Monday meeting, and I reviewed what had been said that morning. Interest rates steady despite some disagreement within the Fed, airline stocks oversold, auto inventories too high, Bill Arden under pressure to resign, Combined Drug about to report higher earnings . . .

Again my thoughts turned dark in the same way they'd been dark before I went to Zürich. Suppose we were wrong. Suppose what we were forecasting didn't materialize.

And presently I was reliving those terrible weeks following Kevin Rand's arrest, when the details of his sale of top secret plans for the Calthorp antenna to an agent of the East German government were being ferreted out and released by the media; when the price of Calthorp stock was dropping; when my friend Donald Calthorp, having collapsed during a board of directors meeting, was hovering between life and death in the cardiac intensive-care unit at Mt. Sinai Hospital; and when I was being questioned by the FBI.

I'd almost come unglued then. Knowing that I'd contributed to a calamity, I'd begun to feel calamity-prone and to doubt my own convictions. Decisions that should have been easy became difficult. I was no longer sure of anything. And the more I wavered, the more errors I made. Securities analysts need strong egos, and my ego was coming unraveled.

At the time, I hadn't realized how shaky I was getting. My partners and everyone else in the company had closed ranks around me—the herd protecting its injured member—and I'd been irritated by all the solicitousness. But in Switzerland I'd come to see myself objectively, to admit that I'd lost my self-confidence and become a detriment to the firm, to face the fact that I either had to pull myself together or quit.

So I'd pulled myself together. And I intended to stay together.

But for a few minutes, thinking about the letter that would go out the next day over my signature—Brockton Potter, Head of Research, Price, Potter and Petacque—I had some of the old hesitations. In my mind's eye I again saw the headline CONVICTED SPY KEVIN RAND SLAIN IN PRISON. I also saw Fred Davies and Lawrence Sortini, the two FBI agents who'd been assigned to discover something sinister in my motives.

I heard Sortini repeat the words he'd uttered so often: "The fact remains, Mr. Potter, that you did recommend Rand for the job at Calthorp. You recommended him highly. You went out of your way to recommend him."

And I heard my honest but somehow unconvincing reply: "I believed he was a good man."

With effort, I was able to drive the dark thoughts away and concentrate on my notes.

At four o'clock I punched some keys on my quote machine to learn how certain stocks had closed. Then Tom came into my office, and presently Mark joined us. We had an end-of-the-day drink and rapped for a few minutes. I suspected that they were checking on my mental state, and I went out of my way to demonstrate that my mental state was O.K.

After they left, I opened the door to Helen's office. "Almost finished?"

She was still typing. "Just about."

Five minutes later, she brought a stack of letters for me to sign. "Er—Mr. Potter," she said in an uncertain tone.

I looked at her. She was a dignified, self-possessed woman of sixty who seldom showed uncertainty about anything. But at the moment she seemed decidedly troubled. "Yes?" I said.

"While you were away, Mr. Potter—" She broke off, squared her shoulders and started over again. "While you were away, there was a telephone call I didn't quite know how to handle. I hope I did the right thing."

"I'm sure you did, Helen. Who was it from?"

"A Mrs. Rand. Adele Rand. She said she was Kevin Rand's mother and you knew her. Oh, Mr. Potter, I didn't mean to upset you!"

I unclenched my hands. "I'm all right. Go on."

"She wanted an appointment with you. I told her you were out of the country. She asked when you'd be back, and I said today. I hope that was the right thing. She said she'd call again, this week. Shall I get you a glass of water?"

"No, thank you. When did she call?"

"Last Friday. I'd seen the article in the paper about her son being killed, the week before—all of us did. But I simply didn't know what else to tell her. I didn't think it was my place to tell her not to call back, and yet . . ."

"Of course. You did what was proper."

Helen shifted her considerable weight from one foot to the other. She appeared not to know whether to go or stay.

"If you don't get those letters in the box," I said, "they'll miss the last pickup."

She nodded and went out, closing the door behind her.

I sat at my desk until almost six o'clock, feeling sorry for Adele and wondering why, after making no attempt to get in touch with me during the investigation and the trial, she wanted to see me now.

2

"Not tonight," Carol said. "I'm tired, and I have to be up early."

Carol was the woman in my life. We weren't married; we had a Relationship—separate homes, separate lives, but weekends at my place. And this wasn't a weekend, it was Wednesday.

"Well, at least come home with me for a nightcap," I urged, in the hope that one thing would lead to another.

She thought it over. "All right. But just a little one."

We walked to my house. It wasn't much of a trip—we'd had dinner at a restaurant two blocks from where I live.

Tiger, my dog, greeted us noisily and followed us into the den.

I produced a bottle of kirschwasser. "I brought this back from Zürich," I said as I peeled the plastic wrapping from the neck of the bottle.

"Looks like vodka," Carol observed.

"Doesn't taste like vodka," I replied, and poured each of us a shot. "Let me know what you think."

She took a swallow. "Good God!" She put the glass down. "If this is what you drank over there, it's no wonder you came home so happy. . . . You do seem ever so much better, Brock."

This was the first time since my return that she'd made even an oblique reference to what she'd been calling my "unhealthy attitude."

"I'm back to normal," I assured her.

She smiled. Her smile didn't last long, however. "But if that woman calls back . . ."

I gathered that she meant Adele Rand. I'd told her, over dinner, that Adele had tried to get in touch with me while I was away, and this was evidently a delayed response, for at the time she'd made no comment. "Let's not worry about it," I said.

"If she does call back, I'd avoid her if I were you."

I took another sip of kirschwasser. "I'd hate doing that, Carol. Adele didn't commit any crime. She's been through hell on account of what Kevin did—I'm sure of that. And now that he's dead . . ."

"Nevertheless. Take my advice."

"She was kind to me, honey."

"She was a surrogate mother, and you didn't need a surrogate mother."

"You're quoting your analyst."

"I am not. I'm quoting my common sense. Your mother died. The Rands, all twenty-seven of them, took you to their bosom—"

"Not twenty-seven. Eight."

"Whatever. You didn't need a surrogate mother or a surrogate father or all those surrogate brothers and sisters. Stay away from her, Brock."

"We'll see."

"Whenever you say that, it means you intend to do as you please."

"No, it doesn't. It means we'll see. So far I've been back three days and I haven't heard from her. Maybe she's changed her mind."

Carol sighed. "You never listen."

"Let's drop the subject."

"It's just that I don't want you to undo all the good you did yourself by going away, Brock."

"I won't undo it. I promise. Now let's talk about something else.

Tell me more about what Perry's been up to."

Perry was Carol's boss and, to her, always a fascinating topic. At dinner she'd told me about his latest quarrel with his wife. Now she told me about his plans to hire a new sales manager—the old one had quit. We then got onto the subject of my itinerary for the coming week. I invariably spend Monday and Tuesday in New York—staff meeting, market letter, discussions with Tom and Mark, conferences with customers—but the balance of the week, more often than not, I'm on the road collecting information, like the members of my staff. And I intended to leave the following Tuesday night for a trip to Phoenix, Los Angeles and San Francisco.

"You'll be home in time for the party, though," Carol said, just to make sure.

"Of course," I replied.

The party was one that was being given by Stiles, Levin and Sullivan, the law firm that represented Price, Potter and Petacque, to celebrate the opening of its new offices. It was going to be a big affair. Carol was looking forward to it.

"I've bought a new dress," she said, glowing. "Chiffon. Pink, with fuchsia here and here. Wait till you see it!" Her glow disappeared. "But about Mrs. Rand—"

I put my hand over her mouth. And, when I removed it, noticed lipstick on my palm. But I'd made my point. Carol didn't mention Adele Rand again.

She didn't allow herself to be talked into a second shot of kirschwasser, either. At eleven o'clock she announced that it was time for her to go, and that was that.

I walked her the short distance from my house, on West Eleventh Street near Fifth Avenue, to her apartment, on Fifth Avenue near Ninth Street, and after giving her a chaste kiss I headed home, reflecting on the advice she'd given me.

She was more right than wrong, I decided.

3

ON THURSDAY AFTERNOON Brian Barth put in an appearance at the office. He'd just returned from Tulsa and was about to leave for Boston, but he had a few hours in between.

He'd checked with his source, he told me. His source insisted that the rumor about Bill Arden was true. Bill was being forced to resign; the announcement would be made any day.

"Who is your source?" I asked.

"A friend at National Guarantee," Brian replied. "He was in San Francisco last week and ran into Sol Arden. The two of them know each other. Sol said Bill's on the way out."

"Any reason?"

"Sol wouldn't say."

I frowned. "Sol—is he the cousin or the brother?"

"The cousin, I believe."

"Strange," I said. There were four Ardens on the board of Arden Electronics: Arden the father, Arden the brother, Arden the cousin and Bill. Bill was *the* Arden, the one who'd taken the small company founded by his father and built it into one of the world's largest manufacturers of semiconductors. The other members of the family were on the board because they owned a lot of Arden stock; Bill was there because he'd made the Arden name famous in connection with those wonderful little memory chips that had revolutionized electronics.

"A family feud?" Brian suggested.

"Why now?" I replied.

"You'd know that better than I."

"Not really." I'd been acquainted with Bill for fifteen years. I liked him and believed in him. At my recommendation, our customers had bought Arden stock early on and had made big profits in it. But I had no idea how the various Ardens felt about one another. "If there are rivalries, they've been there for years. Why let them erupt now? And without Bill, the company will be just another semiconductor firm. The board must realize that—the outside members of the board, at any rate. It would be different if the company weren't doing well, but it is. All those awards, all those government contracts. Terrific earnings . . . It doesn't make sense."

"I could go out to San Francisco and poke around," Brian said. He was always volunteering to go places and do things. And he invariably brought back useful items.

"It won't be necessary," I said. "We haven't recommended Arden recently, and I don't think our customers have a strong position in it. Besides, I'll be in San Francisco myself the end of next week."

Brian eyed me. "You'll do your own poking around?"

I hadn't intended to, but now I reconsidered. "I may give Bill a call while I'm there."

Brian nodded, then glanced at his watch and said he had a few other matters to take care of. He left.

I spent the next hour and a half talking on the telephone with customers, mending fences.

Price, Potter and Petacque doesn't have many customers. We don't deal with the general public, only with large buyers and sellers of securities, such as pension funds, banks and insurance companies. But the customers we do have give us a lot of business. The largest of them, Amalgamated Investors Services, lets us handle roughly $350,000,000 of their investment transactions each year, and there are several other concerns whose accounts don't lag far behind Amalgamated's in dollar volume. So we go out of our way to pamper the handful of portfolio managers and trust officers we call our "client list."

My partner Tom is chief pamperer. He's considered by many to be the best securities salesman in the industry. When it comes to stroking worried decision-makers, no one can match him. But I have to do a certain amount of pampering, too. I'm one of the reasons those decision-makers came to us in the first place and are still with us. The fact that our customers can deal directly with Brock Potter and get his advice is, according to Tom, his biggest selling point.

During the *Sturm und Drang* period I'd recently gone through, our customers knew that something was amiss; I was frequently unavailable, and when I was available I was vaguer than usual. They also knew that I was involved in the Rand case; word had got around that FBI agents had been interviewing me about my association with the Calthorp engineer who'd been arrested as a spy. My name hadn't been mentioned by the media—I was only one of scores of minor actors in the drama, a man who'd known Kevin as a teen-ager and had helped him get the job with Calthorp. But in my state of anxiety over the affair, I'd been terribly worried that my name *would* be mentioned. I saw myself being chased down Wall Street by newsmen with minicams. I all but woke up in the middle of the night shouting, "No comment!"

In Switzerland, I'd come to realize that our customers wouldn't have been terribly upset even if the worst had happened—if the television and newspaper reporters had got on to me. Our customers wouldn't have liked it, they would have said I wasn't very bright in picking my friends, but they wouldn't have lost faith in me as a securities analyst. What did upset them was the fact that I'd gone into some sort of emotional decline that impaired my usefulness. Hardin Webster, our big gun at Amalgamated, summed it up best, perhaps, when he complained to Tom that he couldn't get a straight answer from me, adding that in his opinion I was slipping.

Now I was anxious to prove I was my old self again. So I made the rounds by telephone, chatting with various portfolio managers and trust officers on our customer list and doing my best to sound cheerful, knowledgeable and foresighted.

Apparently I gave some credible performances, for the responses I got were encouraging. Especially Hardin Webster's. He said, "Sounds like you're back in the groove, thank God."

It was almost five o'clock when I decided to call it a day. I hadn't talked to everyone on the list, but I'd talked to the most important eight. The rest could wait until tomorrow. Pleased with myself, I put on my coat and headed for the door. I'd almost reached it when the telephone rang.

My first impulse was to keep going. But then I thought that the call might be from one of our West Coast customers, so I went back to my desk.

I was immediately sorry. For the voice at the other end of the line was Adele Rand's.

4

SYMPATHETIC but not too sympathetic, friendly but not too friendly
—I tried to hit just the right note. And failed.

She was in Stamford, Connecticut, Adele said. Staying with
Sean and his family. I knew that Sean lived in Stamford, didn't I?
Well, she'd been there for a week. They'd insisted she come.

I did know that Sean lived in Stamford, but I'd forgotten. I
hadn't kept up with him. I'd kept up with Adele and Roman, and
with Kevin. The other Rand offspring hadn't figured in my life in
years.

Nice, I said. Good idea. Stamford is pretty. I sounded as if I were
barely acquainted with anyone in the family.

Yes, she agreed, very pretty. Roman had thought she should get
away for a while.

Roman was her husband. I asked how he was.

"I tried to get him to come with me," she said, "but he wouldn't.
You know how he is—ever the stoic. He insists on going to work,
on acting as if the whole thing never happened. But he's hurt,
Brock. He blames himself. He thinks he was too strict with
Kevin."

After that, I couldn't avoid the subject of Kevin's death. But I
could, and did, avoid being specific about it. "I was sorry to hear
the sad news," I said.

"Apparently it was God's will," she replied. "God's way of handling things. After all, Kevin didn't have much to look forward to, did he?"

No, I thought, he didn't. He'd been sentenced to a thirty-year term. "A shame," I said. "How's Sean?" Kevin had been the oldest child. Sean was a year and a half younger; he would be thirty-six or thirty-seven, I calculated.

"Shaken," Adele replied. "As we all are."

I maintained my detachment. "Naturally."

My detachment had a false ring, even to me. Warm up a little, I told myself. But instead of warming up a little, I went to the other extreme. My voice rose. "Christ, Adele, why did Kevin do it? What got into him? How could he ruin his own life and everyone else's, like that?"

Adele hesitated. "Perhaps nothing got into him. Perhaps something was there all along."

"He messed up everyone who knew him, including me!"

"He was fond of you, Brock. Believe that. Don't think otherwise. I know he was."

"He wasn't fond of anyone! He couldn't have been!" I got myself under control. "Anyway, it's sad, and you have my sympathy."

"Thank you, dear. I'd like to see you. Will that be possible?"

I recalled Carol's advice. It coincided with my own feelings. I didn't want to see Adele. I didn't want to rake up memories. But I couldn't bring myself to give her a flat no. "I'd love to get together with you," I said, "but I'm pretty busy right now. I just got back from Europe and all."

"Do say yes, Brock. There are things I'd like to talk over with you, to tell you."

I glanced around the office and wished that someone were there to give me moral support. But I was alone. "It would be painful, Adele. For both of us, but especially for you. After all, what can you say, what can I say, what can anyone say? Our crying on each other's shoulder—that won't change anything."

"I've done all my crying. I'm not looking for a shoulder. Not even yours, my dear."

My voice rose again. "I don't want to talk about Kevin, Adele! Damn it, I *recommended* him for that job!"

There was a longish silence. "Were you damaged?"

"Not as much as I might have been, but my thinking got fouled up for a while. I began not to trust myself. I *believed* in Kevin."

"So did we all, my dear. That's what makes it such a tragedy. Why don't you come up here for dinner tomorrow night or Saturday? I still make a good blueberry pie. Remember how you always liked my blueberry pies?"

"Really, Adele, I don't think it would do either of us any good."

"You're angry, Brock. Angrier than I imagined you'd be. And I don't blame you. But try to remember the good times. Our Sunday dinners, our discussions, the ping-pong games. We *were* one big happy family, Brock. Believe that. Remember it. And do come to see me. Sean has a ping-pong table. I'll bet you haven't played ping-pong in years."

"Don't resort to emotional blackmail, Adele. Yes, I still like blueberry pie, and no, I haven't played ping-pong in years, and God knows, I do remember the family dinners and the discussions and the good times. That's what makes the whole thing hurt so much. We *were* one big happy family—or the closest *I* ever came to one. I'm grateful to you, I've never stopped being grateful to you, I never will. But what Kevin did—to you, to me, to my friend Don Calthorp, to the entire country—that does change things. We can't pretend he didn't do it, Adele. We can't pretend everything's the same."

"I wasn't aware I was resorting to emotional blackmail, my dear. The last thing in the world I'd want is blackmail you into doing anything, ever. But there are certain facts I think you should know. Facts I think Kevin would have *wanted* you to know. I don't suppose there'd be any harm in giving them to you over the telephone, but we've been so harassed by the FBI for so long that I'm leery."

Facts that Kevin wanted me to know? What kind of facts? What difference could Kevin's facts make now?

The FBI? It had certainly harassed me. No doubt it had harassed the members of Kevin's family even more.

"I don't understand," I said.

"It would be easy to explain, face-to-face."

Find out, something told me. If there's something she wants you to know, listen to her.

"It's for your own good, Brock."

"Well, since you put it like that—"

"Good. Then you will come for dinner?"

I thought of Carol. We'd planned a quiet weekend at home. "Why don't you come to my place?" I suggested. "You've never been to the house I'm living in now."

Adele accepted immediately. Saturday night at eight, and I needn't fuss.

5

CAROL AND I spent most of Saturday afternoon quarreling.

Our quarrel was multifaceted. One facet had to do with Adele Rand. Carol insisted that my invitation to Adele sprang from emotional dependence. She strung me a necklace of her analyst's pearls of wisdom, and I rejected it. Her analyst had never met me; he only knew me through Carol's dreams. In my opinion, he was in no position to judge my emotional dependences or my general personality.

The real cause of our quarrel was probably our mutual frustration over being almost, but not quite, in love. We'd never been able to eliminate the "almost."

In any case, Carol objected to being in the house while Adele was there, and this irritated me.

"You're part of my life," I argued. "I want her to meet you."

"It's not a question of her meeting me," Carol retorted. "It's a question of my meeting her, and I have no wish to."

"But why?"

"Because I know I won't like her, and if I don't, I'll show it and you'll get mad."

"You've made up your mind in advance!"

"Well, it's my mind! I'll make it up whenever I please!"

"That's stupid!"

"Don't call me stupid!"

We went on and on like that, making progressively less sense.

In the end, I won—if you could call it winning. Carol agreed to stay, but only because I was so insistent, and because this was our first weekend together since my return. She didn't want to spoil the weekend completely—I'd already spoiled it enough by asking Adele over.

Nevertheless, I was relieved. Carol and I had broken up too often in the past. I was ready for a little stability.

Adele arrived promptly at eight. Sean was with her. So was a blueberry pie.

They entered the house like tourists visiting Westminster Abbey for the first time. What a beautiful doorway. What a charming staircase. And, my goodness, a Chagall.

I gave them the ten-minute tour, explaining how I'd bought a house that had been built when West Eleventh Street was considered uptown and that had been converted into apartments a century or so later. Explaining, also, how I'd converted the house back into a one-family dwelling and restored some of its original features.

The tour would have taken longer if I'd had to identify the various paintings and sculptures I'd acquired over the years, but that wasn't necessary—Adele was up on modern art; she was the one who'd got me interested in it.

"Really, Brock," she said as she sank down on one of the overstuffed cushions of the couch, "it's worth a trip to New York just to see how you're living."

"Better than the last time you were here," I said, although I'd been living all right then, too. It had been sixteen years ago, and I was already earning enough to give her and Roman a trip to Bermuda for their twenty-fifth wedding anniversary. "How about some sherry?"

"You remember my weakness!" Adele looked pleased.

I poured sherry for her and Scotch for Carol and myself. Sean requested vodka.

"I don't think I'd have recognized you," I told him as I gave him his drink.

"Nor I you," he replied.

He was handsome in the firm-jawed, clear-eyed way all the Rand offspring were handsome, but his face was haggard. He, too, had been through a lot, I guessed.

It was Adele's appearance that really shocked me, however. Only two years had gone by since I'd extended a Chicago trip in order to drive downstate for dinner with her and Roman, but then she'd been middle-aged, and now she was old. It was hard to believe, seeing her, that she was just sixty-two.

Carol, who'd been quiet up to this point, gave her a strained smile and said, "Brock's told me so much about you."

Adele returned the smile. "Yes, we were all good, good friends." She turned her attention back to me. "I hope you didn't mean what you said over the telephone about emotional blackmail. That wasn't like you, my dear."

I felt contrite, but not contrite enough to apologize. "You touched a raw nerve," I said.

"I assume you know about my son Kevin," she said to Carol.

Carol gave her another strained smile.

"One bears six children, one raises them, one tries one's best, but something goes wrong, and one of them . . ." Adele shook her head sadly. "My husband blames himself, I blame myself—that's the cruelest part, really: wondering where you made your mistake."

Carol's expression softened. "According to my analyst—"

I shot her a look, and she broke off.

"For four lovely years, Brock was one of my children, too," Adele went on. "You didn't know him then, did you?"

"No," said Carol, her eyes brightening. She was obviously getting interested. She'd never met anyone from my pre–New York days.

Adele smiled. "There was something about him. I don't know what it was. The first time he burst into my office—he'd been at college exactly three days, mind you—he was so filled with righteous indignation, his hair was so disarranged, he was such a bundle of energy, he was like a cyclone. And all because he wanted to take an economics course that freshmen weren't allowed to take without the consent of the professor, and the professor had turned him down. You'd have thought his personal honor was at stake, his whole sense of himself. It took me at least five minutes to get him calmed down to the point where I could explain that all I was was secretary to the Dean of Men, and the Dean of Men had nothing to do with such matters. But Brock was so earnest, so sure he could handle that course or any other course . . . I'd met a good many students over the years, but I'd never met one quite like Brock. He simply wouldn't stop presenting his case, even after I'd told him I wasn't the one he should be presenting it to. . . . Anyway, some part of me responded to this whirlwind, and I said I'd see what I could do. The matter was completely out of my territory, and I had no business interfering, but I knew one of the men in the economics department and I had a word with him. Brock got into the course, and I made a friend—a friend I've never for one minute regretted having. . . . Is he still like that, I wonder: so sure he's right?"

"Yes," Carol said fervently.

I poured myself another two fingers of Scotch and offered Sean more vodka, but he declined. And the women had scarcely touched their drinks.

Brock was a strange combination of introvert and extrovert, Adele continued. He got along well with people, and particularly with the members of her family, but there was an inner Brock that he didn't readily share. He had enormous drive and ambition and, as a college student, had been very mature in some ways. But he had a chip on his shoulder—a chip that wasn't apparent to most observers but that she herself had recognized right away. He'd been wounded as a child, and scar tissue had formed, with the result that he was tougher than many people realized.

Carol nodded eagerly. She'd been waiting years for someone to supply her with such material.

It made me uncomfortable to hear myself described with all that objectivity and lofty insight. Yet I had to admit that Adele was close to the mark. I wasn't always so sure I was right—and recently, thanks to her Kevin, I hadn't been sure at all—but in other respects she was drawing an accurate picture of me as I'd been and, at times, still was.

I recalled the incident of the economics professor. I also recalled my first Sunday dinner at the Rand house. It had been a revelation to me.

My father's father had lost everything in the Depression. My father, who'd grown up thinking the world was his oyster, found himself, on the threshold of manhood, penniless and unskilled. Some men in his position—and during the Depression there were a lot of them—managed to get established. He didn't. And to make matters worse, he took on the additional responsibilities of marriage and parenthood. The burden crushed him. One day, when I was nine, I came home from school to find that he'd hanged himself.

Welfare hadn't been invented, and my mother wasn't the sort who would have taken it if it had been. She worked as a domestic, a cleaning woman, on a daily basis. I helped out by getting odd jobs, afternoons and weekends. It wasn't bad. Or at least I had nothing to compare it with. The only time I ever felt underprivileged was one Christmas, when the Big Brothers of the Poor brought us a Christmas basket and my mother wouldn't accept it —I wanted the damn turkey.

But my father's suicide rankled. I'd been old enough to know what suicide was, and what had led to his. I was determined to make big money someday. And no prima donna of an economics teacher was going to stand in my way.

The Rands weren't wealthy—Roman had a small insurance agency—but that Sunday dinner introduced me to a new way of life. Lace tablecloth. Grace before the bread was passed. Six kids with the vocabularies of adults—kids who'd won swimming trophies and awards for science projects and prizes in statewide spelling bees, who said "Yes, sir" and "Yes, ma'am" and sat up straight.

The Rands were the nicest, the brightest, the best behaved people I'd ever met. Furthermore, they liked me. Especially Kevin, who was then fourteen.

That was in October of my freshman year. The very next month my mother died suddenly. She'd been the only family I had.

I was alone, and it was Thanksgiving.

Adele knew.

I became an honorary Rand. And remained one for the rest of my college career. Brock, the oldest of the brood, the one Kevin looked up to.

"Of course," Adele told Carol, "Brock had quite a few rough edges, at first."

Carol was leaning forward now, absorbing it all. "He still does," she said. Whatever else she was doing, Adele was making a friend of Carol.

"No," said Adele, "I don't think so. He caught on very fast."

"Stop talking about me like this," I said. "You're making me feel as if I'm at my own wake."

In the present company, it was an unfortunate choice of words. Adele's face clouded. Sean looked away. Silence fell.

Carol attempted to restore cheer. "The pie looks lovely," she said. "Let's have some. I'll make coffee."

She and Adele went into the kitchen.

"I'm sorry about Kevin," I told Sean, awkwardly.

"It's been terrible," he replied. "You'll never know. They returned the body to mother and dad for burial. They . . ." He didn't finish.

Although he'd refused more vodka before, I now poured him some, anyway. He sipped it.

"Any idea who did it?" I asked.

"Not so far. But we think we know the motive." He put the glass down. "Kevin was murdered to keep him from talking."

I remembered newspaper stories I'd read. The government had offered leniency in exchange for information. Kevin had refused. He'd gone to prison having revealed nothing.

"What makes you think that?" I asked.

"The timing, for one thing. Kevin hadn't been there long enough to make enemies or get into any serious scrapes."

I gave him a skeptical look. It doesn't take much time to incur enmity, I thought, especially in a crowded prison.

Sean met my gaze. All of the Rand offspring had been taught, as children, to look people in the eye. "Also," he said, "certain things Kevin told me."

Adele returned to the living room with the pie on a serving plate. Carol followed with dessert plates, napkins and silverware. The aroma of coffee wafted in from the kitchen.

"We're talking about Kevin's death," Sean informed his mother.

She put the pie on a table and sat down. Carol sat down, too.

"I was telling Brock that Kevin was killed to keep him from talking," Sean added.

"That's true," Adele affirmed. "After his arrest, Kevin wouldn't see Roman or me. Wouldn't see us, talk to us, have anything to do with us. For our sake, he claimed, although I suspect the truth was, he simply couldn't face us. Except for Sean, he wouldn't see anyone in the family."

Sean resumed. "Why Kevin singled me out, I don't know. Maybe because I'd always stood up to him and he thought I could take it, or maybe he just didn't have the same feeling for me. Anyway, I did visit him. At least a dozen times, before the trial and after he began serving his term. He wasn't very talkative at first, but the last couple of visits . . . He was changing, Brock. I could tell. He wasn't so—unrepentant. He was beginning to realize what he'd done, to have second thoughts. . . . Before the trial, when the government was putting its case together, they tried to get Kevin to open up. If he would, they said—"

"I read about that," I broke in. "He didn't go for the deal. What you're saying now is, he didn't like being in prison. He thought maybe he could get his sentence reduced. He was *ready* to open up. Word got around, and the long arm of East German intelligence reached over the prison wall and snuffed him out."

"Yes," said Sean.

Adele gave me a reproachful look. "You're putting it in the least attractive way, Brock. There is such a thing as genuine repentance."

There's also such a thing as self-interest, I thought. "What makes you think it was the East Germans?" I asked Sean.

"Kevin was in touch with his lawyer," he replied. "He was trying, as you say, to get his sentence reduced. The chances were slim, but nevertheless . . . Anyway, after the murder, I talked to his lawyer—there were things to see to, you know. His lawyer said that Kevin had made friends with certain of the inmates. He'd confided in one or two of them—told them what he hoped to do. I suspect he wanted their advice. It may have been naïve on his part, but then, he hadn't been in prison very long. His lawyer thinks—we think—that word got out and wound up in the wrong ears."

I said nothing. Stranger things had happened, I supposed. Foreign agents had arranged for certain convicts to escape; I'd read about that. I'd also read that contracts had been taken out on prison inmates by people outside the prison. But getting the information to the East Germans—that would have taken some doing, I thought.

Carol glanced from Sean to Adele and back to Sean. "What was it that he *knew?*" she asked.

"The identity of the person who recruited him," Sean replied.

"Among other things," I put in.

"Among other things," he agreed. "But mainly that, Brock. The FBI wanted to know who'd recruited Kevin." He turned back to Carol. "If you followed the trial, you know how Kevin passed the microfilms. The FBI had movies of him in the cemetery, placing the envelope under the tree, marking the headstone . . . Unfortunately, the Germans got away—they're back in East Berlin now, no doubt, wearing medals."

"I remember," Carol said. She'd followed the trial as closely as I had.

"But they weren't really the big fish," Sean went on. "Not according to what Kevin told his lawyer. The person who recruited him is the one the FBI was after. They made no bones about it. They wanted to know how Kevin had been recruited; when, where—and, above all, by whom. That's the person they'd really like to catch."

Carol frowned. "It's all so complicated, it's beyond me." But her next words indicated that it wasn't in the least beyond her. "They think that person may have recruited others like Kevin."

"Exactly," Sean said. "May have, probably did, and is still recruiting more. Calthorp Industries is only one of hundreds of companies doing work the East Germans would like to know about. How about all the others?"

"How much of this is just guesswork on your part?" I asked.

"Some," he admitted. "But it's based on what Kevin's lawyer told me and what Kevin himself said. My conclusions are valid, Brock. Think about them."

I did think about them. And they were valid. The questions put to me by Davies and Sortini, the FBI agents, supported them.

Davies and Sortini had wanted to know every detail of Kevin's conversation with me about the job at Calthorp. What, exactly, had he said? What, exactly, had I said? Had he mentioned any names—any names at all? Had I ever recommended other friends of mine for jobs in companies like Calthorp? Who were the friends? Which were the companies?

Now, for the first time, I understood why Davies and Sortini had been so persistent, so hard to deal with.

"You're right," I said to Sean. "It *would* be important to know who recruited Kevin. He gave no hints?"

Sean and Adele exchanged a look.

"Just one," Adele said. "And that's what I've been wanting to talk to you about, Brock."

"All right," I said, "go ahead. What did Kevin hint?"

Sean took a deep breath, let it out slowly and said, "Kevin told me that the person who recruited him is someone you know."

6

I LEFT CAROL A NOTE. It said: "Taking a walk."

She was still asleep. She'd slept better than I.

Accompanied by Tiger, I strolled slowly up Fifth Avenue. It was seven-thirty, and the sidewalk was deserted. Tiger, at his end of the leash, sniffed at everything that caught his attention, while I, at mine, continued the train of thought that had kept me awake most of the night.

Had Adele and Sean been telling the truth?

I wanted to believe they hadn't been, but I couldn't. Kevin was dead, and the case was closed. They had no reason to lie.

No reason to lie, but a very good reason to tell the truth: to involve me in Adele's effort at atonement. Kevin had done a terrible thing, and she felt partly responsible—she'd failed as a mother. If his deed could be undone, or at least mitigated, her conscience would be eased.

She'd finally admitted this, although she'd put it differently. "I'd hate to think the horror of these past months has been for nothing, Brock. God isn't that cruel. Some small good should come out of it."

She'd blinked back tears when she'd said that, and I'd been touched. I'd wanted somehow to help.

The other question was: Had Kevin himself been telling the truth?

"Don't misunderstand," Sean had said. "Kevin didn't make a big thing of the fact that you knew the person who'd recruited him. And he didn't blame you. No one *could* blame you. He merely mentioned that you knew the person. Your name came up accidentally, I gather. In talking about himself, Kevin happened to say that you'd been a friend of ours when he was in high school. How the conversation went after that, I can only speculate. I suppose the person said, 'Brock Potter the stockbroker? I know him.' And so on."

"That doesn't mean it was true," I'd pointed out.

"Granted," Sean had replied. "But apparently the person knew enough about you to convince Kevin."

"You keep saying 'the person.' Don't you know whether it was a man or a woman?"

"I asked Kevin that, Brock. He wouldn't tell me. He changed the subject."

"Have you told any of this to the FBI?"

"Not personally. But Kevin's lawyer has. They said you've already been questioned exhaustively."

"That's for damn sure. They questioned me about everyone I've ever known."

After that, there had been nothing useful any of us could say. I'd insisted that, to the best of my knowledge, I wasn't acquainted with anyone who went around recruiting spies, and Adele had sighed, and Sean had nodded gravely, and none of us had been able to smile for the rest of the evening.

Kevin had had nothing to gain from falsely linking me with the man who'd made him a spy, I decided as Tiger and I crossed Fourteenth Street. Nothing at all.

Memories came and went. I saw Kevin as he'd been at fifteen, sixteen, seventeen. I saw him at twenty-five and thirty. I recalled fragments of conversations I'd had in the past with Adele, with Roman; when the children were young, and when the children were grown. I thought of the time Sean had lost his temper and punched Kevin in the nose and then gone to his father to confess what he'd done.

Honest, upright people, all of them. Exceptionally so. And yet Kevin . . .

Tiger paused to sniff a discarded wrapper that had once contained a Hershey bar. I watched him make his analysis. It didn't take him long to reach a conclusion. The wrapper represented a treat that had disappeared.

We crossed Twenty-third Street and kept going. This particular stretch of Fifth Avenue, between Twenty-third and Thirty-fourth streets, wasn't one of my favorite pieces of real estate at any time, and on a Sunday morning it was particularly dismal. The buildings, which had been splendid once but no longer were, reminded me of my grandfather's career.

At least I didn't have to worry about the FBI, I thought. According to Sean, the Bureau was satisfied that I knew no more about the Rand case than I'd already reported. I wasn't going to be interrogated again.

Or was I? And what could I tell those unsmiling, gimlet-eyed agents if they did come back?

Although the temperature was in the sixties, I suddenly felt chilled.

With Tiger trotting beside me, I continued along Fifth Avenue. We were the only living creatures on the sidewalk, except for an old man who was poking in a trash bin at the corner of Thirtieth Street. He had a blanket over his shoulders, like a shawl.

As I neared the Empire State Building, I had a sensible idea. Talk things over with Jonie Stiles, I decided. He was familiar with the Rand case. He'd been present when the FBI had questioned me.

It was nine o'clock when I placed the call, from a public telephone on Fifty-seventh Street.

Sure, Jonie said, if I had something important to discuss, he was at my disposal.

Twenty minutes later, I presented myself to the doorman at the building on Sutton Place where Jonie lived. "Mr. Potter to see Mr. Stiles," I said.

This information was duly relayed over the house phone, and

the doorman returned to say, grudgingly, "Eighteen C."

Jonie greeted me in his pajamas and bathrobe. "Come on in, Brock. What an ungodly hour! And what's that odd-looking animal you're holding?"

"He's not odd-looking," I said. "He's a purebred toy poodle. Tiger, this is Jonas Stiles the Third, our lawyer. Is it O.K. if I put him down, Jonie?"

Jonie nodded, and I deposited Tiger on the marble floor. He began to sniff at Jonie's house slippers.

"He's too small for you," Jonie observed. "You should have got a bigger dog."

"He wasn't my choice," I said. "He was foisted on me by one of my staff—Brian Barth. Brian found he couldn't take care of him but didn't want to return him to the pet shop. Be careful how you talk, though; Tiger and I are buddies."

We were joined by Deedee, Jonie's wife. She was wearing a negligee that Marie Antoinette would have envied. "How nice to see you," she said. "I hope you haven't had breakfast. I bought some delicious croissants yesterday. What an adorable dog!"

Tiger allowed himself to be petted and began to explore the living room. I apologized for the untimeliness of my visit. It wasn't untimely at all, Deedee assured me; all she had to do was set another place at the table. She went off to set it.

"You want to talk now or later?" Jonie asked.

"Later, I guess."

He nodded, and we talked about dogs until Deedee summoned us to the dining room.

Jonie's manner was so laid-back that it was easy to underestimate him. Nothing ever seemed to upset his equanamity. Puffing on his pipe, his face a study in detachment, he was invariably an island of calm in the sea of troubled and contentious businessmen who paid him huge retainers. The only time I'd seen him even come close to losing his temper was when a waiter insisted that mayonnaise and vinaigrette dressing were really the same thing.

But he was a man of power and accomplishment. First of all, he was a Stiles, which was something all by itself. Stileses had been active in city, state and national affairs since the nineteenth century. Several of them had been advisers to Presidents of the United States, and one had been an ambassador. Furthermore, Jonie himself had been an editor of the *Harvard Law Review,* an assistant to a justice of the U.S. Supreme Court, and an Under Secretary of Defense. His credentials, including clubs and service organizations, took up three inches in *Who's Who,* and he still had a long run ahead of him—he was only forty-five. All in all, I thought, he was one of the smartest and most effective men I'd ever met.

The dining room, with its crystal chandelier and antique refectory table, made me wish that I'd shaved before leaving home. And while the breakfast itself was no more than Deedee had said it would be—croissants and coffee—it was served on Coalport china that had been fired when Queen Victoria was a teen-ager.

Deedee gave me the latest news of the two Stiles boys. Jonie IV had called shortly before I had, to report that his bicycle had been stolen from one of the racks in the Harvard Yard, and Steve, a senior at Phillips Academy, after trying for three years, had finally made the track team.

We spent a pleasant half-hour at the table. Then Jonie and I retired to the library.

He made a little ceremony of deciding which of the many pipes on the shelf he should smoke, and of lighting it. "All right, now," he said at last, "tell me what you're so fertutzed about."

"Fertutzed" was a word he sometimes used instead of "upset." I had no idea where he'd got it, but it wasn't part of the standard Stiles, Levin and Sullivan vocabulary.

"The Rand case has surfaced in my life again," I said.

He raised an eyebrow. "But the villain is dead. I read it in the *Times.*"

"Maybe," I replied, "but last night his ghost came back to haunt me." I proceeded to tell Jonie about Adele's and Sean's visit.

He listened with half-closed eyes.

"So what should I do?" I asked, at the end.

"Do?" He seemed mildly surprised by the question. "Nothing, of course. The story is unverifiable. Mere hearsay."

"Adele and Sean believe it. I'm sure of that."

Apparently Jonie's pipe wasn't drawing properly. He took it from between his teeth, tamped down the tobacco with a book of matches, then tried it again. "A mother, a brother," he said, "I imagine they would. But what difference does that make to you, Brock?"

"Suppose it *is* true—how much trouble am I in? I don't want to go through the whole rigmarole with the FBI a second time. Once was enough."

"You're in no trouble at all, as I see it, and you needn't worry about the FBI. Even if someone you know *were* working for the East Germans, you wouldn't be the only person who knows him or her. A lot of other people would be in the same boat. And no one could possibly expect you to screen all your acquaintances. The way you get around, the number of people you meet—you come into contact with hundreds of people, Brock. If one of them isn't what he or she seems to be—how would you have any way of knowing? It might be someone you met years ago, someone whose name you don't even remember.

"The FBI wants *hard* information. It isn't interested in the allegations—and I use the word advisedly—the allegations of a dead man whose story can no longer be checked and whose character was, at best, suspect. No, Brock, you're needlessly fertutzed. The Rands are simply making use of you to solve their own guilt problem. It's not pleasant being related to a convicted criminal, I suppose."

"That thought crossed my mind," I admitted.

"No one can vouch for all his friends. We all know people who, if we realized what they're up to, we'd report to the police."

I heaved a sigh of relief. "You've made me feel a hell of a lot better."

"That's what a large part of my work consists of: making folks feel better." Jonie permitted himself a smile. "I should have gone to divinity school. At one time I considered it."

I apologized for having made a mountain out of a molehill, collected my dog, who was in the kitchen nibbling on a croissant Deedee had given him, and prepared to leave.

"See you at our shindig on Friday," Jonie reminded me as I waited for the elevator. "Come early, stay late. We're having quite a crowd."

"I wouldn't miss it for the world," I replied.

The elevator came, and I got in. Riding down to the lobby, I thought: Jonie was right about divinity school. He would have made a great minister. He had a wonderful way of restoring a person's peace of mind.

7

CLAIR GOULD, our switchboard operator, barely acknowledged my breezy "Good morning." This wasn't like her. She was a tiny woman with a booming voice, and her greetings could usually be heard as far away as Central Park.

I hesitated, then went over to her. "Anything wrong?"

She was slumped in her little swivel chair, looking utterly dejected. "Not really," she replied. But then she held up a newspaper, which she'd folded in half lengthwise, and groaned, "My horoscope."

Remembering that she regarded astrology the way Einstein regarded electricity, I kept a straight face. "Bad?"

"The worst it's been in years, Mr. Potter. The last time it was this bad, my purse got snatched."

"Well, now," I said, "maybe you'd better take a cab home this evening."

"Mine's the only one of the signs that's like this. All the others are better." She shook her head sadly. "What sign are you?"

"Gemini."

She consulted the newspaper. "See what I mean? Listen to yours." She began to read aloud.

The forecast for Geminis, I had to admit, was very good. We were entering an up cycle. Money matters and health were both well aspected, and we could look forward to unexpected dividends. Furthermore, romance and adventure were highlighted. The only cautionary note was: "Be circumspect with Taurus individual."

"Not like mine at all," Clair concluded. "Mine's nothing but danger signals."

"Tell you what I'll do," I said. "For this one day, I'll trade you your sign for mine. You can be me."

I'd intended the remark as a joke, but Clair took it literally. "That's impossible, Mr. Potter. People are what they are."

I gave up. "I suppose you're right, Clair. Good luck. Watch your purse." I went down the corridor to my office to begin the day and the week.

But from that moment on, good things began to happen to me. I really did seem to be entering an up cycle.

Take gold, for example. Normally I don't fool around with commodities or precious metals. Too risky, in my opinion. And while gold may not be dependent on the weather, as soybeans are, it's dependent on the actions of inscrutable Soviet bureaucrats and high-strung Arab billionaires who are even more unpredictable than the weather. But shortly before going to Switzerland, in a moment of despair over the fate of Western civilization, I'd bought $100,000 worth of gold bullion.

Since then, the price of gold had dropped seventeen dollars an ounce, and the opinion of the moneymen I'd met in Zürich was that for the foreseeable future gold was not the thing to own.

However, on that Monday morning I learned that the price of gold had inexplicably shot up twenty-six dollars an ounce. My loss had turned into a modest profit. I cashed in my chips and walked away from the table, whistling.

Also, at our staff meeting that morning, Joe Rothland had good news about Halliday Foods.

Some months back, Joe had reported an imminent turnaround in the fortunes of Halliday, which had been doing poorly for the past two years. Three Crowns, the company's new line of frozen entrees, had tested well in Seattle, Dallas and Pittsburgh, according to Joe, and if sales reached the projected figure, Three Crowns would earn enough to offset losses in the company's other divisions. At the time, I'd been swaying with every wind, and in this particular case I'd swayed too far. On the strength of what Joe had said, I'd recommended the purchase of Halliday shares, and some of our customers had taken my advice. But the company's second-quarter earnings statement, which was released shortly after my buy recommendation, had been even worse than expected. I'd been very worried.

Having talked with Halliday's treasurer on Friday, Joe now presented us with new data. Not only had the sales of Three Crowns reached projection, but they'd surpassed it by fifty percent. In the third quarter the company would show a profit.

Joe felt vindicated, and so did I. "Hallelujah, Halliday!" I exclaimed.

A number of other nice things came out at that morning's meeting, too.

Brian informed us that Walker Tool was about to announce a new process for recovering oil from shale, and that Prentice Coal was forming a joint venture with Darby Oil to drill in the Baltimore Canyon. Moreover, this was going to be the best profit year Prentice had ever had. Since both Walker and Prentice were on my buy list, I felt gratified.

Automobile inventories were coming down, Irving said.

Harriet had it on good authority that government economists were revising their estimates of Gross National Product upward.

And, with his usual preoccupied air, George Cole observed that Seaboard Optics was making strides.

"Strides?" Irving inquired dryly. "In which direction—forward or backward?" He didn't like Herb Minton, Seaboard's president, any more than I did.

"Forward," George replied. "Lasers." He paused, and stared into space. At times there was something very remote and otherworldly about him, and this was one of those times. He reminded me of a cleric who was trying to solve a difficult metaphysical problem. "It could be important, you know."

"Follow it up," I said.

He nodded, and all of us proceeded to a discussion of domestic steel producers, about which Irving was preparing a special report. He was discovering, Irving said, that the domestic steel industry wasn't as bad off as he'd been led to believe.

It was, from beginning to end, an excellent meeting. One of our best ever, I thought. Lots of news, all of which was good.

After lunch, I had a long session with Ward Carlton and Tom.

Ward's title is Assistant Sales Manager; he is to Tom what Irving is to me. And his was the principal voice in this particular get-together.

Our topic was the Bay Area Trust and Savings Bank, with emphasis on Bob Gerard. Gerard had recently become head of the bank's trust department. He was the main reason for my going to San Francisco. Ward had been wooing him for a year and a half, in anticipation of his eventual promotion to department head, and he felt that this was the time for us to close in. The bank had given us bits and pieces of its business, but it had never given us a substantial amount.

Ward had been to San Francisco several times during the summer, and Gerard had made encouraging noises. But before dropping some of the other brokerage houses with which the bank did business, he wanted to meet me and review the trust department's entire portfolio. If he liked my ideas, he would make a pitch for Price, Potter and Petacque to his bosses. Once more I was to be our gift offer to a new customer.

I listened while Ward gave me a personality profile of Gerard and a résumé of his career. Nothing he said caused me anxiety. Gerard was apparently a nice man of thirty-seven who'd come up through the ranks and had never worked for any company other than Bay Area Trust and Savings. He was bright, aggressive, an ardent Raiders fan and he loved Chinese food. I should be sure to take him to a Chinese restaurant, Ward said.

Tom confined himself to the single, and largely superfluous, observation that this could be the beginning of something big. We weren't as strong on the West Coast as he would like us to be; and where Bay Area went, others were likely to follow.

After we disposed of the main item on the agenda, our meeting became a bull session. We let our hair down and talked frankly about all our customers. Tom and I had had uninhibited conversations of this sort in the past, but Ward hadn't been included in them. He made some interesting contributions, though. I hadn't known, for instance, that Clifford Jeffries, of the Jeffries Growth Fund, had at one time almost gone to jail for bigamy. Or that Morton S. Saunders, the founder of the Saunders Group, who acted like one of God's special deputies on earth, had certain kinky tendencies.

It was a lovely day, that first day of my alleged up cycle. And it was followed by a lovely evening, for romance *was* highlighted. At four o'clock Carol telephoned to say that she wasn't doing anything after work.

Ordinarily she and I didn't see each other on Mondays. Because of her, not me. Out-of-town buyers usually came to town on Sunday, and on Monday nights she either had to work with them or help her boss entertain them. Besides, Monday was one of the days on which she saw her analyst. On those Monday nights when she wasn't busy with customers, she was busy being introspective.

She arrived at my house shortly after six, and we shared a long cocktail hour. Then we shared the lamb stew Louise, my housekeeper, had left in the warming oven. Finally we shared my bed. And this was one of those all too rare nights when Carol's and my desires meshed. I fell asleep convinced that Casanova could have learned a thing or two from me.

8

THE WAY WE LINGERED over our coffee the next morning, you would have thought it was a Saturday or Sunday instead of a Tuesday.

There was no overhang of tension. Both of us were relaxed. Carol read the first section of the *Times,* while I scanned the financial news. Each of us mumbled headlines and snippets from stories, but neither expected the other to pay attention.

Carol said something about the Secretary of State, but I didn't catch what it was. I observed, without even looking up, that Irving was right, auto inventories were dropping. She told me that someone was getting married, but I missed the name.

Suddenly, however, she raised her voice and said, "When it comes to armed robbery, I agree with you."

I put down the paper. "You agree with me about what?"

"Armed robbery. It says here that armed robbery is up five percent nationwide, and I think you're right. Also when it comes to stealing cars and picking pockets and forging checks."

"How am I right?" I asked.

"You're always saying that crime is caused by greed—greed and envy."

I smiled. It was nice to know she'd been listening all those times when I'd complained about the Washington types who insisted that crime could be eliminated if only Congress would pass some new laws; when I'd said that you can't legislate greed and envy out of people.

"But treason is different," she said, leaning forward, her elbows on the table, her eyes bright. She looked very earnest, very intense.

"What makes you say that, honey?"

"Dr. Yarborough. I told him about the Rands being here Saturday night."

Dr. Yarborough was her analyst. Once more the events of my life had been grist for his mill, it seemed. I was annoyed.

"He says greed and envy *are* at the root of most crimes. But he says treason is unique. It's caused by bitterness."

"Oh?" After my conversation with Jonie Stiles, I'd relegated the Rands to one of the back burners, beside such unpleasant but not really urgent matters as the cyst under my left arm that someday was going to have to be removed and the fact that the house would need a new roof in a year or so.

"I told him about the Rand family," Carol explained, "and he said psychologically it fits. Kevin was the oldest of six children."

"Is there any more coffee?" I inquired.

Carol seemed irritated by the interruption, but she refilled my cup. Then she went on with Dr. Yarborough's theory. "The birth of a new sibling is an insult to the others. Especially to the oldest, who's been insulted the most often. In Kevin's case, it made him secretly bitter toward his parents. Don't look like that. Let me finish."

"O.K., finish."

"His bitterness toward them turned into bitterness toward his employer and his country. Treason, Dr. Yarborough says, is really a crime against parents."

"Finished now?" I asked.

"Not quite. It's a problem with oldest children, and it's also a problem with adopted children. They're bitter toward their natural parents for giving them away. See?"

I drank some coffee and impatiently pushed the newspaper aside with my elbow. "Sounds like you had a real profitable session yesterday," I said. "In addition to reviewing your weekend with me, you figured out how to strengthen our national security. Take all the people who were oldest children in large families and all the people who were adopted children and put them under FBI surveillance, and you'll end the giveaway of classified information. Spies will be caught one, two, three."

"You're making fun of me again, Brock."

"What about all the oldest kids and all the adopted kids who grow up to be honest, responsible citizens? What about—?"

"Never mind. I knew you wouldn't understand. Excuse me, I've got to go. I'm already late."

"Don't get sore, Carol. I just don't like your discussing me with Dr. Yarborough, and I don't like being reminded of Kevin Rand. And I never detected any bitterness in him, ever."

Carol shrugged and said she wasn't sore. Then she told me not to be late on Friday and hurried off to resume her independent life.

I put on my tie, took Tiger for a brief airing, picked up my suitcase and headed for the office. There, at least, I wouldn't have to deal with any of Dr. Yarborough's theories.

I did concede, though, that the doctor was doing Carol some good. Slowly but surely she was changing. It was partly due to Dr. Yarborough, I believed, that she and I had had such a satisfactory night.

9

Phoenix wasn't as hot as I'd feared it might be. The temperature was only a hundred and one.

I'd always had mixed feelings about the Sun Belt. On one hand, I liked it. I liked the optimism, the this-is-where-it's-at attitude of the people. But on the other hand, I distrusted the life-style. In my opinion, there were too many swimming pools, tennis courts, barbecue pits and sports cars; all that easy living could be morally debilitating.

Driving along Camelback Road to the Mojave Insurance Building, I remarked to myself on the vast distances between neighborhoods in Sun Belt cities; on the absence of sidewalks; on the absolute necessity of owning an automobile. If the oil ever stopped flowing, I thought, the population of the northern half of the United States might freeze to death, but the population of the southern half, being unable to get to its grocery stores, would die of starvation.

From my air-conditioned car, I hurried across the parking lot, which was like the inside of a kiln, to Mojave's air-conditioned lobby, and five minutes later I was happily settled in Sam Gage's office, talking business.

Sam was the president of Mojave and an old friend of mine. I'd begun my career as a specialist in insurance companies, and while

I was now devoting an increasing amount of time to other industries, I still considered the insurance industry my special turf.

Sam gave me a rundown of Mojave's financial position and future prospects. Then he began to tell me his troubles.

The troubles weren't his alone; I'd had them told to me often enough before by other insurance executives. I didn't know what the answers were, except to raise premiums, which were already too high, but I was sympathetic.

The tremendous increase in arson was very much on Sam's mind. So was the high degree of sophistication in auto-theft rings. It had reached the point, he said, where cars were now being stolen to fill special orders—you want a new Mercedes or Cadillac, just tell the right person, and within a week one will be stolen for you, with tape deck and sun roof, exactly as requested.

And Sam was particularly bitter about the unconscionable awards being made by juries in personal-injury and malpractice cases. "Juries don't seem to realize," he lamented, "that the public foots the bill. They don't realize that awards which are out of all proportion to the damage done raise the premiums for everybody; that that's one of the reasons why medical costs are so high. What juries are doing, what lawyers are encouraging them to do, is robbing the general public to enrich a single individual who comes across good on the witness stand."

"Everyone thinks insurance companies have unlimited resources," I said.

"Damn it, Brock," Sam exploded, "the way things are going, there won't *be* any insurance one of these days! Not because people won't want it, but because they won't be able to afford it."

With Sam's gloomy prediction ringing in my ears, I drove back to the airport and caught a plane for Los Angeles, where the temperature was a mere one degree cooler than in Phoenix.

Most unusual, the natives said. September is usually ideal.

My appointment was with the supercharged chief executive officer of a supercharged real-estate investment firm that was, in the face of generally adverse conditions, going great guns. My objective was to get a true picture of how the company was doing; his was to paint as rosy a picture as possible, which really wasn't necessary, because the true picture was good enough. But he was one of those people who have more energy than they know what to do with, and he wore me out, ushering me from one office to another to look at big photographs, big charts, big books of figures. And when we finally finished, at seven in the evening, he insisted on driving me all the way from Van Nuys, where the company headquarters were, to Santa Monica for dinner at a restaurant noted for its swordfish steaks and abalone.

The abalone was only so-so, but the martinis were marvelous. I had three of them. After the day I'd put in and the cultural shock that Los Angeles, as usual, had given me, I felt entitled. Los Angeles wasn't Sun Belt, as far as I was concerned; it was Oz. Straw men and tin men and the MGM lion, who, cowardly or not, had always seemed decidedly Oz-like to me. I expected to get off a plane someday and find that Los Angeles and Orange counties had entirely vanished—not as the result of an earthquake, but from a tidal wave of reality.

"Whenever I'm out here," I confided to my host after the third martini, "I'm reminded of what my partner Mark once said: 'Los Angeles is all right, if you like pink stucco.'"

My host smiled the way people do when they're trying to be polite, but I sensed that he didn't altogether appreciate the remark.

San Francisco, after the heat of Phoenix and Los Angeles, was bracing. I didn't allow myself time to savor the air, however. As soon as I'd checked into the Fairmont, I took off for the main branch of Bay Area Trust and Savings, to keep my date with Bob Gerard.

I'd left nothing to chance; I'd called from New York to reserve a table at the Imperial Dragon, which I'd been to before and which I thought served the best Chinese food I'd ever tasted. Table for two, at one; Potter; and make sure *I* get the check.

I wasn't nervous, exactly, but I was keyed up. Like a boxer before a major bout.

As it turned out, however, my anxiety was unwarranted. Gerard and I took to each other like a pair of identical twins who'd been separated as infants and were unexpectedly reunited after twenty years. There was instant rapport between us.

Over lunch, Gerard explained that the bank was attempting to change its image. It was, by California standards, an old and venerable institution, known primarily for the excellent care it took of rich widows and orphans. But now it was trying to get onto the fast track. It wanted a larger number of commercial accounts.

Gerard himself, as head of the trust department, was concerned with the widows and orphans. He was hoping to do things differently in that department, too, however. The bank had been ultraconservative in managing the trusts; the beneficiaries of them had fallen far behind in the race with inflation. He was looking for investments that would yield a higher return and appreciate more in value than the securities that made up the bulk of the trust department's current portfolio, but were nevertheless safe. If the right investments could be found, he believed, the beneficiaries would be better off, and the word would get around—the bank would get more trust business.

We agreed that it wouldn't be easy to come up with just the right mix of safe and profitable, but we felt it could be done. He gave me a printout of the securities in the trust portfolios. I said I would take it back to New York, study it and then make recommendations. Meanwhile, I offered a few suggestions which he said he liked.

By the time we finished the meal, there was no doubt in my mind that Price, Potter and Petacque had a new account and that I'd made a new friend. Gerard even went so far as to say that he expected to be seeing a lot of Ward Carlton.

"And incidentally," he added, "I hope you'll take part in our seminar."

"Your seminar?" Ward hadn't told me about anything of that sort.

The bank was sponsoring a two-day seminar for local bigwigs,

Gerard explained. It was a promotional event designed to let businessmen in the area know that the bank was in tune with their
needs and would like their accounts; part of its overall effort to
change its image. The affair was generating more interest than
anyone had expected. Executives were coming from other parts of
California, even from other parts of the country. Every day new
people were calling up to ask for invitations.

"The theme," Bob said, "is 'Investment Policy for the Decade
Ahead.' It's right up your alley."

I'd been invited to participate in such events before, but I'd
always said no; they took up time that I thought could be put to
better use. "It's nice of you to want to include me," I replied, "but
I don't think I'm the seminar type."

"Oh, but you are," he said eagerly. "You have the presence, the
reputation—everything it takes. Do say yes, Brock."

"It would mean another trip out here."

"No. You could appear on a TV hookup. Several of our speakers
are doing that." Gerard went on to name some of the people who
were going to address the group. It was an impressive list.

Tom would want me to say yes, I knew. He believed that kind
of publicity was good for us. And since the audience would be
primarily West Coast, the demographics of this seminar would
especially appeal to him.

"Come on, Brock," Gerard persisted. "When the brass heard
you were going to be here today, they asked me to persuade you.
You don't want me to look bad, do you?"

I certainly didn't. And I didn't want to displease Tom, either.
"All right," I said at last. "But tell the brass I'm only doing it
because of you."

Gerard grinned. "Terrific!"

We returned to his office on the best of terms, and Gerard
invited me to his house for dinner.

"I'd love to come," I said, "but I have in mind to go down the
Peninsula to see Bill Arden, if he's available."

Gerard's expression changed. It became grave.

"I've been hearing rumors," I said. "Have you?"

He didn't hesitate. "Yes. There's trouble brewing. The other members of the family have ganged up on Bill."

"They're making a mistake."

"Not according to them."

"Any idea why?"

He shook his head. "Nobody will say."

I asked to use his telephone. He handed it to me.

Bill Arden said that he would indeed be available.

"I'll take a rain check for the dinner," I told Gerard, and we began the intricate process of saying good-bye and at the same time cementing our relationship. I assured him I'd be in touch with him about the investment portfolio, and he said he'd let me know about my televised appearance on the seminar.

By a quarter to four, I was skimming along Interstate 280 in a rented Cutlass Supreme on my way to see the embattled head of Arden Electronics.

10

THE ARDEN PLANT looked like a newly built high school in a very affluent suburb, except that high schools, even in affluent suburbs, don't have as much fancy landscaping or as many athletic facilities as Bill Arden had provided for his employees. The long, rambling one-story building of glass and concrete was surrounded by a private park that featured, in addition to all the little date palms and flowering shrubs, an Olympic-size swimming pool, three clay tennis courts, a putting green and the necessary accouterments for badminton, basketball and archery. All that was lacking, I thought as I drove up the two-lane asphalt driveway, was an ice-skating rink and a setup for jai alai.

Yet, I knew, such Club Med features were necessary business expenses in that part of the world. Arden was located in the fiercely competitive band of real estate around San Jose that has come to be known as Silicon Valley, because of all the silicon-related products that originate there—products that have revolutionized electronics.

The companies in that area didn't compete for customers; they competed for employees. No matter how high the unemployment figures elsewhere at any given time, in Silicon Valley they were practically zero. At least for men and women with the right skills, such as being able to understand infinitely complex electrical circuitry or to work their way through mathematical equations that cover entire blackboards.

At first I was puzzled by the amount of activity I saw on the grounds. A dozen or more people were swimming, two of the tennis courts were in use, and a number of men were engaged in an informal basketball game. In addition, several small groups were picnicking on the grass. Was this some sort of holiday in Silicon Valley? I wondered. But then it occurred to me that Arden was probably one of the many employers in the area that let their personnel set their own schedules; it didn't matter when you did your job, as long as you did it. What was going on now went on all day long, no doubt.

The minute I entered the plant itself, however, I sensed that what I'd seen outdoors didn't reflect the mood indoors. I wasn't sure what gave me the feeling that the mood indoors was less than happy. Possibly it was the grimness on the faces of the first three people I came across: a receptionist; a uniformed guard with gunbelt, gun and ammunition; and a stolid man who was standing near the receptionist's counter and who I was almost positive was a security agent. All three of them looked as if they were expecting a terrorist attack momentarily.

The tensions emanating from the executive suite were having their effect throughout the building, I decided.

Bill himself came out to greet me. The change in him was shocking. Shoulders hunched, head thrust forward, he seemed to have developed a stoop. In no way was he the brisk, confident Bill Arden I'd always known.

"Good to see you, good to see you," he said as we shook hands. And then, distractedly, he said it again. "Good to see you."

My God, I thought, he's turning senile at fifty.

But when we reached his office, I learned that this wasn't the case. He was as alert as ever. The only difference now was, he was preoccupied. He evidently had so many things on his mind that it was hard for him to focus on any of them.

His questions about my partners, business trends and the purpose of my trip to San Francisco were lucid and perceptive. As I answered them, I tried to figure out how to proceed with the interview. In the car, I'd decided to take the direct approach—to confront him with what I'd heard and to ask for an explanation —but now I thought that low-key might be better.

In the end, however, I didn't need any approach at all. Bill took the initiative.

"I suppose you're here to find out what's behind all the stories you've been hearing," he said. Then his mind wandered briefly. "Yes, all the stories."

I nodded.

"Who told you?" he asked. "How did you hear?"

"I heard about it from one of the people on my staff," I said. "I don't know exactly who he heard it from. He merely told me that your brother, your cousin, the board—that there's some dissension here."

He snorted. "Dissension. Yes, that's the term, I suppose. Dissension."

"And since the news is out, I came down here to—"

"To find out the details." He smiled, and for a moment he was his old self again. But then the smile faded. "I'm the last person who wants to talk about them, Brock."

"The news *is* out, Bill. At least the central fact. The other family members of the board are trying to force you to resign. One of my questions is: How do the outside members feel?"

Bill took a paper clip from a little dish on his desk blotter and began to fiddle with it. He didn't answer.

"I assume there've been rivalries within the family for years," I went on. "You've run pretty much a one-man show, as far as the family is concerned. But still . . ." I left the sentence hanging.

He unbent the paper clip until it looked like a crooked pin. He said nothing.

"My own feeling is, the board would be making a mistake to let you go. Arden Electronics won't be the same without you. You've made this company what it is." I paused. "Is it possible there'll be a proxy fight?"

He shook his head.

"You don't intend to fight?"

Bill threw the paper clip over his shoulder. It made no noise as it hit the carpet. Finally he let his eyes meet mine. "You're an old friend, Brock, but I'm not going to discuss the matter even with you. The board can do what it wants. As long as I'm here, I'm here. When I go, I won't come back."

I shed my securities analyst shell. "You're right, Bill, I *am* an old friend. What the hell's going on? Tell me."

Bill sighed and shook his head again.

"I'll help if I can."

"Yes," he said, "an old friend. And you look wonderful. Better than you've looked in years. Have you been on vacation?"

"Yes, as a matter of fact."

"Where were you?"

"Switzerland."

A shadow crossed his face. But then he said, "Beautiful country. Especially Gstaad." He took another paper clip from the dish and unbent it.

I tried to interpret what I was seeing and hearing. He just wanted someone to talk to, I decided. He'd been feeling very much alone lately.

It wasn't like him not to put up a fight, though; he'd always been a scrapper. "Your morale is shot," I said. "You ought to take a stand."

He looked across the desk and said, "It ain't worth it, Brock."

"Nonsense," I replied. "I felt the same way you do, not so long ago. My morale was shot, too."

This interested him. "That a fact?"

"Yes. I'd made a mistake and I lost my confidence. Everything I did began to seem wrong. Finally Tom and Mark talked me into taking a couple of weeks off. I came home a new man."

"I've been thinking of going around the world," Bill said. "Six months, a year."

"Sounds to me like you've already given in," I observed. "Like you're reconciled."

"What will be will be."

I felt sorry for him. But frustrated, too. "Damn it, Bill, you've always been a dynamo. Go on being a dynamo. The world needs people like you in the important jobs, not on the sidelines."

He began jabbing the blotter with the paper clip. "A dynamo. Yes, from the time I was a kid, I suppose. I couldn't wait to get into this business and do all the things I thought could be done with it. I saw what was going on in the schools, in the labs, in other businesses. I saw the possibilities. The computer, the mechanical memory, the machine that could do in a minute what human beings couldn't do in an hour—I knew it, I felt it, and, by God, I put this company on the map. But I hurt a lot of feelings along the way. Bruce, Sol, Dad—they resented the way I ran what you called a 'one-man show.' I made them rich, but they resented me anyway. Bruce and Sol, at any rate; Dad was always more or less on my side. But now even he thinks I should be punished. And maybe I should be. You said you made a mistake. Well, I made one too, and nobody knows it better than I." He felt silent.

"What mistake did you make, Bill?"

He didn't reply.

"The stockholders at large aren't going to like your leaving," I said. "Neither am I." I waited for a response, but didn't receive one. "I think you ought to get an impartial referee to intervene. You probably have a good lawyer, but even so, let me recommend mine. He represents some of the biggest corporations in the country, and he's very good at this sort of thing. He's straightened out a lot of internal squabbles that, if it weren't for him, would have led to bloodshed. Jonie Stiles, of Stiles, Levin and Sullivan. Why don't you consult him? It might be worth your while. The firm is giving a big party tomorrow to celebrate the opening of its new offices. I'll mention you to him, if you'd like. It'll all be confidential. You have nothing to lose, Bill, and everything to gain, and so do the stockholders."

Bill continued his stony silence.

"Would you like me to call him now?" I asked.

At last Bill spoke. "I've heard of Stiles, Levin and Sullivan, Brock. They can't help."

I pulled the last arrow from my quiver. "Well, if you've already made up your mind, and you aren't willing to talk about it, there's no reason for me to take up more of your time." I got to my feet. "I will say this, though. In my next market letter I'm going to recommend that anyone who owns Arden stock sell it."

I'd expected the threat to have at least a minor impact, but it didn't. Bill remained impassive.

"Good-bye," I said, and held out my hand.

He looked up at me. "Tell me something, Brock. What mistake did *you* make?"

The question caught me by surprise. I realized that Bill's thoughts had been somewhere else altogether, that he wasn't even aware I was getting ready to leave. "It—it's a personal matter," I stammered.

He nodded. "That's what everything boils down to in the end, doesn't it? Personal matters."

Should I tell him? I wondered. Will it make him change his mind? After all, his knowing can't do me any harm.

I decided to go halfway. "I misjudged a man," I said. "Someone I thought was upright wasn't. A lot of damage was done."

Bill's eyes widened. He seemed amazed. "That's exactly the mistake I made. I misjudged a man. Someone I thought was upright wasn't."

I sat down again.

"It really shakes you up, doesn't it?" Bill went on. "Someone you trusted, someone you would have staked your life on. In this case, it was my right-hand man, the man I trusted more than anyone else in the entire company, including my father."

"What did he do?" I asked in a very low voice, and then held my breath. Would I get an answer or wouldn't I?

I did. The last of Bill's resistance disintegrated. "He turned out to be an East German spy," he said.

11

I THOUGHT ABOUT BILL during most of the flight from San Francisco to New York. Mentally I continued the conversation we'd had in his office after we'd got around to comparing notes.

Your predicament is a damn sight worse than mine was, I told him as the plane reached cruising altitude. If mine was painful, yours must be excruciating.

Bits and pieces of his story came back to me, out of sequence. My imagination played with them, putting them in order, supplying little details. This was as close to the truth as I would ever get, I supposed. And basically it *was* the truth.

The spy's name was Alfred Stone. Bill had hired him seven years ago. Although Stone was only thirty-two at the time, he immediately proved to be a skilled problem-solver, a man who could quickly spot an impending bottleneck and prevent it.

His first job at Arden was that of Assistant Production Manager, but Bill soon made him Chief Production Manager, and within two years Stone had the title of Head of Plant Operations. In this position, he was responsible for overseeing everything that went on in the manufacturing end of the business and reported directly to Bill.

In time, Stone became even more important than his title indicated. He became Bill's personal troubleshooter even in areas that had nothing to do with manufacturing—and Bill's closest friend within the company. His confidant. The man with whom he sat up until one in the morning, sharing his innermost thoughts. There was little that went on at Arden Electronics that Stone didn't know about, and virtually nothing, secret or otherwise, that he didn't have access to.

One morning in August, Bill received a visit from two special agents of the FBI. They showed him a small packet of memory chips that Arden had developed for the Manta missile system and asked him to identify them, which he did. They then explained that the chips had been found in the luggage of a man they'd arrested as he was about to board a plane for Switzerland, a man they'd had under surveillance for months. He'd been under surveillance in connection not with Arden but with two other companies that were also suppliers to the Department of Defense. Microfilms of documents belonging to those companies—the evidence they'd been looking for—were also in his luggage. The packet of Arden chips was an unexpected find, a stroke of luck.

Bill was horrified. He'd believed that security in his plant was airtight. Nothing of this sort had ever happened before. He immediately suggested lie-detector tests for all key personnel, starting with himself, and sent for Stone, intending to have him make the arrangements. Whereupon he learned that Stone hadn't come to work that morning.

And Stone hadn't been seen since.

It was no one's fault, really, that Stone got away. Under prolonged questioning, the arrested courier confessed. Stone had given him the chips, he said, and had been delivering classified material to him for years. But this information didn't come out until several days after the arrest, and FBI agents didn't have it at the time they paid their first visit to the plant. Meanwhile, Stone had been warned. His wife said that he'd got a telephone call early on the morning of his disappearance and had left shortly thereafter. She didn't know where he was and she seemed genuinely distraught.

A comprehensive investigation had got under way almost at

once and was still going on. No one knew how much damage Stone had done, but it was apparent that for years he'd been turning over to the East Germans all the vital information he could get his hands on. Furthermore, he'd had the cooperation of many others in the plant. The others hadn't been knowing accomplices, the FBI believed; Stone's position in the company was such, thanks to Bill, that everyone gave him what he asked for without hesitation. Eventually he'd become so sure of himself that he'd used the regular office personnel to photocopy classified diagrams and specifications, and he'd let the security guards examine them at the door when he left the plant. After all, he was Alfred Stone.

Now Arden Electronics was faced with the cancellation of tens of millions of dollars' worth of government contracts—the Pentagon didn't look with favor on suppliers that allowed a weapon as vital to national security as the Manta missile to be compromised. Bill was also afraid that if the affair became public knowledge the company would lose civilian business, too; no one wanted to buy from a source that was suspect.

So far, no public disclosure had been made. The Pentagon was even less anxious than Arden for the world at large to learn what had happened. But other companies in the area knew that something was up; scores of Arden employees had been questioned by the FBI and were talking about it.

Bill held himself responsible for the entire catastrophe. He'd trusted and allowed himself to grow dependent on the wrong person; in his own way, he was as guilty as Stone. He deserved to be fired, he felt. The board of directors was scheduled to meet on Monday. He expected it to request his resignation, and he intended to oblige. Family rivalry wasn't the real problem; he'd placed the company in serious jeopardy and he himself felt he should go.

And perhaps you should, I told him mentally as the DC-10 swept eastward at an altitude of 35,000 feet. Emotionally you're in no shape to manage a business, let alone see it through a crisis of this magnitude.

I debated with him, and with myself, what I should do with the confidences he'd given me. It didn't take us—me—long to decide, however. I couldn't make them public; the way things stood at the moment, that, too, would be a breach of national security, as well as a violation of friendship. All I could do was put an item in Tuesday's market letter recommending that Arden stock be sold. The reasons: policy disagreement at the top level and Pentagon dissatisfaction with recent Arden products.

No, I went on, picturing Bill, the question isn't what I should do but what you yourself should do. Take the damn trip around the world, if that's what you want, but don't pursue an independent investigation.

Here I had to do a lot of guessing, because Bill had only hinted at the steps he'd taken.

He did plan to take a long vacation, but first he intended to act out his own little drama of expiation and revenge. He didn't believe the FBI was trying to catch Stone. In his opinion, they'd given up on that—they were convinced that Stone was already on the other side of the Iron Curtain. What they wanted to know was how much he had given away or sold, and who, inside or outside the company, had collaborated with him. The collaborators within the company, it was turning out, were unwitting ones. And the courier, as Bill referred to him, had little to contribute other than the names of the people who turned material over to him and the Swiss company for whom he worked. The FBI was sure that the Swiss company was an arm of East German intelligence, but the Swiss government refused to believe this or, if they believed it, to do anything about it.

Al wasn't born a spy, Bill had told me; someone had talked him into becoming one. Someone had also given him orders. And someone had assisted in his escape. If he'd fled the country, as the FBI insisted, he'd had help. The State Department had no record of anyone leaving the United States with his name or his passport.

Bill had hired outside investigators. They'd already cost him $20,000, but he didn't care. Money was no object. He wanted to know where Stone had gone, how he'd got there and who had helped him. If he had to follow the trail all the way to East Berlin, he said, he was prepared to do so.

You don't know what you're doing, I told him. Let the FBI handle it—that's what they're there for. Or the CIA. All you're going to do is make a bad matter worse.

Bill was stubborn, though. A Taurus, he'd called himself at one point. A bull. And his investigators had already found out more than the FBI. The FBI had lost the scent at the San Francisco airport. They'd located Stone's car in a parking lot near Market Street and they'd learned that he had taken a taxi from there to the airport, but no one they'd questioned remembered his buying a ticket or getting on a plane. As far as the FBI was concerned, he might have gone north, south, east or west; he'd vanished, and that was that. But Bill's investigators, at a thousand dollars a day, had been more thorough. They were positive that Stone had boarded a plane for New York. They were now combing New York, still at a thousand dollars a day, and Bill said that he intended to join them there as soon as he could.

It was a misguided effort, I'd told him in his office. But I hadn't got anywhere with him then, and now, on the plane, even though I could arrange the conversation to suit myself, I still couldn't get anywhere with him.

And after a while—over Kansas, perhaps—I quit trying. Instead, I began mentally to discuss with him the other aspect of the situation that he found interesting: the similarity between his experience and mine. He believed that the two experiences were related, that both of us were victims of a conspiracy that was larger than we realized.

I didn't disagree, exactly. The espionage efforts of the Warsaw Pact countries did, indeed, amount to a global conspiracy, and industrial espionage was an important part of it. Yet to my way of thinking, the fact that Kevin Rand and Alfred Stone had been working for the East Germans didn't mean that there was any other relationship between them. I doubted that they'd ever heard of each other. All they had in common, it seemed to me, was their service to East Germany.

By chance, I told Bill, he and I had discovered that both of us had been victims of spies who worked for the same government, but that didn't even constitute a coincidence. Everyone knew that the East Germans wanted American industrial secrets and were paying people to steal them. Bill and I were merely two among hundreds who'd been directly affected.

In a way, I said, I was sorry I'd mentioned my own experience; I'd pushed a man who was already too close to the edge one step closer. All the energy, the pride, the single-mindedness and, yes, the neuroses that had gone into building a great company were now going to be used to chase the ghost of a man whose potential for harm was already at an end.

Over Pennsylvania, the plane began its descent, and I stopped thinking about Bill. I set my watch ahead three hours and adjusted my state of mind accordingly. I began to wonder whether I would have time for a quick shower and change of clothes before picking up Carol.

12

MARK AND HIS WIFE were entering the building as Carol and I got out of the taxi. We caught up with them in the lobby and had a little reunion. I hadn't seen Joyce Price since before going to Switzerland, and Carol hadn't seen her in even longer.

"How was California?" Mark asked me.

"Bay Area is in the bag," I told him.

He gave me one of his thin smiles. "Nice work."

Other people trooped into the lobby, obviously headed for the party. One of the men stopped to study the directory on the wall. "They ought to call this place Tax Haven," he said to his friends. "It's all accountants and corporate lawyers."

The Prices, Carol and I followed the crowd into an elevator. We all piled out at the sixth floor, where we were greeted by a bevy of female attendants who were in charge of checking coats and, beyond them, a receiving line of Stiles, Levin and Sullivan partners and their wives. The line appeared to have no end.

Although the firm was called Stiles, Levin and Sullivan, the name was misleading. There were sixteen senior partners, not three, and most of them weren't Stileses, Levins or Sullivans. The full complement, including junior partners, assistants and trainees, added up to about fifty. The firm's new quarters, I'd been told, occupied three entire floors of the building and had cost a million and a half to furnish. As I looked around, I didn't doubt this figure. There was even an interior staircase to connect the three floors, with a balustrade that looked like something from *Gone With the Wind.*

Jonie and his wife were in the first third of the receiving line. We exchanged hellos, and I wished him well in his new lair. There wasn't time to say more, for the line was moving right along.

When Carol and I finally finished all the handshaking, we went in search of drinks, and on the way we encountered Tom's wife, Daisy. She had a highball in her hand.

"Where'd you find the booze?" I asked.

"On the second floor," she replied. "There are half a dozen bars."

I left Carol and Daisy to discuss Carol's new dress, which was as pretty as she'd said, and climbed the stairs. Daisy was right. Six of the largest offices had been converted into bars, and at least six others were being used as buffets. The bartenders and waitresses were in maroon uniforms, and all of them seemed to have been to charm school. I'd never run across such gracious help anywhere. Or been served such large drinks. Stiles, Levin and Sullivan was really laying it on.

After getting Scotches for Carol and myself, I spent a few minutes browsing. Each of the buffets was devoted to a particular type of food. One offered nothing but pâtés, another seafood, a third Chinese appetizers. All of them were doing a brisk business. Although the party had been under way for no more than thirty minutes, the crowd was already large. I saw a number of familiar faces—top executives of major corporations. Stiles, Levin and Sullivan represented at least a dozen companies that were among the *"Fortune* 500" and many more in the category just below it. Represented the companies and/or the individuals who ran them.

Without knowing quite how it happened, I got cornered by a lovely waitress who insisted I try the egg rolls and, when I said I wasn't yet ready to eat, handed me one on a little plate, urging that I "just have a taste." She was so charming about it that I did have a taste, and immediately wolfed down two more egg rolls on the spot.

I carried the drinks downstairs to where Carol and Daisy were. Tom had joined them.

"Now we know where our money went," he remarked.

"Ours and everybody else's," I said.

"Let's go on a tour," Carol suggested. "Daisy says the place is gorgeous."

Tom and Daisy had already seen all they wanted to see, they said, so Carol and I went off by ourselves to inspect the premises.

It took us an hour to make the rounds of the three floors, not because there was so much square footage to cover, but because Carol kept pausing to inspect the furnishings, and I kept stopping to talk to people I knew.

"There must be ten billion dollars' worth of stock wandering around here," Carol observed.

"I wouldn't be surprised," I said.

"You'd think there'd be a conflict of interest."

"The partners try not to take on competing clients," I said, "but sometimes it happens."

And just then, in a minor way, it did. A man tapped me on the shoulder and said, "How's things in the brokerage business?"

The man was Martin Zweifert, one of the heads of Zweifert, Hadley, Jones and Scott, which was known around the Price, Potter and Petacque offices as Big Z. Technically, Big Z wasn't a competitor of ours; it had branch offices in all major cities and catered to the general public. But it also did a large volume with the funds and with banks and had several customers we wished we had, and vice versa.

"Passable," I said. "How're you making out, Marty?"

"We're surviving," he purred, with a patronizing smile. "I heard you were sick or something."

"I recovered," I said airily. "Looks to me like you've put on a bit of weight."

His smile faded, and he moved on.

"I don't think I like that man," Carol murmured.

"There're a lot of people here you wouldn't like if you really knew them," I replied, and added, "and a lot you would."

We worked our way a few yards farther along the thronged corridor and entered one of the small conference rooms. Carol examined a chair, and I examined a picture. The picture was a watercolor by an artist I knew personally.

"Guess how much this fabric costs," Carol said in an awed tone.

"I couldn't," I said, "but that picture set them back at least eight hundred."

"Sixty dollars a yard. I priced it. Let's have another drink."

We started to leave the conference room, but at that moment Nicholas Buck and his wife came in. He was chairman of the board of Prentice Coal. I'd known him when he was treasurer of the company, before he'd moved up to the presidency and then to his present position, but I hadn't seen him in several years.

"Aren't you Brock Potter?" he growled, peering at me nearsightedly.

"Yes," I said, "and this is Miss Fox."

"My wife, Clara," he growled. "Who told you we were going into a joint venture with Darby?"

I'd put Brian's item about Prentice and Darby in last Tuesday's market letter, along with the information that Prentice was going to have the largest profit in its history. "One of my staff," I replied. "Isn't it true?"

He harrumphed.

"What do you think of that picture over there?" I said. "It was painted by a friend of mine."

"Can't see a damn thing with these new glasses," he replied. But he went over to look at it anyway, and while he was doing so, Carol and I slipped out of the room.

"I've never seen a bald-headed teddy bear before," she remarked.

"Teddy bear nothing," I said. "He's a grizzly."

We made our way toward the stairs and ran into General

Quigley, U.S. Army (Retired), who was now what was euphemis-tically called a "liaison man." He worked for King Corporation, which manufactured, among other things, armored vehicles. His main function was entertaining old friends at the Pentagon. I knew him through Tom; he'd attended West Point with Tom's father. We said it was nice to see each other, and he introduced me to his wife, who looked more like a general than he did.

"Do you know everybody in New York," Carol said as we descended the stairs to the second floor, "or does it just seem that way?"

We edged up to one of the bars and got fresh drinks. Tom and Daisy were in the room, along with Mark and Joyce and about twenty other people.

"Mark says you and Gerard got along fine," Tom said. "He says you think it's in the bag."

"Definitely," I said, and added, "I'm going to be on television."

"You *are?*" Carol squealed.

"To a very limited audience." I gave the group an account of the bank's plans for its seminar.

Tom was delighted. Mark was pleased. Carol said I'd have to find a new barber—the way my hair was cut wasn't good enough for television.

"Apparently the receiving line's disbanded," Joyce observed. "I see some of the people I shook hands with, out there in the corri-dor."

"And I'm hungry," Daisy put in. "Let's get something to eat."

"Let's," I agreed. "And let me recommend the egg rolls. They're marvelous."

The six of us went to the Chinese buffet. The waitress who'd served me before served me again—and remembered me. "You must try the baby ribs, too," she said. "In China, this is the year of the pig."

"What do you do when you're not doing this?" I asked her.

"Play the violin," she replied. "I concertize."

I was about to make an appropriate comment, but I was distracted by the grip of a hand on my elbow and a voice that said, acidly, "And here we have the eyes and ears of Price, Potter and Petacque."

It was Herb Minton, and the acidity was typical of him.

"Herb!" I exclaimed with a heartiness I didn't feel.

I felt about Minton the way Irving—and many others—did. In the seven years he'd been president of Seaboard Optics, Minton had made more enemies than most company presidents make in a lifetime. He was a brilliant man, and under his stewardship Seaboard was doing well, but he had a reputation for being the worst son of a bitch in America to work for. He paid top dollar to hire the best talent away from competitors, and then abused it.

Minton stories abounded. Stories about how he telephoned Seaboard executives in the middle of the night to hector them, how he deliberately kept them late at meetings when he knew they had appointments elsewhere, how he humiliated them in front of their co-workers. Some of the executives put up with it, because they couldn't make as much money anywhere else, but many of them didn't. The turnover of hundred-thousand-dollar-a-year types was exceedingly high at Seaboard.

"I didn't know you were a Stiles, Levin and Sullivan client," he said, "or are you merely one of the gate-crashers? I understand a number of them got in."

I forced myself to smile. "We've been with Stiles, Levin and Sullivan from the beginning. Our beginning, that is, not theirs."

"Let me introduce you to Ronald Carris," he said, indicating the man beside him. "Brock Potter—Ron Carris."

"We've met," Carris said, and held out his hand.

I transferred my plate to my other hand, and we shook. I couldn't place him.

"We met at the Seaboard offices five years ago," he reminded me.

Suddenly I remembered. "Of course. You're the headhunter."

"Career consultant," he said affably. "It has a better sound."

"Carris Associates," Minton put in.

Carol, who'd been talking with Daisy and Joyce, joined us. I introduced her to the two men.

"You have the kind of haircut I wish Brock would get," she told Carris.

I looked at his hair. It was nice and long and wavy. Carol is right, I thought. I should get a new barber.

"Actually," Carris said, "I'm the one who's the gate-crasher. Herb and I were having a meeting, and he brought me along."

Now the entire incident came back to me. I realized why I hadn't been able to remember it before. It had been too unpleasant.

Irving Silvers had been following Seaboard in those days, and he'd infuriated Minton. From one of his sources at Seaboard, Irving had learned that NATO wasn't happy with a new Seaboard night-scope for automatic rifles—during field exercises in Germany, the troops had found the scope unsatisfactory. Irving had checked the story with sources outside the company, who said it was true. He reported it at one of our staff meetings, and since the NATO contract involved a lot of money, I mentioned the story in a market letter. Minton found out and was livid. He demanded that Irving tell him who the source was. Irving refused. Minton threatened to bar him and all Price, Potter and Petacque people from Seaboard facilities.

In an attempt to straighten things out, I went to see Minton. He kept me waiting in the anteroom outside his office for an hour and a half, and it was during this time that I met Carris. Carris also had an appointment with Minton. The two of us got acquainted. Then Carris, who'd arrived after I had, was summoned into Minton's office, while I was left to cool my heels—a deliberate act of rudeness on Minton's part.

I'd appeased Minton by letting him tell me off and agreeing to have someone else—George Cole—keep up with Seaboard. I'd been furious at myself afterward for doing so, but the results had been good. On the basis of material George had gathered, I'd recommended Seaboard stock, and our customers had profited. But I still didn't like Herb Minton. In my opinion, he was living proof that bad guys often win.

Having thrown his little dart about gate-crashing, he was now prepared to be nice. He hoped to have some interesting news for me soon, he said.

Recalling what George had reported at our last staff meeting, I was tempted to ask whether the good news concerned lasers. I didn't, though. I merely said, "Fine."

Jonie Stiles appeared in the doorway, saw us and came over. "Having a good time?" he asked.

"It's a lovely party," Carol replied.

Minton introduced Carris to him and said, "I hope you don't mind my bringing a freeloader."

"The more the merrier," said Jonie. "Today's freeloader may be tomorrow's client."

Carris smiled. "Thank you. And since I'm freeloading, I think I'll have some of those ribs." He went over to the buffet table.

"Speaking of clients," I said to Jonie, "I almost got you a new one last night. Bill Arden."

I hadn't seen Martin Zweifert standing nearby. But now, drink in one hand, plate in the other, he turned around and came a step closer. "Bill Arden?" he inquired.

I ignored him. "Unfortunately," I said to Jonie, "I wasn't able to pull it off."

Unfazed, Zweifert said, "I've been hearing rumblings about Arden."

Carol tugged on my arm and said, "Come on, let's get some seafood."

I allowed myself to be led out of the room.

"Did you see how that man looked at you?" Carol asked.

"Which man?"

"The one you said has put on weight. I just know he was getting ready to pump you, and I didn't think you wanted to be pumped." She paused. "Who's Bill Arden?"

"A man I was with yesterday. It was kind of depressing."

We went into the room where the seafood was being served and spent ten minutes nibbling. Since there was no one around whom I knew, we talked without interruption. About Carol's activities. She'd reorganized the closet in her bedroom, and it was much better now. Perry, her boss, had interviewed two more people for the job of sales manager but hadn't hired either of them. Then she fell silent.

"You're thinking," I said.

"About you," she confessed. "You're so obvious at times, Brock. Anyone can read your face. Like a little while ago."

"Oh?"

"You don't like that Mr. Minton, do you?"

I shook my head. "Did it show?"

"And how!"

"Well, I don't. He's a confirmed sadist."

Mark wandered into the room. "I've been looking for you two," he said. "Tom and Daisy are coming over to our place. How about joining us?"

Carol and I said we would love to.

So presently the six of us left the party and went uptown to the Prices', where we took off our shoes and passed an enjoyable two hours talking about the people we'd seen and discussing whether, to keep up with the Joneses, we should buy new chairs for the foyer at our office. Tom and I thought we should. But Mark, who has more money than most of the people who'd been at the party, was opposed. His argument, as usual, was that it would cost too much.

The party had been nice, I thought, but this was nicer. I felt none of the crosscurrents of hostility here that I'd felt there.

13

My up cycle, if that was what it was, continued into the following week. Everything went right.

On Monday, Davis Computer, which I'd recommended in July and then begun to worry about, went up three and an eighth and led the "Most Active" list; Amalgamated Investors Services gave us sell orders totaling 75,000 shares and buy orders totaling almost as many; and, to Tom's and my utter astonishment, Mark announced that he'd changed his mind about chairs for the foyer—he thought we should get some new ones.

At our staff meeting that morning, I took up twenty minutes of the group's time with an account of my trip. Reporting on the situation at Arden was tougher than I'd imagined. I didn't feel I could tell the whole truth even to my staff, yet I didn't want to lie. So I presented the same story I intended to include in Tuesday's market letter—policy disagreements and Pentagon displeasure.

But I spoke more slowly than usual and hesitated frequently, and my staff wasn't taken in. Joe Rothland seemed to be voicing the opinion of all five when he said, "Isn't there more to this than you're telling us, Brock?"

I leveled with them. "Yes, there is. But I've given you the gist. Everything else is incidental." I then went on to the next point. I said I'd seen Herb Minton on Friday and he'd told me he would soon have some interesting news.

"It's lasers," George said. "I've been checking. He's hired a man named Jerome who's supposed to be a genius when it comes to mirrors and light refraction."

"Can you be more specific?" I asked.

George became dreamy-eyed. "Seaboard is working on a helium-neon laser. The light is reflected around the tube by an unusual placement of mirrors, not like it is in conventional lasers. To get the light to move in exactly the right way requires people with special talent."

"What's the object?" Brian asked.

"Greater precision," George replied.

"I don't mean that," said Brian. "I mean, what's it for?"

"Any number of things. Aircraft and missile guidance systems, to name two. To sense variations in altitude."

"I feel sorry for the guy who got hired," Irving said sourly.

"Any big contracts involved?" I asked.

"I should think so," George replied.

"Stay on it," I said. "It may soon be time to recommend Seaboard again."

George nodded, and we proceeded to another topic.

All in all, it was a productive session, I thought.

That afternoon I tried to put some time in on the list of securities Bob Gerard had given me. I was repeatedly interrupted by telephone calls, however, so I took the computer printout home with me and worked on it after dinner.

With Tiger at my feet and a snifter of cognac at my elbow, I studied the list until almost eleven o'clock and came up with some ideas I believed were sound. Then, after putting the printout back in my attaché case, I poured myself a final ounce of cognac and leaned back in my chair. I had a feeling of satisfaction. I'd come a long way since the end of August, I thought. And things might just as easily have gone in the opposite direction. I might have become a victim of burnout, like a number of men I knew. Instead, here I was, back in the mainstream, as involved as ever—and having a good time.

A good time? I asked myself. Is that really what this is?

And, for once in my life, the little voice that answers such questions came back with a firm yes. I was doing what I liked to do, among people I was fond of, and I was doing it well. Nothing could be better.

Even my relationship with Carol was improving, I acknowledged. We would never be the ideal couple, but what we had was above average.

The work I did on Monday night paid off on Tuesday. Gerard telephoned, and I gave him my ideas. He seemed genuinely enthused about them.

After we'd talked for a while, he asked me to transfer the call to Ward Carlton, which I did. Five minutes later, my telephone rang again; Gerard had asked Ward to transfer the call back to me.

"I got so carried away," he said, "that I forgot to tell you. Everything's set. We've leased half an hour for you on ManSat. Six to six-thirty, New York time, October the fifth. Jonathan Dickson will be your director."

"Director?" I repeated, dazed.

"Television director. We've hired him to handle your segment. He'll be in touch with you to work everything out."

Still dazed, I said, "All right," and the conversation ended.

Ward and Tom burst into my office. Both of them were flushed with excitement. Gerard wanted Ward to be in San Francisco the first of next week, and was talking big figures.

I was too preoccupied to share their excitement fully. "They've leased a half hour for me on a satellite," I said. "I'm going to have my own director. What the hell am I going to say?"

"You'll think of something," Tom said confidently.

He and Ward returned to the sales department to continue congratulating each other.

I went on thinking about the seminar. Satellite time cost plenty.

And television directors didn't come cheap, either. I would have to give an especially good performance to make it all worthwhile.

And later, on the way home, instead of studying the closing stock prices in the afternoon paper, as I usually did, I found myself wondering where I could find a really good barber.

14

"INMATE CONFESSES TO PRISON SLAYING," the headline said.

Apparently, now that Kevin Rand was dead, he was no longer considered newsworthy. You had to read the text of the article to learn that he'd been the victim, and the entire piece, including the headline, was hardly more than a filler—an inch and a half at the bottom of a page, next to an ad for men's topcoats. I might not have even seen it if I hadn't needed a new topcoat.

But I did see it. And it did affect me. When the cabin attendant came down the aisle with the beverage cart, I ordered a double Scotch.

There were few facts in the article. The murderer's name was Jimbuck Kincaid, and he was already serving a term for murder. The other particulars pertained to the FBI, which had conducted the investigation, and to Kevin—his crime, the date of his conviction, the length of his term, the date of the stabbing.

Since no specifics about Kincaid were given, I made up my own. I decided he was a country boy from the South who'd robbed a gas station or a grocery store and shot the proprietor. I pictured him as a tall, rangy man in his twenties with stringy blond hair, mean little eyes and arms like a gorilla's. Also as mentally unstable. A psychopath who smiled while killing.

The Scotch didn't help. I arrived in Atlanta feeling depressed. And the three hours I spent there didn't do anything to improve my mood.

The purpose of my trip was to meet with the President of Barton-Brickstein, a manufacturer of emission-control devices that was under siege—Herndon International was trying to take it over. I wanted to find out how good Herndon's chances really were.

They were very good, I learned. The President of Barton-Brickstein was beside himself. He talked nonstop the entire time I was with him about the treachery of the Herndon people, the infidelity of stockholders and—reluctantly—his own mistakes. Once or twice his voice broke. I felt sorry for him, but I was glad to get away.

Instead of making notes on Barton-Brickstein, I reread the article about Kevin several more times on the flight back to New York and let my thoughts wander.

They didn't wander anyplace nice. I saw Kevin on the day he won the state swimming meet; Adele and Sean in the living room of my house; Kevin learning to drive a car; Roman carving a Thanksgiving turkey; and a tall, rangy man with a sick smile.

It was pouring when I got back to New York. I had to stand in line for thirty minutes at La Guardia to get a cab, and when I did get one, the traffic was terrible. I arrived home tired, hungry and dispirited. To make matters worse, the fricassee of veal Louise had made wasn't as good as usual.

A telephone call from Carol interrupted the lackluster meal. She'd seen the item about Kevin's murderer and wanted to know whether we should do anything.

"Like what?" I asked.

"Call Adele, maybe. Express our—I don't know, I just thought maybe we should let her know we know."

I recalled what Jonie had said about Adele's spreading the guilt. "I intend to keep my distance, Carol. Now and forever more."

"Well, it was just a thought."

I changed the subject. "How about dinner tomorrow night? I'm going to be in town."

"I don't know if I'll be through in time," she said. "I'll call you tomorrow afternoon."

We left it at that.

I went to bed early, and when I woke on Thursday it was still raining. I didn't mind, though. The depression I'd felt the day before was gone. I was prepared to provide my own sunshine.

15

THE FIRST TELEPHONE CALL I received that morning was from Hardin Webster. The second was from Martin Zweifert. Both men were probing. They wanted to know about Arden Electronics.

Hardin had received my market letter the previous morning and ten minutes after reading it he'd heard that Bill Arden had resigned. "That's more than coincidence," he said.

"Of course it is," I replied. "I spent some time with Bill last week. He told me what was going to happen." And I couldn't resist adding, "When it comes to being in the right place at the right time, nobody beats Price, Potter and Petacque."

With Zweifert it was different. For one thing, he'd never called me before. For another, he tried to be cute. He said I seemed to have been hiding under some strange boardroom tables lately and mentioned three other companies before getting around to Arden. But at last he swallowed his pride and asked, "What's really going on out there, Brock?"

I told him what I'd told everyone else. After all, he had his own research department, and it was a lot bigger than mine. Let it hide under a few boardroom tables itself.

The truth was, I suspected, that Zweifert had a large position in Arden and was worried about his investment.

At noon I knocked off for a long lunch with Bruno Langleider.

Bruno was one of the top investment analysts at the private banking firm of Malther, Zimmer, in Zürich. I'd met him at the conference there and had liked him. The two of us had swapped some ideas, and when he'd mentioned that he would soon be in New York, I'd invited him to have lunch with me so we could continue swapping.

I told him about my upcoming talk on investment policy for the decade ahead, and picked his brains. He felt, as I did, that the actions of governments were the key to understanding the future, and this was something he was well equipped to talk about. The Swiss had always had to go abroad to do most of their investing —there weren't enough investment opportunities in their own country. For years they'd been viewing elections, revolutions and coups with a dispassionate eye, calculating the effect of these events on their money. Bruno's own particular bent was more psychological than political, however. He believed that the actions of governments were the result of the actions of people. If enough people wanted something—right or wrong—and wanted it badly enough, they would eventually get it.

"How many forecasters twenty years ago predicted that Japan would become the world's largest producer of automobiles?" he asked, rhetorically. "Very few. Or that New York City bonds would be a cause for anxiety? Or that your American landscape would be dotted with unfinished and abandoned nuclear power plants? Yet in terms of psychology all of these events were predictable. Prosperity made Americans self-indulgent and immature."

"We landed men on the moon," I pointed out.

"True," he admitted. "But today, in the bathrooms and parking lots of some of your beautiful new factories, one smells marijuana. We are not talking about what Americans are capable of doing, Brock. We are talking about what they may soon be incapable of doing." He paused. "I wouldn't be on this trip if I didn't think America has a good future. But I do worry at times. When I read of the millions of tons of narcotics that are sold in your country each year, I wonder how stable the American people really are."

When we finally separated, at three-fifteen, I felt refreshed. I didn't agree with everything Bruno had said, but he'd stimulated my thinking. Investment policy for the decade ahead, I realized, depended not only on economic trends but also on moral ones—I would have to take that into consideration.

Shortly after I returned to the office, I heard from Jonathan Dickson. He wanted to know about my living quarters. It would be more interesting, he believed, to do the telecast from my house. Could he look the house over?

I gave him the address and told him my housekeeper would show him around.

Then, at four o'clock, Carol called. She was still tied up with the same customer, she said, but she expected to be through around five. If I wanted her to come for dinner, she would.

"Great," I said, and after hanging up I called Louise, to check on the food situation.

The food situation was only fair, Louise reported. She'd made some of her special cornbread, but she'd only defrosted one steak. "Bestest thing I can do, if Miz Fox be comin', is run out an' buy 'nother," she said.

I accepted this solution and hoped that the butcher shop wasn't crowded. Louise was an excellent housekeeper, but she was inflexible about her hours. Four-thirty was quitting time, and if she hadn't bought the steak by then, we wouldn't have it. "By the way," I said, "a man named Jonathan Dickson will be stopping by in the next few days. He's a television director and he wants to look around. It's all right to let him in."

Louise uttered an "um" that indicated limited approval, and put down the telephone.

Brian Barth popped into my office, looking pleased. "We got in just under the wire," he said. "Arden Electronics dropped two and three-quarters yesterday and another one and seven-eighths today."

"You were on the ball," I acknowledged.

"So were you," he replied.

We exchanged a smile, and he popped out of my office as abruptly as he'd popped in.

I thought of Martin Zweifert and wondered how much the past two days had cost him.

The rain had stopped by the time I left the office. I had no difficulty in getting a cab and arrived home shortly after five.

There were two steaks on the kitchen table, and in the refrigerator I found a platter of sliced tomatoes and onions. But evidently the clock had run out before the second potato was completely ready for the deep fryer; instead of being peeled and cut into strips, it was merely disfigured. I picked it up and finished the job.

Carol arrived at exactly five-thirty. "I need a drink," she said as she came through the doorway. "I'm absolutely done in. I couldn't have stood it another minute."

I returned to the kitchen for some ice cubes, and while I was taking them from the tray, the telephone rang. I answered it and immediately recognized the voice at the other end of the line as Bill Arden's.

16

"THERE'LL BE SOMEONE joining us," I said as I handed Carol her drink.

"Oh, no!" she groaned. "I look awful."

"You look fine. We'll have to go out to eat, though. There isn't enough for three."

She stooped to pet Tiger. "Is it anyone I know?"

"No. His name is Bill Arden."

"Sounds familiar," Carol said, frowning. She stood up.

"He's one of the people I spent time with last week, on the Coast."

The frown disappeared. "Now I remember. You said it was depressing."

"Did I? Well, it was. And it's liable to be again. He's kind of disturbed emotionally."

"Really?" Carol's face lit up. "Maybe I can give him some insight. Depending on the problem, of course."

"The problem is, he just got fired."

"Oh."

We carried our drinks into the den. Tiger followed us.

I thought about what Bill had said.

He'd sounded very agitated. "God, Brock, I'm glad you're home! We have to talk! The two cases are related—I'm almost positive! Tomorrow I'm going to the FBI!"

"Where are you?" I'd asked. "Are you in New York?"

"Of course I'm in New York! I said I was coming, didn't I? I'm at a pay phone on Fifth Avenue and Forty-ninth or Fiftieth or something. Near Rockefeller Center. I can be at your place in fifteen minutes. Wait there. We'll compare notes. The whole thing is very big, I think." With that, Bill had hung up.

I dropped into my favorite chair. Tiger planted himself at my feet, with one paw on my shoe.

The evening was going to be difficult, I thought. The two cases Bill had spoken of were undoubtedly those of Kevin Rand and Alfred Stone. He'd been overwrought—he was liable to blurt out something crazy in front of Carol. I wished I'd had the presence of mind to put him off.

"Try to be understanding," I said, by way of preparing her. "He may talk a bit wild."

It was the wrong remark to have made. Carol began to look even more interested than before. "Wild—how?" she asked.

I ducked the question. "Think of a place we can go for dinner. I'll make a reservation. Someplace quiet."

"Wild—how?"

"I don't know. We'll just have to wait and see. He said he'd be here in fifteen minutes. Ever heard of Jonathan Dickson?"

"Wild—how, Brock?"

"Jonathan Dickson is a television director. He's going to direct me on that television thing I'm doing. They've leased time for me on a satellite."

The diversion worked. "How exciting!" Carol exclaimed.

"He wants to do the filming here at the house."

Carol eyed the room critically. "You ought to be sitting at your desk, I think. You'll have to clear it, though—it looks terrible. And you'll have to hide that dreadful whiskey decanter. People will think you're a lush."

"It belonged to my grandfather."

"Even so." Carol glanced at her watch. "I'd better see what I can do with my face."

She left. However, instead of going to the upstairs bathroom where she kept a supply of cosmetics, she went to the powder room on the first floor. I guessed that haste was responsible for the choice; she didn't intend to miss a single minute of Bill's visit. After all, he was emotionally disturbed.

I had a sudden sense of foreboding. "I wish he weren't coming," I told Tiger.

Tiger gave the rug a couple of thumps with his tail. I picked him up. He licked my hand.

"I won't let him involve me," I said as I put Tiger down.

Carol soon reappeared. "Now I feel better. Why so glum?"

I shrugged.

"Let's go to Linguini," she suggested. Linguini was an Italian restaurant on Fifty-second Street. It was named after its specialty.

"O.K.," I said. "I'll make a reservation."

I got up to go to the telephone, but at that moment the doorbell rang.

Carol followed me into the foyer.

"Brock! Christ! Am I glad to see *you!*" Bill's eyes were aglow, his face was flushed, and he sounded slightly out of breath.

"Come in," I said. "Calm down. Give me your coat. This is Miss Fox—Carol."

Bill's face fell. "I thought—" He recovered. "How do you do."

The two of them shook hands. I escorted Bill into the den and offered him a drink.

"Good idea," he said. "I need one." He glanced uneasily at Carol, who'd joined us. With a third party present, he seemed at a loss.

"It's so nice to meet you," she said in her warmest tone. "Brock and I were just talking about where to eat. I hope you like Italian food, but if not . . ."

Bill turned back to me. I'd put ice cubes in a glass and was waiting for him to tell me what to pour on top of them. "Er— bourbon," he said. Then he noticed Tiger. "A poodle. My wife breeds poodles."

I gave him a large drink, and he sat down. Things might work out after all, I thought. He won't confide in me as long as Carol is here. And if he doesn't confide in me, I can't become involved. "Cheers," I proposed.

We drank. Then Bill put his glass down and held out his hand to Tiger. "Come here, little guy."

Tiger went over to get acquainted. Bill's expression became less intense.

I started to mention his resignation, but decided not to—it might trigger something.

His glance traveled from me to Carol and back again. "Terrible weather today," he said, obviously inhibited by Carol's presence.

"Brock tells me you're from California," she said. "What part?"

"We have a house down the peninsula from San Francisco," he replied.

"I've been to San Francisco," she said. "It's a delightful city. So cosmopolitan. Tell me about your house."

Her voice was different from usual. So was the expression on her face. She seemed to be making a conscious effort to appear sympathetic, interested and detached all at the same time. At first I was puzzled. Then I realized what was going on; she was conducting her version of a psychiatric interview.

I smiled. And felt a sudden rush of affection for her. She was really trying to help.

Bill allowed himself to be drawn out. He told her about his house, his wife, her poodles. I sensed that he was functioning on two levels simultaneously. On one, he was the old Bill Arden, in possession of himself, socially adept; on the other, an unstrung, excited man with something urgent on his mind. But the latter came through only at intervals, when he shot me looks that begged me to get rid of Carol so that we could talk confidentially.

I didn't intend to do anything of the sort. The less I knew, the safer I was. Let him take his troubles to the FBI. That was the place for them.

But as Carol went on playing psychiatrist, I found myself

becoming increasingly curious about what Bill wanted to tell me. Evidently he'd learned something about Alfred Stone that he considered important to me as well as to himself. Evidently he'd found, or thought he'd found, some link between Stone and Kevin. What could the link be? Perhaps I should let him tell me. It wouldn't hurt to listen.

I began to vacillate.

From time to time Carol gave me furtive, and puzzled, glances. I guessed that she wasn't finding Bill as disturbed as I'd led her to believe.

I refilled our glasses, and the charade went on, with Carol doing her best to be Dr. Yarborough and Bill struggling with his split-level self. I stayed on the sidelines and continued to debate whether or not to break my promise to myself and hear Bill out.

After a while, my curiosity won. After dinner, I decided, I would take Bill aside and give him a chance to unburden himself.

Carol eventually brought the conversation back to its starting point. "There's a lovely little Italian place Brock and I sometimes go to," she said to Bill. "They serve a linguini with clam sauce that's out of this world. We were planning to go there tonight. If you don't like Italian food, though, they have very good steaks."

"After dinner, you and I'll talk," I told him.

He heaved a deep sigh of relief. "Any kind of food's all right with me," he said.

We went into the foyer and began putting on our coats.

"It's almost theater time," I said. "It may take us a few minutes to get a cab."

"Our best chance is on Sixth Avenue," said Carol. "It's northbound."

I opened the front door. West Eleventh Street was dark and quiet.

"Did you make a reservation?" Carol asked, as a reminder that I hadn't.

"It probably isn't necessary," I said. "They know us there."

"Even so," she said. "Remember last time."

The last time we'd gone to Linguini, we'd shown up without a reservation and had had to wait nearly an hour.

"All right," I said. "You two go ahead and see if you can get a cab. I'll catch up with you."

The two of them went down the front steps. I returned to the den, looked up the number of the restaurant and dialed.

Mario, the owner, said, "No trouble, Mr. Potter."

"We'll be there in a few minutes," I assured him. I put down the telephone and headed out of the house for the second time.

And that was when I heard the screams. They were coming from a figure who was sitting on the bottom step of a house near Sixth Avenue. One high, piercing feminine shriek followed another.

Stretched out on the sidewalk near the woman were what appeared to be two human forms.

I raced down the steps and turned toward Sixth Avenue.

The shrieks continued.

A man emerged from the doorway behind the woman, rushed to her side and put an arm around her. Several people had stopped at the corner of Eleventh Street and Sixth Avenue to see what was happening, but no one approached the bodies.

I reached the spot where they lay. One was Bill, the other was Carol. Carol saw me and tried to raise her head, but couldn't. I dropped to my knees and took her hand.

The woman on the step stopped screaming and began to moan. "Someone tried to kill me, someone tried to kill me, take me home, please take me home."

Bill's eyes were open, but there was no sign of life.

"Take me upstairs," the woman moaned. "Please take me upstairs. Someone tried to kill me."

Carol made another attempt to raise her head, and again failed. I slid my arm under her shoulders and felt it becoming moist. She murmured something, but I couldn't hear what it was. A froth of blood came from her lips. I put my ear close to them.

"Don't let me die," Carol said, and a moment later she went limp.

I looked around. The woman was still sitting on the step, holding her head. The man was trying to get her to stand up. The crowd at the corner had got larger, but no one came to lend a hand.

I jumped to my feet, ran to the corner, pushed my way through the crowd and rushed into the traffic on Sixth Avenue, waving my arms and calling for help.

Two cars swerved to avoid me and kept going. The driver of a third jammed on his brakes and stopped his car inches from my hip. He flung the door open and jumped out. "What's the matter?" he shouted. "You crazy?"

"Call an ambulance!" I yelled. "There's been a shooting!"

He went into the deli at the corner and used the telephone.

17

Dazed, I looked around. There was a huge bridge to my right. Approach ramps. Cars. Old buildings with stores on the ground floor. Beyond the old buildings, high-rises.

Suddenly I realized where I was, and was astounded. I was at Fifty-ninth Street and First Avenue, with no idea how I'd got there, except that I'd walked. My last clear recollection was of leaving Saint Vincent's Hospital in the predawn.

Five minutes to eight, my watch said. Evidently I'd been walking for three hours. Just walking. And this was where I'd ended up.

I was very tired. And hungry. And I wanted to go to the bathroom. Someone at the hospital had brought me coffee not once but twice. I hadn't had anything to eat, however, since . . . I couldn't quite remember.

The doctors—one doctor in particular—had been quite nice. I couldn't remember the names of the doctors, either. Not even the nice one. I guessed he was one of the surgeons, though; he'd been wearing a green gown and cap, and the gown had been stained with blood.

Unexpectedly, his name popped into my head. Feinstein. He'd had a peculiar look on his face. Almost exalted. The look of a man who'd spent hours doing battle with death and felt that, for the time being at least, he'd won. It had been a difficult operation, he'd said. They'd removed fragments of the scapula, the big bone against which one of the bullets had lodged, and they'd removed the bullet, and they'd reinflated the lung, and replaced the blood loss.

I remembered, now, what I'd said when he'd told me. I'd said, "You look too young to have done all that."

And I remembered his reply: "I didn't do it by myself."

I wondered what had prompted my remark. I supposed it was because I was older than he, and because I'd been so aware of my own helplessness. Carol had said, "Don't let me die." Yet I hadn't been able to do anything to keep her alive. If she lived, it would be because of Feinstein and the other doctors.

There was no assurance, however, that she would live. All Dr. Feinstein had told me was "She has a fighting chance" and "She seems to be a strong woman." But he'd also told me that she'd sustained a terrible injury. Two bullets in the left lung. One had gone all the way through her; the other had lodged against the scapula. It was a miracle that she'd survived the operation. Luckily St. Vincent's was only two blocks away from the scene of the shooting; the operation had been performed with a minimum of delay.

Bill hadn't been that lucky. He'd been shot four times, and two of the bullets had punctured his heart. He'd probably been dead before hitting the sidewalk.

Gazing at the Queensboro Bridge and all the cars, I wondered what I should do, where I should go. I couldn't just stand there. After a moment, I began to walk again. Presently I came to a coffee shop, went in and sat down at the counter. When the waitress asked me what I wanted, I said, "Strawberry cheesecake and coffee, and where's the men's room?"

Returning to the counter, I saw the coffee and cheesecake waiting for me and I was puzzled. I couldn't understand why I'd ordered strawberry cheesecake; I didn't really like it. The power of suggestion, I supposed. I'd seen the cake on the shelf behind the counter and hadn't been able to think of anything else.

I wanted to tell the waitress about Carol and Bill, and ask her opinion. Would it have made any difference if Carol and Bill had walked toward Fifth Avenue instead of Sixth? I also wanted to ask her opinion about human nature. Why was it that with a dozen people looking on, no one had volunteered to help or even to approach the two victims?

The waitress was busy, however. She was putting a new filter in the coffee machine. So I merely mumbled, "People are strange," not expecting a reply and not receiving one.

Most likely, Carol's mother was already at the airport, I thought. She'd said she would take the first plane. She'd been calmer than I'd imagined she would be. But then, I'd been unnaturally calm myself at that point. I'd merely said, "Mrs. Fox, this is Brock Potter. There's been an accident. Carol's been hurt. They're operating on her right now. She's at Saint Vincent's Hospital, on West Twelfth Street. You'd better come." And she'd said, "Thank you for calling, Brock. I'll take the first plane." That had been the extent of our stunted conversation.

Why, I wondered, if I'd been clearheaded then, did I feel so confused now? How could I have walked so far without noticing where I was? Why couldn't I make up my mind about what to do next? When had the confusion set in?

"More coffee," I said to the waitress.

She refilled my cup and added another fifty cents to the check.

My memory of events at the hospital was unclouded. I'd been coherent the whole time I was there. I'd even volunteered to call Bill's wife, to break the news. The call had been a difficult one, but I'd coped.

I'd coped with the policemen, too. I'd given my version of what had happened, and had answered as many questions as I could. I'd suggested that they get in touch with the FBI for more information on Bill, and had told them why.

Sylvia May, the woman who'd been sitting on the step screaming, had been the only eyewitness, it seemed, and she wasn't a good one. She was convinced that she'd been the intended victim. She'd had an altercation with a terrible-looking man on the subway a short time before. He'd pushed her, and she'd told him what she thought of men who pushed women. She was sure that he'd followed her from the subway station at Fourteenth Street and had shot at her as she reached the building where she lived. The shooting never would have occurred, she insisted, if her husband had been with her or if she'd taken the bus.

Mrs. May had been questioned in her apartment; I, at the hospital. But after a while a Detective Lindsey, who'd been part of the team questioning her, had come to the hospital to talk with me. He'd given me her story. It didn't exactly jibe with such evidence as there was, he'd admitted. Mrs. May, as near as could be determined, had been fifteen or twenty feet away from Bill and Carol; it wasn't likely that a person shooting at her would have hit them —not six times, and not at such close range.

Mrs. May had described the man she'd had the run-in with on the subway—and had already changed the description twice. With each revision he'd become taller and more menacing. Lindsey was hoping that Carol would be able to provide a more accurate description—if she lived.

If she lived.

I finished my second cup of coffee and sat there, thinking. Scenes from my life with Carol kept appearing in my mind. And I remembered various occasions when Bill and I had been together.

Questions occurred to me. I couldn't answer any of them. I did reach one conclusion, however; that there was nothing random about what had happened on the sidewalk down the block from my house. It was merely one link in a chain of events. And I had a hunch that the chain had been started many years before, when a professor of economics told me I couldn't take his course.

I considered the chain of events for a few minutes. Then I got up from the counter, paid my check and left the coffee shop.

From Grand Central Station, I called my office to say I wouldn't be in and to ask Helen to cancel my appointments for the day.

There was a local leaving for Stamford in twelve minutes, the man at the information kiosk told me.

I went to the platform and boarded the train.

18

A SLENDER WOMAN with a young face and prematurely gray hair opened the door on its safety chain and eyed me with doubt. "Yes?"

"I'm Brock Potter," I said. "May I come in?"

She considered the request for what seemed a long time. I supposed I didn't match her conception of what Brock Potter looked like. Finally she unhooked the safety chain and opened the door wider. "I'm Rosalie Rand," she said.

A man's voice, somewhere in the house, made a statement about clogged drains.

Rosalie kept eyeing me as if she didn't believe I was who I said I was. But then Adele came into the foyer and saw me.

"Brock!" Adele cried. "My dear! I've been trying to reach you!"

Rosalie stepped aside.

"I read in this morning's paper," Adele began. "I—heavens, your eyes are all red—you must be exhausted." She took my arm and led me into the living room.

"I know I should have called first," I said, "but I just, well, got on a train and came."

I discovered the source of the statement about clogged drains: The television set was on. Now a young woman was talking about a cooking oil that was low in saturated fats.

Rosalie turned the set off.

Adele escorted me to a sectional sofa, and we sat down. I was extremely weary.

"I read about Carol, about your terrible experience," Adele said. "I called your house, your office. I'm dreadfully sorry, my dear."

I sighed. Adele took both my hands and held them. I tried to organize my thoughts. Finally I said, "I stayed at the hospital until they moved her from the recovery room to intensive care. But that's not what I want to talk about. I want to talk about Kevin."

"Of course," said Adele. "We'll talk about anything you'd like. But first let me make you some coffee. You look awful."

"I had coffee a few hours ago. Let's just talk."

She nodded.

Rosalie seated herself on another section of the U-shaped unit.

Again I tried to organize my thoughts. On the train I'd framed questions and put them in order; my head had been clear. But now the confusion was back. I kept seeing Carol being wheeled out of the operating room. "About the man who killed Kevin," I said. "I was on a plane, going to Atlanta. You see, I needed a new topcoat. I mean, the article was there, in the paper. I . . . Excuse me, I'll be all right in a minute."

"I think we'd *better* have some coffee," Rosalie said. She got up and left the room.

I started over. "The man who killed Kevin—what can you tell me about him?"

"No rhyme or reason," Adele said sadly. "He just—killed him. Or so the FBI would have us believe. Sean spoke to Kevin's lawyer, asked him to find out what he could. For our peace of mind. But the FBI doesn't seem to feel it's any of our business."

I forced myself to concentrate. "Jimbuck Kincaid. Sounds like a hillbilly."

"Not exactly," said Adele. "He's from Texas—a small town in Texas. Apparently he's been in and out of prisons for years."

"Then you do know something about him?"

She shrugged. "A little. It hasn't caused me to change my views any, though. They'd have us think he had a grudge against Kevin for some reason, but I still believe it was a deliberate murder planned outside the prison to keep Kevin from telling what he knew."

"You'd expect, then, that money would be involved. Yet what good is money to a man who's serving a long prison sentence? Was he due for parole soon? The article didn't say."

Adele released my hands. She frowned. "I don't know, but I doubt it—he's only twenty-nine. Suppose he did receive money —then what?"

"If he received money, and I could find out where the money is, I might be able to trace it back to where it came from."

"Ah." Adele smiled. "You haven't changed, Brock. You still see solutions in terms of money, and simplistically. I don't know how one goes about tracing money back to its source, but I should think it's very difficult and, when foreign governments are involved, almost impossible."

Rosalie returned with a coffeepot, mugs and all the accessories. She began to pour, but Adele went on talking.

"The man who murdered my son is what we used to call a 'ne'er-do-well,' " she said, "but even ne'er-do-wells have weak spots. I don't know what crimes he committed in his twenty-nine years, what he got caught at or didn't get caught at, but I do know that somewhere he has a wife and child, and I'm willing to believe he loves them. Perhaps they're the only people in his entire wretched life he ever has loved."

"So the money could have gone to them. Is that what you're saying? Well, it doesn't make any difference. I may see things simplistically, but I do know something about tracing money, and what I don't know I can find out. I—"

"What I'm saying, Brock, is that money may not be involved at all. Someone may have threatened to harm his wife or child. How do you intend to trace *that?*"

I had no answer.

Adele handed me a mug of coffee. "Here. Drink this." Her

expression softened. "Apparently you've had a change of heart. You now want to know how Kevin came to do what he did. I'm glad. I'd like some good to come from all the bad. But I don't think you'll get anywhere by trying to trace money. I think what you'll have to do is examine your friendships."

"That's what you said before. But I can't, Adele. I know too many people. I wouldn't know where to start."

There was a long silence.

"Tell me about what happened last night," Adele said at last.

I gave her an abbreviated account of the shooting. "It could have been a random crime," I concluded. "Some demented character might just have walked up to Bill and Carol and shot them because God told him to, or something. There's no evidence to the contrary. But I have a hunch that wasn't the case."

The two women looked at me.

"Why?" Adele asked.

"I'd told Bill about Kevin. He knew something about spies."

"So, because of that . . . ?"

"More or less." She was right about tracing the money, I decided; that road was littered with too many obstacles. But there was another road. "Tell me about Hattie Sargent," I said. "Does she still live in Boston?"

Both women appeared surprised.

"As far as I know," Rosalie said.

"She and Kevin broke up, then?" I asked.

"Yes. Before Kevin moved to North Carolina."

I'd only met Hattie twice. Once, briefly, in New York, when she and Kevin had come there for a weekend; and once in Boston, at Kevin's apartment. They'd been living together for some time. Hattie was a scholar and, I recalled, she'd been writing a book about another scholar—an obscure seventeenth-century French philosopher.

"With Kevin," Rosalie added, "none of them lasted more than a few years."

"There've been others since?" I asked.

She nodded. "I didn't care for Hattie, but I thought she was more right for him than some of the others. Cold, intellectual, absorbed in herself. Not my type, but the type Kevin himself was."

"Really, Rosalie!" Adele protested.

Rosalie, it seemed to me, was pretty much on target. "Who was his latest?" I asked.

"A woman named Flora Dexter," Rosalie said.

"What was she like?"

"Another Hattie, I believe." Rosalie glanced uneasily at her mother-in-law. Then she plucked up her courage. "When it comes to Kevin, Mother Rand and I don't see eye to eye. Kevin was never my type of person. He took everything so seriously. He took *himself* so seriously. His jogging, his swimming, his work—the emphasis was always on *him, his* schedule, *his* interests. Hattie was the same way. You'd think two people like that wouldn't get along, but sometimes people like that get along better with each other than with people who are different.

"That book Hattie was writing. Sean and I went up to Boston for a weekend, some years ago. Kevin invited us to dinner. Hattie was going to cook—Sean and I brought a bottle of wine—but when we got there, Hattie hadn't even started to fix dinner; she'd been reading or writing or something all afternoon and hadn't thought it necessary to stop. It ended up, we went out to eat, and she didn't even go with us—she stayed home, in the bedroom, doing whatever it was she was doing. She never did come out of the bedroom, even after dinner. I don't know what you call someone like that, but I call her selfish."

"Did you ever meet Flora Dexter?" I asked.

"Once," Rosalie replied. "She, too, was very wrapped up in her career. She was nicer, though, I thought."

"But birds of a feather?"

Rosalie smiled. "Kevin also."

Adele bit her lip.

"I'd like to talk to both women," I said. "Do you have the addresses or phone numbers?"

"I used to," Rosalie said, "but I threw them out."

"I wish . . ." Adele began, but she didn't finish.

"Don't worry," I said. "I'll be careful."

She managed a smile.

"And now," I said, "if you don't mind, I'd like to call the hospital."

Adele showed me where the telephone was.

The information I received about Carol wasn't reassuring. Her condition was unchanged.

The taxi was one of those spick-and-span jobs you never seem to find in Manhattan. The driver was spick-and-span, too, a silver-haired old gent with a problem: The elm tree in his backyard was sick, and he hadn't been able to get anyone to come and cut it down. All the way to the station he talked about the economics of tree surgery.

I'd just missed a train and had to wait a long while for the next one. I went to the telephone and called Jonie Stiles.

He'd read about the murder. With characteristic understatement, he said, "You seem to have had a spot of trouble last night. How's Carol?"

"Pretty bad, Jonie."

"I'm sorry as hell, Brock. Anything I can do?"

"Yes. That's why I'm calling. I'd like a complete transcript of the Kevin Rand trial. How long does it normally take to get something like that?"

"Days, weeks—it depends. And it's expensive."

"I don't care what it costs," I said, "but I do care how long it takes. I want a copy right away."

Jonie began to tell me about the difficulties involved.

I cut him off. Carol had been shot twice through the lung, I said. I wanted the transcript, and that was that.

"Very well," he said, demonstrating the spirit that set Stiles, Levin and Sullivan apart from most other law firms. "I'll try to get it for you this afternoon. Shall I have it sent over to your office?"

"Please."

"Is there any connection between the Rand trial and what happened last night?"

"Maybe," I said, and hung up before he could ask any further questions.

I dropped some more coins in the slots and called Louise. I might have to go out of town unexpectedly, I said. Would she board Tiger at her place?

She said she would. Then she launched into a long lament about how she hadn't been able to get any work done, because the telephone had been ringing every five minutes. Everyone in the world had been trying to get in touch with me, I gathered, and message-taking wasn't Louise's strong point.

I sympathized, and explained the circumstances. But Louise already knew the circumstances all too well; she'd been hearing about them from everyone. She hoped Miz Fox be better, she said, and with that our conversation ended.

I bought a copy of a New York newspaper and sat down on a bench to read about the shooting of Bill and Carol.

The case was treated as an ordinary street crime. William Arden, a prominent California industrialist who had resigned as Chief Executive Officer of Arden Electronics Corp. earlier in the week, had been shot to death while walking on West Eleventh Street with a female companion, Miss Carol Fox. Miss Fox had been wounded and was in Saint Vincent's Hospital, where her condition was listed as critical.

The facts were accurate, but the story was misleading. Anyone reading it would assume that Bill and Carol had been out on a date. My name wasn't mentioned until the fourth paragraph. "Mr. Arden and Miss Fox had been visiting New York stockbroker Brockton Potter, a mutual friend."

Mrs. May's experience with the man on the subway was treated at some length.

I marveled at how facts that were essentially right could lead to a conclusion that was essentially wrong.

Exhausted, I fell asleep as soon as the train left Stamford. I didn't wake until it reached 125th Street. The nap did me good, though, for when I woke I had an idea.

From Grand Central Station, I walked over to the public library. There were a lot of books written by people named Sargent. Eventually I found the one I was looking for, however. The library owned three titles by Sargent, H(attie) B(ates). The first was *Jean Robert Cirnaud: Deism and the Rights of Man*. The two later ones were *Theocracy and Oppression* and *Woman and Free Will*. All three had been published by the Konklin University Press.

I spent a few minutes leafing through the book about Cirnaud. He'd been a man ahead of his time, I concluded. He'd questioned orthodox beliefs at a period when it wasn't smart to do so. He'd been burned at the stake.

After returning the book to the desk, I hurried downstairs, flagged a taxi and went to my office.

19

My ARRIVAL caused something of a stir. I'd said I wouldn't be in but hadn't said where I could be reached. My partners had been calling my house, the hospital, then my house again, trying to locate me. Everyone had read about the shooting and wanted to know how Carol was. Also how I was—emotionally, that is.

I gave them the latest report on Carol. As for me, I said, I was kind of tired.

No one asked where I'd been, although I felt the question hovering in the air. I let it hover and went to my desk.

There were telephone messages from everybody I'd ever had anything to do with. Glancing at them, I couldn't tell who had called for business reasons and who hadn't. Some names I didn't even recognize.

I put the messages aside and buzzed Helen. "Get me Philip Quick," I said.

"Oh, dear!" she muttered. She didn't like Philip Quick; his telephone manner was abrasive. But then she said, "Yes, sir."

I tilted my chair back, closed my eyes and waited. Presently Helen rang to say that Mr. Quick wasn't available but would get back to me. I glanced at my watch. In Chicago, it was three-fifteen. Everything else being equal, I knew, Quick would return my call within an hour. I closed my eyes again and thought about him.

Originally I'd picked his name from among the many listed under "Detective Agencies" in the Chicago telephone directory. I'd known nothing about him. I'd been in Chicago at the time and I'd chosen him simply because his listing wasn't in boldface type and wasn't accompanied by any sort of advertisement—I'd wanted someone obscure. But the lightface type was misleading; without realizing it, I'd latched onto one of the most flamboyant, and costly, private detectives in America.

The task I'd given him was what he called "a nothing sort of job." I'd wanted him to locate a man who was trying to avoid me. He'd done so in no time at all. I'd been impressed, and on several subsequent occasions I'd used him to obtain information I couldn't get otherwise. He'd never let me down.

In a way, my feelings about him were like Helen's. His abrasiveness annoyed me. So did his boasting and his habit of building himself up at other people's expense. But on the other hand, there was something about him I admired. He had the same dedication to his work, the same do-or-die attitude, that the members of my staff had. And I wasn't the only one who appreciated it; some of Chicago's most prominent lawyers referred their clients to him. His income, he'd once bragged to me, was "well over two hundred Gs a year."

To him, he claimed, I was a hobby. There was no real money in me—I wasn't getting a divorce and I never seemed to want a stolen necklace found. My children didn't run away, because I didn't have any, and no one had any photographs of me that needed to be recovered. I was unprofitable. But I was kind of a nice guy and, what the hell, the things I wanted didn't take up much of his time.

The fact was, the things I wanted took up hardly any of his time. Usually, the information I was after wasn't available in Chicago; he got it from correspondent agencies in other cities. All he had to do was make a few telephone calls. But his correspondent agencies were the best in their particular locales, and I'd never had reason to complain.

The jangle of the telephone interrupted my thoughts.

"There's a Mr. Bakersfield on line one," Helen said. "He's with the, ah, FBI."

I was disappointed. I'd hoped it was Quick. I flipped through the pile of messages. Bakersfield had called earlier in the day and had left his number, but he hadn't said he was with the FBI. "Put him on," I said, "but hold all other calls except Quick's."

"Mr. Potter?" Bakersfield's voice was very FBI. Deep, dry and unrevealing.

"Yes."

"I'm calling in regard to the shooting incident involving Mr. Arden and Miss Fox. We'd like some further information from you. Would it be possible for you to come in for an interview sometime this evening?"

"I'll be glad to give you whatever information I can," I said, "but this evening . . . I don't know how much sense I'd make. I've been up since yesterday morning and I'm in sort of a fog. How about tomorrow morning?"

There was a ponderous silence. The FBI, I'd learned, liked to do things at its convenience, not yours.

But in this instance the FBI gave in. "Very well," said Bakersfield. "Nine o'clock."

"Nine o'clock," I agreed.

He told me where to come, and I promised to be there.

"Mr. Quick on line two," Helen said, before I could put down the telephone.

I punched the line-two button and said, "Hello, Phil."

Quick was in a better than average mood. "Potter? Long time no hear. I thought maybe you'd got yourself a new agency. What's on your mind?"

"I need some information, Phil, and I need it in a hurry."

"You always need it in a hurry, Potter. One of these days I'm going to start charging you double. But I got to be honest with you, I don't think I got time for any small stuff right now. I'm handling twelve cases as of an hour ago. Finished one this morning—big one, too; twenty-five Gs, I'm charging—and took on two more this afternoon. I'm not getting hardly any sleep."

He was telling the truth, I knew. It wasn't unusual for him to juggle a dozen cases simultaneously—and do all the work himself; he used what he called "stringers" only on rare occasions. But I also knew he didn't intend to turn me down. "I'm pretty tired myself," I said. "I didn't get to bed last night and I feel like hell. So let's not play games."

"Who's playing games?" But then Quick relented. "What kind of information you want?"

"The present whereabouts and whatever else you can pick up on two women: a Hattie B. Sargent and a Flora Dexter. The Sargent woman used to live in Boston, on Commonwealth Avenue, and she taught at Falmouth College. I don't know where she is now. She's written several books that were published by the Konklin University Press. Flora Dexter, as of a few months ago, was in one of the Triangle cities in North Carolina—Raleigh, Durham or Chapel Hill. She may still be there. She was a friend of a man named Kevin Rand."

"Kevin Rand?" said Quick. "That name rings a bell. Wasn't he mixed up with the Russians?"

"The East Germans."

"And you—?"

"Just get me the information, Phil."

"It's none of my business, Potter, but aren't you getting kind of far from home? You're out of your league."

"Just get me the information."

"O.K., soon as I get some free time, but I can't promise when that'll be."

"Thank you, Phil." I knew he would be making the necessary calls within an hour. "You may not be able to reach me tomorrow, so I'll check back with you."

"Don't look for much tomorrow. It's Saturday."

"It's also urgent." I put the telephone down.

A few minutes later, Helen rang me to say that a large package had arrived by messenger from Stiles, Levin and Sullivan.

I went to her office to inspect it. It was large, all right. The size of the one-suiter I took with me on most of my trips. It was heavy, too. But then, the trial had lasted for two weeks. I couldn't even begin to estimate how many words the transcript contained. It was no mean feat for Jonie to have got it for me so fast, I realized.

"This is what I was waiting for," I told Helen. "Now I can go home."

I carried the package down to the street, hailed a taxi and was driven to my house. Then, after depositing the package in the den, I walked over to the hospital, pausing at the spot where the shooting had occurred.

West Eleventh Street, with the late afternoon sun slanting into it over the rooftops, seemed very different now from what it had been the night before. A youngster was practicing turns on a skateboard, homeward-bound residents moved briskly along the sidewalk, and there was a flow of automobile traffic.

I glanced at the steps where Sylvia May had been sitting. And forced myself to recall the scene. And felt a cold little knot in the pit of my stomach.

Carol's mother was standing in the corridor outside the intensive-care unit. At first she didn't recognize me. When she did, she lost whatever composure she'd managed to hang on to throughout the long and difficult day that had begun with my telephone call. Her eyes filled with tears. Her chin quivered. "Oh, Brock . . ." She dabbed at her eyes with a wadded-up handkerchief.

Finally she pulled herself together. She'd spoken with the doctor a short while ago, she said. According to him, Carol was slightly better than she'd been earlier. The big danger was pneumonia. At present Carol was heavily sedated and was hooked up to a machine that was helping her breathe.

"Have you seen her?" I asked.

Mrs. Fox nodded. "Twice, but only for a few minutes. She looks—" Her chin began to quiver again.

"Does she remember anything?"

Mrs. Fox shook her head. "I don't know. I didn't ask. I—" She cleared her throat and squared her shoulders. "We must be strong. I *will* be strong."

I introduced myself to the nurse who was in charge of the unit. Would it be all right for me to see Carol? I inquired.

It would not, the nurse replied. Miss Fox had been given a sedative of considerable strength and mustn't be disturbed. Tomorrow, perhaps.

I peeked into the room but couldn't determine which of the beds was Carol's.

Mrs. Fox accompanied me down to the lobby. I told her she could stay at my house if she didn't have a hotel room, but she declined. She had a key to Carol's apartment, she said; she would stay there. She did consent to go out with me for something to eat, however.

We talked about the shooting. She kept shaking her head and saying, "This wicked city." I didn't tell her much about Bill Arden. Merely that he was a friend of mine from California.

After dinner, she returned to the hospital, and I went to my house, where I began to read the transcript. I was repeatedly interrupted by the ringing of the telephone, however. Friends of Carol's. Friends of mine. Business acquaintances. They all wanted to know the details.

At last, in desperation, I took the transcript up to my bedroom, unplugged the bedroom extension of my telephone and closed the door. But weariness got the better of me, and by nine o'clock I was sound asleep.

20

THE NATIONAL DEBT NOTWITHSTANDING, the federal government ought to spend some money on redoing its FBI offices. All those seals and flags and pictures of the Director are nice enough, but something else is needed. Something to remind the agents that after all they are human beings and do have personalities. The surroundings they now work in discourage the sort of give-and-take that is often necessary in order to arrive at truth.

I did my best. Bakersfield did his best. So did the other two men who were present, Agents Dillon and Schuster. They asked, I answered. But little was accomplished.

To my surprise, none of the agents knew of my connection with Kevin Rand. At first I wondered whether the information had been fed into the computer, but then I decided that it had been—the agents simply hadn't thought it necessary to consult the computer. At any rate, I held nothing back. I told them about my role in the Rand case, about the conversation I'd had with Bill in California, and about the telephone call from him that had preceded his visit to my house.

At no point during the interview were the agents anything but courteous, and at no point did they give me a feeling that they didn't believe me. They accepted my reason for not letting Bill tell me what he'd found out; that it wasn't the sort of thing I wanted to discuss in front of Carol. My actions were understandable, they said, but, as things turned out, unfortunate.

Actually, what was wrong with the hour and a half I spent in Bakersfield's office was the formality of it all. The FBI men never forgot their role or let me forget mine. They were the interviewers, I the interviewee. If they'd let their hair down for even a few minutes, if they'd answered more of my questions, if we'd spent part of the time just batting ideas around, something useful might have emerged. But that didn't happen.

They wanted what the police had wanted: a description of the killer. And I couldn't give them one.

I, on the other hand, wanted to explore the possibility of a link between Kevin Rand and Alfred Stone. But this, they indicated, was strictly a Bureau matter. When I tried to find out whether they knew where Bill had been before telephoning me, I got nowhere.

I drew the only conclusion I could: They already knew everything I was telling them about Bill and his suspicions.

"I hope I've been helpful," I said dubiously, as I was getting ready to leave.

"We appreciate your cooperation," Bakersfield replied briskly. "Too bad you didn't have a chance to see who fired the shots."

"If I had," I said, "I'd probably be dead, too. But about Bill's telephone call—"

"We'll work on it. Thank you very much, Mr. Potter."

"I hope so. I—"

"We'll check with Miss Fox, of course, as soon as we're able." Bakersfield went to the door and opened it. "Thank you again."

I felt, and was, dismissed.

From the FBI office I went to the hospital. Mrs. Fox was there. She'd seen Carol, she said, and Carol had been awake. "I think— I pray—she's going to make it," she added.

This time I was the one who got choked up.

"They've taken away the breathing machine for a little while," Mrs. Fox said. "They want her to breathe on her own. It's so painful, though." She paused. "She asked about you."

The nurse who was in charge of the unit wasn't the one who'd been there the night before. I gave her a verbal résumé of myself, and Mrs. Fox told her that Carol did want to see me. The nurse wasn't one to make hasty decisions. She considered the matter for a full minute before pointing to her wristwatch and saying, "All right, but not for long."

I found the bed. Carol was awake. There were so many wires connected to her that she resembled a puppet. A wan, limp puppet with dull eyes and a tube in its nose.

I kissed her on the forehead. Carefully, so as not to disconnect anything. "You look great," I said, "but I'm not crazy about that dress."

She smiled. But her smile became a grimace. She was obviously suffering a great deal. "The pain comes . . . in waves," she said in a voice that was scarcely more than a whisper."

"Don't talk," I said.

"Must tell you," she said. "Man in a . . . black raincoat. Collar . . . up. Hat . . . pulled down. . . . Gloves and a . . . ski mask . . . All I . . . remember." She bit her lip and clutched the side of the bed. "So fast . . . Didn't see enough. . . . Sorry . . . You . . . must try, though."

"I will," I promised.

A groan escaped from her. She writhed. "Go," she said. "Come back . . . later."

I stood there a few moments, then left.

Mrs. Fox was waiting at the nurse's desk.

"Keep watch," I said to her. I didn't trust myself to say more; I was feeling too shaken.

21

IF THERE HAD BEEN dramatic moments in the trial, they didn't come through in the transcript. It was one of the dullest documents I'd ever tackled.

In part, the dullness was due to bickering over points of law; in part, to the repetition—one witness saying what another witness, or he himself, had already said. And to the emphasis placed on technicalities—the distance between the fence and the tree; the procedure for signing the logbook in the room where the classified material was kept—that really didn't matter.

At first I read every word, but I soon began to skim, picking out bits of testimony here and there.

The trial centered around Kevin's sale to two East German agents of wiring diagrams for the antenna that would be attached to Calthorp Industries' new CSX-1 communications satellite. The first witnesses called were three executives of Calthorp's research center in Research Triangle Park, North Carolina. One after another, they described Kevin's position in the company and the means by which he'd come into possession of the diagrams.

There wasn't anything unusual about the means, I gathered. As chief electrical engineer on the antenna team, Kevin had security clearance to take them from the room where they were kept; some of them represented his own work.

Nothing the Calthorp men said gave any clue as to why the antenna was so important. For that, I had to rely on my own sketchy knowledge of communications satellites, most of which I'd acquired from George Cole, who knew more about them, and about the Calthorp antenna in particular, than anyone else at Price, Potter and Petacque.

These days, George had told me, there is nothing extraordinary .about the satellites themselves. In fact, so many of them are parked out there, 22,500 miles above the earth, that that band of outer space is getting to be like a garage. Today's miracles have to do with the devices attached to the satellites, and in the case of the CSX-1 the device was a revolutionary new antenna.

The telephone lines now in existence, George had gone on to say, are no longer adequate—they can't handle the enormously increased long-distance traffic from people and computers—and it costs too much to put up new ones. Besides, telephone lines can be sabotaged. So satellites are necessary—satellites with antennae that are small, lightweight and can shift direction with tremendous speed. Big, heavy antennae are unsatisfactory; it takes too much fuel to get them to where they're going, and there's too much chance that the launch will be inaccurate.

Demonstrating the ability to simplify that was one of his greatest assets, George had said when I'd asked him what made the Calthorp antenna so unique. "Look at it this way. A man in Dallas is talking by telephone with a man in Seattle. The call is being transmitted by satellite. The antenna on the satellite picks up the voice signals from Dallas, then shifts direction to pick up the signals from Seattle, then shifts again to pick up Dallas. Now suppose the satellite has to handle a second call at the same time. This one is between a lady in New York and a man in Tucson— or, maybe, between a computer in New York and one in Tucson. The antenna is now shifting between Dallas and Seattle and New

York and Tucson. It has to do it fast enough so that there are no interruptions in either conversation."

"I follow you," I'd said. "But I still don't see why the Calthorp antenna is so special."

"Because," George had said, with a little smile, "the Calthorp antenna, although it's small and lightweight, can handle a hundred thousand calls simultaneously. It can shift direction in one one-hundred-millionth of a second. No one, until now, has been able to produce anything that comes close to that."

I'd whistled. Then I'd reflected, and said, "Even so, I don't understand why the antenna is of strategic importance. After all, the CSX-1 is for domestic use. It can only span an east-west range of eight thousand miles—roughly the distance between New York and Honolulu, with a couple of thousand miles left over."

"True," George had said. "But there are other factors. In the first place, Communist countries have the same need for good communications we do, and that's one field in which we still have a decided edge. If they can duplicate the Calthorp antenna, they'll be as good as we are. In the second place, even in peacetime our military will use the CSX-1, along with telephone companies, television networks and everyone else who relies on communications satellites. But in time of war, the military would preempt it."

I'd begun to get the drift. "You mean if, say, an enemy had a copy of the wiring diagrams, it could tune in on our military conversations?"

"Yes. But the greater danger is that the enemy could jam the transmissions. Can you imagine the chaos there'd be in a national emergency if suddenly no one could get in touch with anyone else! With the wiring diagrams of the Calthorp antenna, an enemy could knock out a huge chunk of our communications capability in a matter of seconds. We'd be paralyzed."

It was then that I'd realized the enormity of Kevin's act. An act which, in a small way, I'd helped him commit.

And, unaware of how much salt he was rubbing into my wound, George had added, "Nuclear warheads notwithstanding, Brock, the real key to world domination lies in communications. Military information has to be passed back and forth across great distances. Instructions must be issued and received. If either side could gain absolute control of the airwaves, that side would win. No doubt about it."

With a camera, Kevin had done more to sabotage America's future communications capacity than a thousand men could ever do by hacking away at telephone lines with knives.

None of this was spelled out at the trial, but enough was said to persuade the jury to bring in a verdict of guilty on all counts.

Nor was the nature of Kevin's previous sales to the East Germans detailed, for the evidence related only to the antenna. But the prosecution did manage to put across the idea that Kevin had been working for the East Germans ever since he'd taken the job at the Calthorp Research Center, and the Calthorp executives did say that he'd had the opportunity to obtain blueprints, diagrams and computations for other items.

Another reason for his being murdered, I thought. To keep him from revealing what else he'd compromised.

To me, the most interesting testimony in the transcript was that of the FBI agents who'd worked on the case, for they described the techniques Kevin had used. The techniques were interesting not because they were bizarre but because they were so ordinary.

One of the East Germans had operated out of New York, collecting the microfilms from the various spots where Kevin had deposited them. The other had established himself in Durham as, of all things, a physical therapist—Kevin, presumably, had trouble with his back from time to time.

Both of the East Germans had used assumed names, according to the FBI; their real names weren't known. The one from New York had called himself Gerald Egan; the one in Durham, Leslie Michaels.

Kevin would telephone Michaels to ask for an appointment, and Michaels would give him one; Michaels would call Kevin to change the time of an appointment that had never been made in the first place, and Kevin would agree to the new time. No business was ever discussed over the telephone. The appointment routine was merely a means of making contact. The instructions were given in face-to-face meetings in the therapist's office, and the money was handed over in the same way.

A number of sites were used for the drops. There was nothing unusual about any of them. A roadside telephone booth near a gas station, a particular bush in a botanical garden, a cemetery. At no time would Kevin have appeared to an observer to be doing anything strange. The observer would never have guessed that Kevin was engaged in selling out, bit by bit, a communications instrument that was vital to the future of the company he worked for and to his country.

Egan, Michaels and Rand—three men quietly going about their jobs. Yet their combined efforts had been mighty valuable to some highly placed men in East Berlin. It was unfortunate, I thought, that the FBI had caught only one of them.

After several hours, I put the transcript aside and made myself a ham sandwich. Sitting at the kitchen table, I considered what I'd read.

As far as I was concerned, the trial testimony was significant not for what it contained but for what it left out. There was no discussion of what enabled the antenna to perform so remarkably. Yet this was important.

I remembered what George Cole had had to say on the subject. "I don't know how the damn thing works, Brock, but I do know this: The secret lies in microtechnology."

Microtechnology. The placement of tens of thousands of tiny particles on a surface smaller than a postage stamp. The key to the Calthorp antenna. Also the specialty of Arden Electronics.

No wonder Bakersfield, Dillon and Schuster hadn't been interested in my speculations. Every branch of the news media had mentioned the efforts of the Warsaw Pact countries to steal the secrets of our microtechnology. The FBI men had been fully aware that the Calthorp and Arden cases were related.

Another thing that the trial hadn't dealt with was the whereabouts of Egan and Michaels. All that had been said was that they'd vanished and were believed to have fled the country.

That was probably true of Michaels, I thought. He'd lived in a small city, dealing with a limited number of people, any of whom might remember him if he or she saw him again. But was the same true of Egan?

I thought about the two men. Egan was certainly the more shadowy. New York had been his base of operations. In New York it was easy to remain unnoticed. Was it possible that he was still in the city, still doing what he'd been doing before? Was he the one who'd recruited Kevin?

There was no way of knowing. But the possibility did exist.

Presently I got up from the table and went to the telephone.

"Mr. Quick isn't in right now," said the woman at his answering service. "I expect to hear from him, though. Would you care to leave your name and number?"

I cared to and did.

Thirty minutes later, my telephone rang.

"It's Saturday," Quick said irritably, before I could get a word in. "I told you Saturdays are bad days. Too many places are closed."

"You've got nothing at all?" I asked.

"Nothing worth calling you about. The address and phone number of the Dexter woman, if that'll do you any good, and the place she works at. Monday I'll have everything complete."

"I'll take what you have, for a start."

He gave me Flora Dexter's address and telephone number. Then he said, "I got to admit, Potter, I learned something from checking on her. I learned what a roboticist is. Bet you don't even know that yourself."

I didn't, I admitted.

"It's someone who designs robots," Quick informed me. "That's what Flora Dexter does."

"Well, now," I said.

But Quick didn't hear me. He'd already hung up.

I dialed the number he'd given me.

Flora Dexter answered.

22

ON MY ONE PREVIOUS VISIT to Research Triangle Park, I'd felt as if I'd been catapulted into the year 2001. That was my feeling this time, too.

The Triangle is the wedge of land defined by the close-together cities of Raleigh, Durham and Chapel Hill and their universities. The Park is a 5,500-acre tract within the Triangle where an assortment of private- and public-sector enterprises have research and light manufacturing installations. Enterprises such as IBM, Monsanto, the Environmental Protection Agency and the United States Army Research Office. There are probably more computer terminals per acre in the Park than anywhere in the United States, and more people of scientific bent. The whole place is tomorrow-oriented.

The roads that run through the Park are seldom crowded, and on a Sunday morning they're all but deserted. I spent a half hour driving about, reacquainting myself, noting the sturdy little pine trees, the avenues of young magnolias, the futuristic buildings, the incredible stillness in the air. One of the lures used to attract talent to the area, I knew, was the quality of life in it, and from what I could see, the quality of life was all that it was cracked up to be. I myself preferred more hustle and bustle, but I could imagine

Kevin, who'd grown up in a small university town, being happy here.

From the Park I headed west toward Hope Valley, the suburb of Durham where Flora Dexter lived. There had evidently been a dry spell recently; the lawns of most of the houses were scorched.

I tried to follow the directions Flora had given me, but I took a wrong turn and arrived fifteen minutes late. Apparently she'd been anxious. The front door was open, and she was standing in front of the house, watching the street.

I parked the car in the driveway and got out. Flora came across the lawn, and we shook hands. Her grip was firm, like a man's. There was an air of competence about her.

Rosalie was right, I thought. Another Hattie Sargent.

"It's nice to meet you," Flora said. "I never really expected to."

"My pleasure," I said.

A boy peeked from behind the open door, then disappeared.

Flora and I walked into the house. As we entered the living room, I decided that Rosalie had been wrong, after all. Hattie hadn't been a nest-builder, as this woman was. There was a bowl of fresh flowers on a commode, clusters of family photographs and hand-painted china on an étagère. The atmosphere was one of coziness.

Flora nodded in the direction of the coffee table, where there was a pitcher of Bloody Marys, two large glasses and a plate of celery stalks. "I didn't know how you felt about Bloody Marys," she said, "but I took a chance."

"I like them," I said, and went to the sliding glass door that opened onto the backyard.

The yard needed watering. The flowers along the fence appeared to be dying, and the grass was the color of sand. But there was a well-constructed tree house in the crook of a small oak.

Flora joined me and handed me a drink. Looking out at the yard herself, she said, "This hasn't been the best of summers. In many ways."

We sat down on opposite sides of the coffee table.

The boy who'd peeked from behind the front door now peeked into the living room. "Can I go over to Jimmy's?" he asked.

"Come in and shake hands with Mr. Potter," Flora said.

The boy hesitated, then reluctantly came into the room. I guessed that he was eight or nine.

"My son, Dick," Flora said. "Dick, this is Mr. Potter."

The boy and I shook hands. He was a good-looking youngster, but shy. He avoided my eyes.

"Can I, Mom?"

"If you've finished straightening your room."

Dick took off.

I wondered whether Kevin had had a hand in building the tree house. And to what extent he'd shared in the overall domesticity. It was hard to imagine him as a substitute husband and father, helping with the dishes, playing with the boy, and then going out to keep his appointments with Leslie Michaels. Yet that was the way it must have been.

Flora sipped her own drink and eyed me over the rim of the glass. "You're not what I expected," she said. "You don't look stockbrokerish. You remind me of the tennis pro at the club."

"I wouldn't if you saw me on a tennis court," I said, and wondered whom she reminded me of. No one, I decided. She was large-boned but not really large, and I got the feeling that there were other contradictions about her, as well. "And you," I said, "I understand you're a roboticist."

"Roboticist? Really, now! I prefer to think of myself merely as an engineer who's struggling to catch up to my counterparts in Japan."

"What aspects of robots do you deal with?"

She seemed to swell. Evidently she liked to talk about her work. "I'm trying to make them smarter by giving them three-dimensional vision. You see, they don't have it yet. They only respond to length and breadth; they can't distinguish between certain kinds of tools or surfaces. I'm also developing a way to make them sensitive to complex voice commands. That's more difficult." Suddenly the swelling disappeared. Her shoulders sagged, and her face puckered with anxiety. She actually appeared to shrink. "I'd like to relocate, Mr. Potter. Can you help me?"

"Brock," I said. And I realized why she'd agreed so readily to a meeting.

"I feel like a leper in this community," she went on, unhappily. "No one trusts me."

I could understand. The social life in the Triangle cities was probably business-related. And every outfit in the Park had secrets to guard. The reverberations of the Rand case would go on for years, and she was associated with it. "It must be difficult," I said.

"These past months are the worst period I've ever lived through. At times I feel like a robot myself. Someone pushes a button and I go through the motions, but I'm not really alive anymore."

"I can imagine."

"I've sent out I don't know how many résumés, but the word has spread. No one seems interested." She drank some more of her Bloody Mary.

"Kevin hurt a lot of people," I said.

There was a silence. Flora gazed toward the glass doors. She seemed to be studying the tree house.

"I'm not good at choosing men," she said at last. "I knew Kevin didn't have much ability to love. I knew there was something cold inside of him. I kidded myself. And it was the same with Dick's father—I had a bad experience with him, too." She sighed. "My mother was right, I think. She always said I shouldn't have been a girl. I don't have female intuition." A note of hardness had crept into her voice.

"Intuition is sexless," I said.

She managed to smile. "Thank you, but I'm afraid you're just being kind."

Her contradictions ran very deep, I thought, and must have caused her a great deal of suffering over the years. "I don't know how you feel," I said, "but I can tell you how I feel. I feel betrayed. I'm sorry Kevin died the way he did—there's something so sordid about it—but I'm not sorry the way I should be. I feel too betrayed for that."

I waited for a reaction.

None was forthcoming.

"I only wish they'd caught the other two men," I prodded.

Still no reaction.

"I can't understand how the FBI let them slip through its fingers."

The reaction finally came. "I'm glad you called," Flora said. "I mean it. I'm glad you're here. All these weeks, all these months I've been so alone. There was no one I could talk to. No one . . . Betrayed? Yes—God knows! Betrayed, betrayed, betrayed. But sorry? How can I be sorry? I still can't believe he's dead." She put her glass on the table and drew herself up. Once more she seemed to get larger. "I *hate* Kevin! Hate the part of him that's still with me! The part of him that will always *be* with me! If I could go to an exorcist, I would!"

I wanted to console her, to tell her that time was the best exorcist. But I fought off the urge. "The other two men shouldn't have been allowed to get away," I said.

"You can thank Birdy Norwood for that."

There had been no mention in the trial transcript of anyone named Birdy Norwood. "Who's she?" I asked.

"Does it really matter?"

"To my peace of mind it does."

Flora regarded me thoughtfully for a moment. "Yes, I can see where it might," she conceded presently. And she began to tell me the local version of what had happened. The local version consisted of gossip that had circulated among people who'd been interviewed by the FBI after Kevin's arrest and news items that had been in the papers and on television in the Triangle area but not beyond it.

Birdy Norwood was Leslie Michaels's landlady. She'd inadvertently tipped Michaels off by saying that she'd seen some suspicious-looking men in the neighborhood. Right after that, he'd disappeared. No one knew how he'd managed to get through the FBI net, but he'd done so. Two days after his disappearance, a stolen car was found in a parking lot near the bus station in Raleigh, and an attendant there identified an FBI picture of Michael's. It was believed that Michaels had succeeded in warning Egan, and it was known that one or the other of them had tried to warn Kevin—Kevin's secretary reported that he'd received several urgent telephone calls on the day of his arrest. Unfortunately, from Kevin's standpoint, the warnings hadn't reached him—he'd had to go to Atlanta that day, unexpectedly, with some other Calthorp people.

The information about Kevin's unplanned and unavoidable trip to Atlanta agreed with the testimony of one of the FBI agents that I'd read in the transcript. Kevin had been arrested leaving a cemetery where he'd placed an envelope containing microfilms. He'd just returned from a short business trip to Atlanta. With the coolness that was characteristic of him, and that the prosecution made a big point of, he'd had the envelope in his pocket the whole time he was away.

Realizing that they'd lost Egan and Michaels, the FBI had arrested Kevin before he too could disappear. They'd hoped he would reveal the whereabouts of the other two, but he hadn't.

Having started, Flora couldn't stop. She told me far more than I wanted to know—all of it, she admitted, based on rumors that had circulated in the area. According to her, the FBI had learned of the penetration of Calthorp's research center from an East German intelligence agent who'd defected. The agent hadn't known much about this particular operation—he'd had nothing to do with it—but he'd heard that his agency had successfully planted a man in the facility and was regularly receiving data from him. It had taken the FBI many months of checking and cross-checking to pinpoint Kevin as the supplier of the data.

The story about the defector was plausible, I thought, but immaterial. So were many of the other things she said. All that was really important was the essence: An FBI surveillance had been detected by a little old lady with sharp eyes, two of the three spies had escaped, and the third was now dead.

"This man Egan," I said, "did Kevin ever mention anything to you about him?"

Flora shook her head. Until the day of Kevin's arrest, she said, she'd never heard of anyone named Egan. Kevin had spoken of the therapist—he did have trouble with his back, she insisted; it was the result of a fall he'd taken in a Boston health club—but she'd never met the therapist and couldn't describe him. "I'm like everyone else," she concluded. "I didn't suspect a thing." She leaned forward and gave me a beseeching look. "You do believe me, don't you?"

I didn't answer right away. Instead, I finished my drink. "Yes," I said at last.

That didn't satisfy her, though. "You sound skeptical," she said. "I believe you."

"Everyone *says* they believe me. The FBI questioned me for days. They checked with everyone who's ever known me. I almost lost my job. Finally they cleared me, and I didn't lose my job, but people keep wondering. God, how I'd like to leave this place!"

"One man can create an awful lot of victims," I said, and glanced about the room. The man who'd created all those victims had sat where I was sitting, drunk from the glass I'd been drinking from, seen the objects I was seeing. For a moment I had the feeling he was still alive.

Flora picked up a celery stalk, swirled it around in what was left of her drink and said, "My mother was right. . . . Can I give you another drink?"

"No, thanks." I got up and strolled over to the étagère. There were a dozen photographs on it, but none of Kevin.

Presently, Flora joined me. She, too, looked at the photographs.

"Kevin's been removed?" I said.

She shook her head. "He didn't like having his picture taken. I never used to understand why. Now I do. The only likeness I have of him is an old one, from a magazine. Do you want to see it?"

She left the room and returned with a dog-eared magazine. She turned the pages until she found the one she was looking for. "Here."

The magazine was called *Age of Circuitry* and was highly specialized. The article that included Kevin's picture was titled "Integrated Circuits and Microelectronics." The picture was part of an insert dealing with his role in the development of a circuit for a small computer. It had been taken when he was living in Boston and working for Dean & Haskins.

The kid I remembered, clear-eyed and grave, was present in the adult. "He never really changed much," I said as I gave the magazine back to Flora.

"He must have," she said. "At some point he must have."

We returned to where we'd been sitting. Flora invited me to stay for lunch. "It's been such a relief to be able to talk," she said. "I feel a hundred percent better. I feel almost human."

"I wish I could stay," I said, "but I have a plane to catch."

Her face fell.

"I'm anxious to get back to New York. A friend of mine is very sick. I'm worried about her. But I'll be back one of these days."

"I hope so. And if you know of anyone who needs a good electrical engineer . . ."

"I'll keep you in mind," I promised.

She gave me directions on how to reach the expressway that led to the airport, and this time I didn't get lost. I turned in my car at the rental desk, checked in for my flight and waited for the boarding announcement.

I thought of the tree house and of the collection of photographs. And of a man who'd grown up with five brothers and sisters, all younger than himself. A man who didn't like to have his picture taken.

I recalled my question to Adele, and her reply. "What got into him?" I'd asked. "Perhaps nothing got into him," she'd answered. "Perhaps something was there all along."

She was right, I decided. Something had been there all along.

None of us had recognized it, though.

My flight was announced. I boarded the plane and settled back in my seat. And suddenly, as the plane taxied away from the gate, I had a sudden, overwhelming feeling of depression.

It came without warning and was very intense. I couldn't account for it, but I couldn't dispel it, either. The flight back to New York took only an hour and a quarter, but seemed longer than any flight I'd ever been on.

There were a dozen taxis lined up, waiting for passengers, when I emerged from La Guardia. I got into the first one and gave the driver my address, but as the taxi moved away from the curb, I changed my mind.

"Take me to Saint Vincent's Hospital instead," I told the driver. "It's on West Twelfth Street."

The driver took me to the hospital.

Carol's mother was in the corridor outside the intensive-care unit. So was Carol's father, who'd been summoned that morning by telephone. Both of them were terribly downcast.

The thing the doctors had been most afraid of had happened, Mrs. Fox said. Carol had developed pneumonia.

23

TOM AND IRVING were standing in the doorway of my office. They looked decidedly anxious. I'd never been late for a staff meeting before, yet here it was, ten o'clock on a Monday morning, and I was just arriving.

"I was at the hospital," I said. "Carol's in a coma."

Irving groaned.

Tom put his hand on my arm. "I'm so sorry."

"Get the group together," I told Irving. "Let's start the meeting."

He must have given the other members of the research department the news; all of them were subdued when they filed in. Everyone waited for me to say something about Carol, but I couldn't do it. I merely said, "Sorry I'm late. Let's begin. What did the Dow close at on Friday? I can't remember."

There was a lot more I couldn't remember, as well. My staff kept having to remind me of points that had been brought up at previous meetings. I even forgot points that had been brought up a few minutes earlier at this one.

I did function, in a limited way. A part of my mind clung to its familiar concerns. I was even able, once or twice, to question figures that had been cited. But for the most part I was vague. My thoughts kept drifting back to the hospital.

They'd let me see Carol for a few moments. Her face had been flushed, and she'd been restless. Her temperature, they'd told me, was a hundred and five.

Dr. Feinstein had put in an appearance while I was there. He'd explained the situation to Carol's parents and me. Carol was getting big doses of antibiotics, but he couldn't guarantee that they would do the job. Medicine could accomplish only so much.

I'd wanted to remind him of what he'd said after the operation: She had a fighting chance; she was a strong woman. I'd kept my mouth shut, however. Reminding him of what he'd said wouldn't change anything.

Remarks that Carol and I had made to each other at one time or another came back to me. "We're more compatible in bed than out of it." "We're not in love. We'll never be in love." "We're a couple of emotional cripples who aren't really handicapped."

One statement in particular kept running through my mind. Carol had made it. "This may not be the real thing, but I think it's as close to the real thing as either of us will ever come."

I'd agreed with her at the time, and I still did. But now I asked myself how many couples did achieve the real thing. Although Carol and I had always considered ourselves to be in the minority, maybe most people were like us.

Every time we'd broken up, we'd got back together. Because we'd missed each other. Better together, we'd decided, than apart —even though we sometimes got on each other's nerves.

I tried not to think about a world without Carol in it, but the thought came anyway. If she died . . .

She wasn't going to die. They would figure out a way to save her.

If she did die, though . . .

I pictured a man in a black raincoat with the collar turned up, the brim of his hat covering his forehead, his face hidden by a ski mask. He'd taken no chances, that man.

It might have been an ordinary street crime, I reminded myself. There'd been holdups and muggings in my neighborhood before.

Yet nothing had been stolen from Bill and Carol. Nothing at all.

No, I couldn't believe it had been an ordinary street crime. I believed it had been a deliberate murder. And if Carol died, a double murder. Furthermore, I was partly responsible. I'd gone to see Bill Arden. I'd told him about Kevin Rand. Because of that, he'd come to my house.

Not wholly responsible, but partly.

If Carol died . . .

"Must try," she'd said. Well, I was trying. As long as there was breath in my body, I would try.

The staff meeting seemed to last forever. Eventually it ended, though. Ended with the usual routine: scheduling for the week ahead.

I told Irving that he would have to write the Tuesday letter. I asked him to have the other members of the team fill in for me. I had other plans, I said; I couldn't be counted on.

He nodded. "Sure, boss. Whatever you say." And with that, he left my office.

A moment later, my telephone rang.

Philip Quick reported that he had some information on Hattie Sargent.

24

"OF COURSE I REMEMBER YOU," Hattie had said on the telephone. "You're the man who thinks God has a sense of humor."

I'd had no idea what she was talking about. Apparently I'd once made a remark to that effect and she remembered. "That's me. I'm in Boston with time on my hands and I'm looking up old friends. How about our having a drink together about six?"

I hadn't placed the call from Boston; I'd placed it from New York, figuring it wouldn't take long to get to Boston.

"I'd like that," Hattie had said. "I've often thought about you. Your concept of divinity fascinated me. It was so in-our-image."

"The bar at the Ritz?"

"Out of the question. I'm working. You come here." She gave me the address, which Quick had already given me. To my surprise, she was still living in the apartment she'd shared with Kevin.

"Fine. Looking forward to it. Six."

On the plane, I tried to recall what I might have said about God's sense of humor. And to dope out what my concept of divinity really was. Evidently I was going to need one.

My mind rebelled, however. It wanted nothing to do with concepts. It wanted to dwell on concrete matters, such as the unexpected visit I'd had from two Homicide detectives before leaving the office and the brief stop I'd made at the hospital on the way to the airport.

The detectives had questioned me further about the events on Thursday night. Unfortunately they hadn't been able to interview Miss Fox, they'd said, so they had to rely on Mrs. May and me. Did I recall anything more?

I didn't, I'd answered, but Miss Fox had given me a description of sorts. And I'd passed along to them what she'd told me. They'd made me repeat it three times.

They hadn't come up with any additional eyewitnesses, I gathered, and except for recovering the bullets had made little progress of any sort.

The stop I'd made at the hospital hadn't lifted my spirits one damn bit. Carol's condition was unchanged. Her temperature continued to fluctuate between a hundred and four and a hundred and five. At noon they'd performed a tracheotomy.

The plane landed in Boston on time. As the taxi sped through the Sumner Tunnel and along the Esplanade, I reviewed the facts Quick had given me about Hattie.

Not much had changed since I'd last seen her, it seemed. She was still on the faculty of Falmouth College, which had always struck me as an improbable place for someone like Hattie to be employed, but where she evidently felt comfortable. A finishing school for young ladies, Falmouth was a haven for those female offspring of the affluent who weren't bright enough to get into schools such as Wellesley, Smith or Bryn Mawr and whose parents wouldn't be caught dead sending one of their kids to a state university. It offered a two-year program that kept the young ladies occupied between the ages of eighteen and twenty, providing them with as much English literature, French, music appreciation and world history as they could handle. It had bowed to the times by changing its name from Miss Falmouth's to Falmouth College, and no one had yet sued it for practicing sex discrimination, but it was an anachronism.

Hattie was one of its main attractions; she had a reputation as a scholar. At the time I'd known her, her first book hadn't yet come out—she'd been working on it. But even then she'd been known in academic circles for some monographs she'd published. Now, with several books to her credit, she was a true luminary. She taught only three days a week, but the school's advertising brochure mentioned her prominently. According to Quick, she was "a big deal." Or, as I saw it, a large fish in a small pond.

The building in which she lived was a converted brownstone on Commonwealth Avenue. It looked exactly like the brownstones that flanked it, but to me it was different from them—it brought back memories.

I pushed the button that had SARGENT beside it. A buzzer sounded. I walked into the inner vestibule and immediately felt transported backward in time. Everything was as I remembered it.

Hattie was standing in the hall outside the door to her apartment. She, too, was unchanged. For a moment I almost expected Kevin to appear behind her and speak to me.

"How nice," she said. "How strange, but how nice. I should have thought you'd forgotten about me. Come in."

The feeling I'd had of everything being the same evaporated when I walked into the living room. Kevin had been neat and orderly, and his surroundings had always reflected that side of him. But now every flat surface was covered with books and papers. Here and there, unwashed mugs and coffee cups served as paperweights. The desk, which was the central piece of furniture in the room, had a high-intensity lamp clipped to one side of it, and the arm of the lamp stood at an odd angle, blocking access to the typewriter. Another high-intensity lamp menaced the lounge chair, on which, at the moment, was seated an enormous dictionary.

"As you can see," Hattie said, "I'm hard at it. Much has changed for me, recognition-wise, since you were last here. I'm taken more seriously."

I noted the pictures on the walls: a large etching of the Colosseum in Rome and some Van Gogh reproductions that seemed to be requesting the etching to go away. Evidently Kevin hadn't wanted to take the pictures with him; I was almost certain they'd been there before.

"What are you writing?" I asked.

"I'm plowing an old field in a new way. Are you sure you're interested?"

"Very much so."

"Well, I'll tell you, then. But first—drinks. I can't offer the same selection as the Ritz, but I have a nice Chianti."

I'd never had much of a palate for wine, but I'd finally learned to enjoy it. With the exception of Chianti. "Swell," I said.

She went into the kitchen, and I heard cabinet doors being opened and closed. I put the dictionary on the floor and sat down.

Hattie returned with two glasses of Chianti, gave me one and carefully moved some books to make room for herself on the daybed. *"À votre santé,"* she proposed.

I managed to get some of the wine down.

"You asked what I'm writing," she said. "It's a study of an abbess of Saint-Esprit de Monfleur. But really what I'm dealing with is convent life in the seventeenth and eighteenth centuries. Or, to put it differently, how people disposed of unwanted daughters." She went on to tell me at some length about the treatment of girls at a time when they were regarded as mere pawns to be moved about in the game of getting ahead. This particular abbess, it seemed, had bucked the system.

I studied Hattie as she spoke. She was an attractive woman, tall, dark-haired, with clear skin and violet eyes. But there was an edge to her voice when she talked about unwanted or exploited daughters that detracted from her good looks and made me suspect that she'd been, or thought she'd been, an unwanted or exploited daughter herself.

I remembered what Dr. Yarborough had told Carol: Treason sprang from bitterness.

Had Kevin sensed in this woman a kindred spirit? I wondered. Was that what had drawn him to her?

My thoughts went back to Flora Dexter. Her mother had told her she should have been a boy. Also, Flora had had a bad experience with the father of her child. Was there a kernel of bitterness in her, too?

"Tell me, though," Hattie said, changing the subject, "do you still travel so much?"

"Even more," I replied. "I've branched out."

She gave me an arch smile. "I'd like to think that what you said is true, that you called me because I'm an old friend, but I can't. We were never what you call 'friends.' We never really got to know each other."

I forced myself to drink some more wine. "You made an impression on me. And I must have made one on you—or at least my concept of divinity did. But you're right, I do have an ulterior motive. The daughter of a good friend of mine is interested in going to Falmouth."

"Oh? Who?" Hattie immediately became businesslike.

"The father's name is Irving Silvers. He works for me."

"Give me the address. I'll get in touch with them the next time I'm in New York." She hurried to the desk for a pencil and paper.

I gave her Irving's address and made a mental note to warn him. He had two daughters and a son. All three children were so bright that it was scary. The oldest, Elaine, had expressed a desire to go to Harvard and would have no difficulty whatsoever in being admitted.

Hattie gave me a sales pitch. Falmouth had updated its curriculum. Now the emphasis was on relevance. The sciences were being stressed. There were courses in social psychology and urban planning.

I waited for an opportunity to introduce the subject of Kevin, but as it turned out I didn't have to. Hattie, again sending the conversation off in a different direction, introduced it herself.

She said, "You know about Kevin, I suppose. You must."

"A terrible shock," I said.

Her expression darkened. "The FBI thinks I had something to do with it."

"Oh?"

"They descended on me like the Vikings on Ireland. They were checking on Kevin's background, they said." Her eyes flashed. "The hell they were! I wouldn't have minded, except that it jeopardized my position at the school. For a few weeks I was thoroughly upset. I still get furious when I think about it."

"What did they say that led you to believe—"

"I'm no fool. They didn't have to *say* anything."

The FBI had probably treated her no differently from the way it had treated me, I thought. "At any rate, Kevin's dead now," I said. "It's all over."

The anger went out of her eyes, but that was all. There was no sign of grief.

"Do you ever find yourself thinking about him?" I said. "I do."

Hattie reflected. "When I was being investigated, I did. But before that, and now—seldom. Kevin was a phase in my life. A chapter. He furthered my development."

"In what way?"

"He taught me to be more disciplined. In that respect he was very good for me."

"He was a disciplined person himself."

"Yes. And nothing was allowed to interfere with his schedule. His jogging, his swimming, his work, his anything."

"That must have made for a difficult social life."

Hattie nodded. "It did. But in all candor I must admit that ordinary social talk has never appealed to me. So much of it, even among academics, is concerned with the best way to poach a salmon or what kind of soap to use if you're allergic. Kevin's friends, the few I met, seldom had anything interesting to say. I preferred not to waste my time with them, so he rarely brought them to the apartment. He saw them elsewhere, when he saw them at all."

So different from Flora, I thought, and yet . . .

"I was an exception, I take it," I said.

Hattie shrugged. "You were from his past."

"And the friends who weren't from his past?"

"Bores, mostly. Men he worked with. Men he met at the health club. Not my type, certainly."

"The health club," I said. "He had a bad fall there, didn't he?"

"Not that I know of."

"But he spent a lot of time there?"

"Twice a week. Religiously."

"And made friends?"

"Some. One was a friend of yours, too, I believe."

I tried not to react. "Oh? Who?"

"I don't remember his name. He knew you, though. Kevin said so."

"Kevin never mentioned it to me," I said. "Are you sure you don't remember the man's name?"

Hattie frowned. "Ott—could that be it? Do you know anyone named Ott? No, that wasn't it. I really don't remember." But suddenly her frown disappeared. "Cottly! Pete Cottly!"

"Ah, yes," I said. "Pete. I believe he did go to a health club. The Brookline Health Club, wasn't it?"

"No. Jackson's it was called."

"Nice fellow—Pete. Did you know him?"

"No. Kevin suggested inviting him over, but I couldn't imagine having anything in common with a manufacturer of surgical instruments."

"Surgical instruments?"

"Surgical instruments, precision instruments, instruments of some kind. I mean, that isn't my orientation, and Kevin knew it. *Must* we talk about Kevin, though? Tell me more about the Silvers girl."

I told Hattie about Elaine and was given another sales pitch.

Even the art department had become relevance-conscious.

At last I managed to get in a few words of my own. "I'm sure Elaine will be interested in hearing all that," I said, "but now I'm afraid I have to go."

Hattie pulled a face. "So soon?"

"Perhaps we'll get together again, the next time I'm in town," I said. "I'd love to hear more about your new book."

"But of course," Hattie said, with a pleased smile. "So few men really understand."

I squeezed her hand as I said good-bye, and congratulated myself on not having had to explain my concept of divinity. The thought occurred to me, however, as I walked down the stairs to the lobby, that I might have been right when I'd said that God had a sense of humor. For, along with everything else, He'd created vanity.

But my thoughts immediately shifted to a more urgent concern: how to track down the man who'd called himself Pete Cottly.

25

WHILE WAITING FOR QUICK to get back to me, I called Adele.

"Cottly?" she said. "The name isn't familiar. Let me ask Sean." She put down the telephone.

Evidently Sean was nearby, for I heard their voices. Hers inquired whether Kevin had ever mentioned anyone named Pete Cottly. His answered no, he didn't think so, but he would ask Rosalie.

Adele returned to the telephone. No one could recall Kevin's having spoken of such a person. Was it important? And how was Carol?

I didn't know whether it was important or not, I said, but it might be. And Carol was barely hanging on to life.

Both statements were true. I'd paid another visit to the intensive-care unit on the way home from the airport. Carol was having to fight for each breath.

Adele expressed appropriate sentiments, and I hurried the conversation to a conclusion by saying I was expecting a long-distance call.

A needle in a haystack, I thought wearily.

Quick didn't call until eleven-thirty. He'd had a tough day, too, apparently; he wasn't as sanguine as usual, and when I told him that Cottly was probably an assumed name, he became downright nasty. "Damn it, Potter, what do you expect me to do with an *assumed* name? I need a *real* name, or a real address, or a real something. I don't know why I even bother with you."

"The man belonged to Jackson's Health Club. I imagine he had a membership card under the name of Peter Cottly. In order to get it, he had to fill out an application. The information on the application—"

"I know all about applications. Don't try to tell me my business. And don't 'imagine,' either. People use all kinds of different names in all kinds of different places and put all kinds of things on applications."

"At any rate, Phil, I very much need whatever you can pick up. The man claimed to know me, and I haven't the slightest idea who he is."

"That's the whole trouble with you: Too many people know you." Quick slammed the telephone down without saying whether he would or wouldn't try to get the information.

He would, I hoped. He'd never yet disappointed me. This time I wasn't sure, though.

Dejectedly I went upstairs and crawled into bed. Tired as I was, however, I couldn't fall asleep. I kept thinking of Carol. If she died . . .

Other thoughts came and went, as well. Some had nothing to do with Kevin or the man he'd met at the health club. Others did, but only in a remote way. I recalled the conversation I'd had with Sam Gage, in Phoenix, and the things Bruno Langleider had said. The increase in the number of arson cases, the tons of marijuana and cocaine consumed in the United States—had the moral climate in America changed? Were people who committed acts of treason really different from other people?

That question, somehow, seemed important.

Finally sleep came. A deep and troubled sleep. I dreamed I was at a party. Sam Gage and Bruno Langleider were there, too. They warned me not to drink the Chianti. Adele appeared. "You're not drinking," she said. "The wine is poisoned," I told her. I had a sense of danger and wanted to leave the apartment, but couldn't find the exit. There were a lot of rooms with pictures on the walls, but none of them had a door that led to the outside. A man tapped me on the shoulder. "I know you," he said, "you're Brock Potter. Have some wine."

I woke and turned on the light. The bedside clock said three-thirty. My mouth was dry, and my heart was beating rapidly.

The party had been merely a dream, but the sense of danger persisted. I knew that no one had really tried to poison me, but I had the feeling that someone was very angry at me.

Eventually I fell asleep again, and dreamed of something else. But when the alarm clock went off, at seven, it was the first dream, and not the second, that I remembered.

26

"BACK AT WORK?" Tom asked hopefully.

"No," I replied. "Merely back at the office."

"And Carol?"

"They're doing everything possible, but her chances aren't good."

Tom looked stricken.

I took a deep breath. "Tell me something: Did I ever know anyone with a name like Peter Cottly?" Tom was my oldest friend; we'd begun our careers at the same time, with the same company.

"Cottly? I don't think so."

"Or anyone named Egan?"

"Egan? There was Dave Egan. Remember him? He drowned in the Bahamas, scuba diving. Had a heart attack or something and went down like a rock. Is that who you mean?"

"I don't know who I mean."

"About Carol . . . "

"I can't talk about her, Tom. Forgive me. I just can't."

Tom nodded sympathetically.

I cleared my throat. "Someone who said his name is Peter Cottly told Kevin Rand he knew me."

"Kevin Rand? You're not still—?"

"It's because of Kevin, in a way, that Bill Arden and Carol got shot." I gave Tom a capsule version of the story.

"My God!" he exclaimed.

"So you see," I said, "if Carol dies, it'll be partly my fault, as Bill's death is."

"I don't see it like that, at all. You're being too hard on yourself. You're doing what you always do: bearing other people's burdens."

"And whose burden is it?"

"Not yours, certainly."

"So I should just forget about the whole thing? Go on with my life? I *can't* forget about it, Tom. I *can't* go on with my life. Bill is one thing; I liked him, but he wasn't really important to me. Carol is something else. She *is* important. And Kevin—apparently I haven't yet paid in full for what I helped him do."

"You're starting to come apart at the seams again. Don't let it happen. Take it from me, nothing is worth that."

"I'm not. I almost did before, but I'm not now."

"You're blaming yourself without cause."

I began to get angry, and I didn't want to. So I said nothing.

Tom must have sensed what I was feeling, however, for he said, "Everyone has to follow his own blueprint, I guess. At any rate, what I came in to tell you is, Ward called from San Francisco last night. Bob Gerard has made a commitment. Between fifty and seventy-five million, to start. Not bad, eh? And it's all because of you. If you insist on blaming yourself for the bad, take credit for the good, as well." He got up and started for the door, but then he turned around and came back. "If there's anything Daisy or I can do . . . "

I tried to smile. "Thank you."

He left.

My thoughts went back to the day I'd spent in San Francisco. Tragedy on the one hand, profit on the other.

I tapped the symbols for Arden Electronics on my quote machine. The screen showed that the stock had dropped another two points.

The number of telephone messages on my desk had grown. I leafed through them. Martin Zweifert had called twice, I noted. Once on Friday, and again on Monday.

"Get me Martin Zweifert, at Zweifert, Hadley, Jones and Scott," I told Helen.

"I'm returning your calls," I said when he came on the line.

He didn't beat about the bush. "Terrible about Bill Arden," he said. "I'd like to ask you some questions."

"Not over the telephone," I replied.

"O.K. Where? When?"

A bar would be best, I thought; no point in starting unnecessary rumors by my being seen at his office. "The Oak Bar at the Plaza," I said, and glanced at my watch. "An hour from now."

"I have a luncheon date. I— All right; an hour from now, the Plaza."

We hung up, and I went to tell Irving about Hattie Sargent and Falmouth College. He agreed to cooperate.

On the way back to my own office, I stopped to check on the other researchers. George was the only one who was in. He was reading a magazine called *Advanced Optics*.

"Any hot items?" I asked.

"An article about Sid Jerome," he replied. "How's Carol?"

I told him.

A hard glint appeared in his eyes. For once he didn't look like a cleric with a problem. He looked like what he was, a very tough pragmatist with no illusions. "The world is full of sons of bitches," he said. It was his way of consoling me.

"Jerome," I said. "I dimly recall the name."

"He's the man Minton's just hired. Highly talented, it seems." The glint in George's eyes became even harder. "What happened to Bill Arden and Carol is bugging all of us," he said. "We'd like to help. Why don't you level with us, Brock?"

"You are helping," I said. "You're doing my work in addition to your own."

George wasn't about to be put off, however. "You'd talked to

Bill Arden in California. He'd just been to your house. What really happened?"

I was tempted to tell him. But then I decided that the crimes of Kevin Rand and Alfred Stone weren't a Price, Potter and Petacque problem; they concerned me personally. "All I can say is this," I told him. "Bill Arden trusted the wrong stone."

George blinked. Then his expression became dreamy. I'd given him what he liked best: an enigma.

I left him to work on it and headed back to my own office to get my coat. I didn't want to keep Zweifert waiting.

The Oak Bar at the Plaza, before the noon rush, is clubby. It's also free of stockbrokers, who at that hour are busy with their quote machines, the opinions of their in-house gurus, and their telephones.

Zweifert and I had one whole corner to ourselves. And the management didn't exactly get rich on us; each of us ordered a Perrier with lime and nursed it as if it were a dangerously intoxicating beverage.

Under ordinary circumstances, I would have enjoyed a few rounds of sparring with Zweifert. For two reasons. One, he was smart. Two, I knew he didn't like me. Price, Potter and Petacque was an annoying upstart that had taken away some of his business, and I was Price, Potter and Petacque's most aggravating member—people quoted me. I was a mosquito that Zweifert couldn't quite manage to swat.

My feelings about him were less clear-cut. I admired his intelligence and drive, but I thought life had been good to him for too long; he'd begun to believe his own myth.

Antagonists can be allies, though, and it was as allies that Martin Zweifert and I sipped our Perriers that morning. After a few initial thrusts and parries, that is.

"You're elusive," he charged.

"It depends on who's trying to catch me."

"You have a penchant for messy situations."

"Well, now, Marty, the lady who was with me at the Stiles, Levin and Sullivan party said you looked as if you wanted to pump me. My guess is it was one of those messy situations you wanted to pump me about."

We continued like that for three or four minutes and then got down to business. With candor on both sides.

"You were just about the last person Bill Arden talked to before he was killed," Zweifert began. "I want to know what he talked about."

"Why?" I asked.

"I own a hundred and twenty-five thousand shares of Arden Electronics, Brock. I personally. This past week has cost me three-quarters of a million dollars. Shall I try to recoup by selling short or hang on and wait for a turnaround?"

It was as straightforward a statement as I'd ever heard him make, and I admired him for it. No pious comments about his obligation to his customers or the welfare of the semiconductor industry. Simply, he personally had lost a bundle and was afraid of losing more. "It depends on how long you can afford to wait, Marty. The stock will drop another few points, I think, but eventually it will come back. If you can afford to wait—O.K. But you'll have to wait quite a while. Without Bill at the helm, it'll take two or three years for Arden to recover."

"Why did he let himself get pushed out?"

"He felt guilty."

Zweifert's eyebrows rose almost to his hairline. "Guilty? Of what, for God's sake?"

"You knew him as well as I did. Probably better, since, if I remember correctly, your company was one of his original underwriters. You knew him, you knew the other members of the family. You shouldn't have to ask me a question like that."

"I shouldn't, but I do. I let things get away from me. I delegated Arden to our semiconductor man, whom I fired last Thursday. He goofed, so I goofed. What did Bill feel guilty of, and how did you find out?"

"An alert member of my staff reported a rumor of trouble in the Arden family. I happened to be going to California. I made a point of driving down to chat with Bill. I got there at the psychological moment. He needed someone to talk to."

"I see. And the other part of my question?"

"Did you ever meet Alfred Stone, Bill's right-hand man?"

"Yes. Why?"

"Tell me about him."

"All right. I met him twice, and once we had dinner together— Bill, Al and I. At Al's house, incidentally. Bill was very much smitten by the guy. He liked the entire Stone family and, from what I could see, felt more comfortable with them than with his own. Bill and his wife were—well, we all change as we get older. At any rate, Bill thought the world of Al, and I was rather impressed by him myself. A quiet type, but a doer."

"Where did he come from?"

"The Charlton Corporation, as I recall. Made a bit of a name for himself there, young as he was. Bill showed me an article about him, one time. Charlton had won an award of some sort, and Bill was mentioned in connection with it."

"I see. Would you be able to get me an appointment with Stone's wife? As an old friend of yours, or something."

Zweifert considered. "Probably. Is that what you want?"

"Yes."

"Done, then. Now what about the second part of my question?"

"Stone was a traitor, Marty. He sold Arden secrets. That's why Bill felt guilty, and that's why the stock is dropping. The public is selling because Bill quit, and the Arden family is selling because the company's in the doghouse with the Pentagon."

Zweifert turned the color of ashes. "I see. Pressure on two fronts. Thank you for telling me. When do you want to meet Clarice Stone?"

"The sooner the better."

"I'll arrange it and get back to you this afternoon." He signaled the waiter, asked for the check and paid it.

I remained at the table after he left, to finish my drink and watch a little old lady who was seated a few tables away. She was at least eighty, I guessed, and she had the stern face of the farmer's wife in Grant Wood's *American Gothic.* But she was belting down martinis one after another and was putting the olives in her pocketbook. It was a fascinating performance and I might have watched longer, but the room began to fill up and get noisy, and I'd had all the Perrier I wanted.

The crisp September air and the traffic on Fifty-ninth Street made me forget about the old lady and the olives. My thoughts returned to Martin Zweifert. I had the annoying feeling that he'd casually said something important and I'd missed the point, but I couldn't think what it was.

27

DOUBTS AND A TROUBLED CONSCIENCE made the flight seem endless. I kept glancing at my watch and thinking it wasn't working right —hours couldn't possibly last so long.

My doubts weren't limited to this trip; they embraced everything I'd done since Thursday. Stamford, Durham, Boston and, now, the suburbs of San Francisco—I was a man who'd jumped on his horse and ridden off in all directions. I was doing what I'd always tried not to do: playing a hunch without asking myself whether it was a good one.

I'd taken the murder of Bill Arden as proof that there was a connection between Kevin Rand and Alfred Stone. Did the connection really exist? Granted, the East Germans and their big brothers in Moscow wanted our microtechnology; but this didn't mean that Kevin and Stone had been recruited by, or worked for, the same individual. Bill might have learned something about Stone that didn't apply to Kevin at all.

What impulse was driving me to question the women who'd been closest to the two men? Wasn't it probable that the women were the least likely to know?

What the hell was I doing on this airplane, anyway? I belonged in New York, no more than ten feet from the intensive-care unit at Saint Vincent's Hospital. When asked about Carol, the doctors had shaken their heads and refused to make predictions. Carol's parents had gone to the chapel in an attempt to tilt the balance in her favor and had asked me to join them, but I'd said I couldn't —I had a plane to catch.

And here I was, five miles above the ground, heading toward the other side of the continent. Was I doing Carol any good? Was I doing anyone any good?

Brock Potter, man on the move. Man with a mission.

On the move toward what? Define "mission." To catch a spy? To avenge a murder? To make America safe forever?

I came to the conclusion, after a while, that I didn't know *why* I was on the plane, but that, being me, I couldn't be anywhere else. I'd learned something from Hattie Sargent, and maybe I would learn something from Clarice Stone, too. Each little piece added to the picture. But regardless of whether or not I accomplished anything on this trip, I had to make the effort. Because many years ago an economics professor had told me I couldn't take his course and had started a chain of events that, for me, hadn't yet ended.

Twenty years after leaving New York, or so it seemed, the plane began its descent, and thirty minutes later I found myself negotiating with a sleepy-eyed young lady at one of the car-rental desks in the San Francisco airport. Only a few cars were available, I was told. It had been a busy day. I should have made a reservation in advance.

"I didn't know I was coming," I explained.

I was at last awarded a subcompact that had been passed by an inspector who didn't give a damn. There was a loose screw under the floorboard, and with each start or stop the screw rolled noisily from one end of the car to the other. But anything is better than nothing, at times, and in the clattering little automobile I headed out into the misty California night to find a place to sleep.

28

It was a beautiful house on a street of beautiful houses, no two of which were alike. This one was of redwood, glass and fieldstone, with a breezeway connecting it to a two-car garage. The garage had a basketball net attached to it, and there was a row of ceramic pots in the breezeway. The pots were brimming with red geraniums.

A woman whose gauntness made her seem ethereal opened the door, brushed a loose strand of hair from her forehead and made a valiant attempt to smile. "Mr. Potter?"

"Mrs. Stone?"

"Come in. I hope you didn't have any trouble finding the place." She glanced over my shoulder. "Were you followed?"

I turned around to check the street. I didn't see anything unusual. "I don't think so. By whom?"

"We've had so many police officers, FBI men, I don't know whatall hovering about that I'm never sure anymore whether we're being watched or not."

I was reasonably sure that no other car had pulled out of the motel's parking lot at the same time as mine. "Marty Zweifert and I—"

"He explained," Clarice Stone said, cutting my explanation short. "You were a friend of Bill Arden's. Dear Bill. We loved him so."

She led me through a large living room with a hooded fireplace to a family room that was even larger. One side of the family room faced the backyard, in which there was a swimming pool.

Arden Electronics paid well, I reminded myself, and Alfred Stone had been one of its top executives. Nevertheless, I couldn't help wondering how much of this spread had been paid for by the East Germans. "Lovely house," I observed.

"But such an unhappy one these days," Clarice Stone replied. "Can I offer you something? I've let the maid go, but I've never been helpless in a kitchen. Coffee, tea?"

"No, thanks."

We seated ourselves on a fifteen-foot sectional unit with a frame of imitation bamboo. The cushions were upholstered in a yellow and green fabric that depicted parrots. Clarice Stone went through the motion of brushing a strand of hair from her forehead, but this time the strand hadn't been there. A nervous mannerism, I concluded.

"I'm afraid I don't know Mr. Zweifert very well," she said, "but Bill did speak highly of him. I understand you want to talk about my husband. I must tell you, though, that I've been warned not to discuss the case." Again she ran her hand lightly across her forehead. "God! That we should be referred to as a case! Watched. Questioned. Our house searched. I don't know what to do. I feel so abandoned."

"A terrible situation," I agreed.

"Are you married, Mr. Potter?"

"No, I'm not."

"I don't suppose you'd understand, then. Al and I were husband and wife for seventeen years. We were married while we were still in college. We were, I thought, a happy couple. I'm not one of those people who take happiness for granted. I was always mindful of the fact that happiness can vanish into thin air. But I never expected mine to vanish like this. When you've been married to a man for seventeen years . . ." She sighed. She seemed fragile enough to be blown away by her own breath.

I recalled the basketball net. "You have children, I take it."

"Two boys, fourteen and nine. I'm terribly worried about them. Especially the younger one. He's become so withdrawn. If only he'd talk to me!" Her eyes filled with tears. "I don't know what to do." She squeezed the bridge of her nose.

"Bill told me part of the story," I said. "Your husband got a telephone call and said he had to leave. He left in a hurry, and no one has seen him since."

"I'm afraid he's dead, Mr. Potter." Her eyes overflowed. She wiped the tears away.

"According to Bill, he went to the airport. Drove to San Francisco, parked his car, then took a taxi. That doesn't suggest murder, Mrs. Stone."

"But it does! He must have been afraid of someone, and that person must have caught up with him. Not in San Francisco, but somewhere else."

"The same person who caught up with Bill?"

"Quite possibly. I wouldn't know. Dear Bill. I still can't believe he won't be coming for dinner, ever again. But my husband . . . It's the not knowing, don't you see? I can't believe he'd simply go away and make no attempt to get in touch with me. He *must* be dead."

I wasn't sure whether she was putting on an act, but I strongly suspected she was. "Did your husband ever mention anyone named Peter Cottly?" I asked.

She shook her head, without even giving herself time to think about it.

"Or Gerald Egan? Or Leslie Michaels?"

"My husband never discussed his business friends with me, Mr. Potter."

"I didn't say they were business friends."

She sighed. Again tears came to her eyes.

Damn good at it, I thought.

"Bill told me your husband was very capable," I said. "So did Marty Zweifert. I'm interested in your husband's career. Both of you were in college when you got married, you say. Where did you and he go, after college? What was his first job?"

"I'd love to tell you, Mr. Potter. I'd love to talk about my husband. Talking about him is all I have left, it seems. But the FBI was very explicit: I'm not to discuss the case with anyone. Case, mind you. I'm part of a case now. So are my children."

"Surely the FBI wouldn't object to your talking about your husband's first job. After all, it was a long time ago. It has nothing to do with what happened recently."

"They were very explicit."

I thought of my conversation with Zweifert. And suddenly remembered what he'd said that hadn't seemed significant until afterward. "Marty mentioned an article about your husband. He said your husband was working for the Charlton Corporation at the time and won some sort of award. I'm curious about that article. I'd like to see it."

"I'd be happy to show it to you, if I had it. Unfortunately, I don't know what article you're talking about, or what award, and my husband didn't keep a scrapbook."

"Have you any idea what magazine the article might have appeared in?"

"I'm afraid not. It must have been some technical journal, though; my husband was never written up in any really big magazine. And in those days we were just starting out. To think that it should come to this! Really, Mr. Potter, I don't know which way to turn."

The "we" might mean something, or it might not. In either case, I'd had enough. She wasn't convincing.

A bird with red-tipped wings lit on the branch of a eucalyptus tree, paused there, then took flight again, passing over the swimming pool. The bird and I felt the same way about this particular plot of ground, I thought; neither of us liked it.

Clarice Stone went on talking. She'd never had any reason to believe her husband didn't love her. Happiness was transient. Her husband was dead—that was the only possible explanation. How else could his silence be explained? I seemed to know more about his activities than she did.

Finally, I got to my feet. "There's no point in our continuing the conversation, Mrs. Stone. A lady I care for very much is in a New York hospital at this moment and may not live, simply because she was walking down the street with Bill Arden. And Bill—dear Bill, we loved him so—was shot because he was on your husband's trail. I admire good liars, Mrs. Stone, but you don't fall into the 'good' category; you're just a run-of-the-mill liar. I'm sorry about your kids—they really *do* have a problem. And I'm glad you're handy in the kitchen, because I see a lot of dirty dishes in your future. Don't bother to show me out—I'll find my own way."

I took a last look at the swimming pool and left the room.

She didn't follow me.

And, as far as I could determine, no car tailed mine to the airport.

In its own way, I thought, the trip had been successful. The pieces were beginning to fall into place.

29

Dr. Yarborough agreed to come in early. He would see me for a half hour before his first patient was due. Be on time, he said; Thursday was his busiest day.

I arrived promptly at seven-thirty. His office was on the ground floor of an apartment building on East Sixty-fifth Street. He admitted me himself; his receptionist didn't come in until a quarter to eight, he explained. He was a medium-size man with spectacles and a neatly trimmed beard; he reminded me of an art dealer I knew. The art dealer came from Wisconsin and described his youth as having been Twentieth-Century Dairy Farm, but you never would have guessed this by looking at him.

We went into the inner office, which was smaller than I'd expected, and cluttered. There was a picture of Freud on one wall and half a dozen diplomas on another, and across from the diplomas stood the couch on which Carol had spent so many hours trying to understand herself.

"Sit down," the doctor said, indicating the chair at the head of the couch, where, I supposed, he sat when he was dealing with his regular patients.

He seated himself at the desk and said, "Now then, what's on your mind, Mr. Potter?"

I hadn't thought I would be tongue-tied, but for the first few minutes I was. I kept wondering what Carol had told him about me and whether I ought to refute some of it. "I, er, well, let me put it this way, Dr. Yarborough: I want to ask you about something you told Carol. . . . This is confidential, isn't it?"

The doctor nodded.

"Because if it isn't . . . At any rate, I was out in California yesterday, talking to the wife of a man who did what Kevin Rand did—sold classified information to the East Germans—and I've been thinking maybe the two men had something in common. That's why I want to ask you about what you told Carol. You said treason is different from other crimes—it's caused by bitterness."

"Go on."

"That's what I want to know: *Is* treason caused by bitterness, and, if so, how do you detect bitterness? I mean, Kevin didn't come through to me as bitter, but maybe deep down inside he was. How does a person recognize it? I mean, you can X-ray the head for a tumor, but you can't X-ray it for an attitude."

The doctor smiled. "Sometimes even the tumor doesn't show up."

I glanced at the picture of Freud and wondered whether I'd brought my questions to the right place.

"What Carol said is an oversimplification," Yarborough went on. "My fault, perhaps. I oversimplified, to her. Bitterness is a very complicated feeling, with many aspects. It can be a powerful force, though, and if you're asking me whether I stand by what I said, the answer is yes. Kevin Rand, I believe, was motivated by bitterness more than anything else, and so are most other people who do what he did. They're trying to get even."

"For what?"

The doctor gave the arm of his chair a little slap and said, impatiently, "Mr. Potter, if I canceled the rest of my appointments for today and devoted the entire day to you, I still couldn't give you a complete answer to that."

"Carol said Kevin's being the oldest child in a big family might have had something to do with it. She also said something about adopted children."

"Did she? More oversimplifications. Not necessarily incorrect, but open to debate." Yarborough reflected, and relented. "Bitterness, like everything else that affects how we see things, begins early. The child—rightly or wrongly—feels unwanted, unloved, rejected, whatever. Resentment is kindled and smolders, often for the rest of the person's life. And occasionally erupts in the form of a criminal act, as in Kevin Rand's case."

"A permanent chip on the shoulder?"

"A chronic sense of injustice, of the wrongness of things. At any rate, there's a need to take it out on someone, even on an entire population. And the person who has that need feels justified. In his eyes, the world must be changed."

I looked at the clock and reminded myself that I'd been limited to thirty minutes. "Could you, Dr. Yarborough, spot that quality in a person? Just by talking to him, could you tell whether he's a potential spy?"

The doctor frowned thoughtfully.

"What I'm saying is, are there symptoms you'd look for?"

The frown disappeared. Behind the spectacles, the doctor's eyes brightened with amusement. "Mr. Potter, I'm not an authority on spies. I've never treated one."

"I'm serious, Dr. Yarborough. Are there symptoms? What would you look for? What questions would you ask?"

The amusement faded. "I wouldn't ask him whether he favored nuclear disarmament, if that's what you mean. Or what he thought of Russia. I suppose I might ask him how he felt about subway fares or how he liked his next-door neighbor. But you have to understand, Mr. Potter, I'm concerned with the total personality, not with particular facets of it."

"Suppose you weren't a psychiatrist, though. Suppose you were just an ordinary person, trying to find out whether someone has the sort of chip on his shoulder that it takes to betray his country."

Again the doctor slapped the arm of his chair. The impatient tone returned. "Mr. Potter, I *am* a psychiatrist, and I *don't* specialize in traitors."

"O.K., you are, and you don't. But someone who isn't does. And that person shot Carol."

The doctor stared at me.

"Now let's start over again," I said. "I believe that someone who works for the East German government reads our advanced-technology magazines. They're available on newsstands; anyone can buy them. I believe that this person pays special attention to those articles dealing with our military hardware, although he doesn't confine himself to that. I believe he notes the names of people who are mentioned in the articles—engineers, physicists, mathematicians, even people like the man whose wife I saw yesterday, who wasn't a scientist but an expediter. I believe he makes it his business to meet them and talk to them, and by talking to them he's able to determine how willing they'd be to sell secrets. Ninety-nine percent of them aren't—probably more than ninety-nine percent—but every now and then he runs across one who is, and that's the person he works with. He doesn't need many; he simply needs the right ones in the right places. Do you understand?"

The doctor continued to stare at me. He didn't answer right away.

"Do you?"

He pursed his lips, leaned back in his chair and contemplated the ceiling. Finally he spoke. "I understand, Mr. Potter. What you're really asking me is whether there's such a thing as a good natural psychologist, someone gifted with keen insight. The answer, of course, is yes. Everyone who's successful in getting along with other people has insight, and some individuals have a great deal of it. As to whether someone could spot a potential traitor, I don't know. I suppose it would be a trial-and-error process." Dr. Yarborough stopped gazing at the ceiling and sat up straight. "The person would know what he's looking for, he might have had specialized training, he probably has a likable personality—yes, I can see it. But the results wouldn't be perfect. There'd always be the possibility of failure."

"He doesn't have to be successful all the time," I said. "Only part of the time."

The doctor's eyebrows came together. For a moment he appeared quite Mephistophelian. "And you believe that such a person shot Carol?"

"Yes. First Bill Arden, then Carol. Bill, I'm convinced, had discovered who the man was and what he did. How Bill arrived at this conclusion, I don't know, but evidently he was right. At any rate, he accidentally tipped his hand, and the man followed him and shot him. Then the man shot Carol." I took a deep breath. "It wasn't necessary for him to shoot Carol, Dr. Yarborough. She wouldn't have been able to identify him—he was wearing a ski mask—but he shot her anyway. Evidently that's the sort of person he is. Thorough."

There was a silence. I looked at the clock. My time had almost run out.

"You know who the man is?" the doctor asked, at last.

"Not yet," I said, "but I'm beginning to get a handle on him."

"I've been in touch with Carol's doctors on a daily basis," Yarborough said, after another silence.

"So have I. They don't offer much encouragement."

"We mustn't give up hope. Miracles do happen."

I sighed. "Occasionally." I saw that I had two minutes left to go, but decided I didn't need them. "Thank you for your time, Dr. Yarborough."

We shook hands, under Freud's watchful eyes.

I'd brought these particular questions to the right place, I felt, but the remaining questions would have to be answered elsewhere.

30

"Where's George?" I demanded impatiently.

"On his way to Cleveland," Irving replied. "Or at least he should be. He has a date with Allied this afternoon."

"See if he's left home yet. If he hasn't, stop him. I want him here." I went down the corridor to my own office.

"Mr. Quick called," Helen said.

"Get him back for me. I don't want any other incoming calls, though."

I hung up my coat, sat down at my desk and looked at the mail and telephone messages, but didn't do anything about them.

"Mr. Quick isn't available," Helen reported. "I left word."

Irving came in. "I caught George just as he was leaving. He'll be here as soon as he can. Someone should keep the date with Allied, though. It's important."

"Who's on deck?"

"No one but me, and I—"

"To hell with it, then."

"Yes, boss." Irving beat a hasty retreat.

Ward Carlton strolled in, beaming.

"I don't want to hear about it," I said.

Ward, too, beat a hasty retreat.

I closed my door and waited for the call from Quick.

It came through at ten-thirty.

"I told you I can't do anything with assumed names," Quick began, pugnaciously.

"What about—?"

"Don't give me any what abouts, Potter. No Peter Cottly belonged to any Jackson's Health Club when you said. Three men worked on it and cost you a bundle. They not only checked out Jackson's, they checked out every health club in the whole damn area. And they're good men, too. No Cottly. Either you got to give me the right name or forget it." Quick was silent for a couple of seconds, which was longer than his silences usually lasted. When he spoke again, it was in a different tone of voice; he sounded almost humble. "I'm sorry, Potter. Most of the time I can come through for you. This time I couldn't."

"In a way you did, Phil. Thank you."

I put the telephone down, thought for a little while, then buzzed Helen. "Get me Adele Rand," I said, and gave her the number.

"Mrs. Rand on line one," Helen informed me presently.

"Adele?" I said. "Brock. Let me ask you a couple of questions. When Kevin was living in Boston, did he ever mention a friend of his named Peter Cottly? Presumably, it's someone who belonged to the same health club he did. And did Kevin hurt his back?"

"Hurt his back?"

She followed the trial, I thought. She knows about the therapist.

"I'm not sure," she said, after a moment. "If he did, it couldn't have been serious. Why do you ask?"

"Because I've heard that he did and heard that he didn't. What about my other question?"

"The name isn't familiar to me. Let me ask Rosalie."

I waited.

"Rosalie says the name isn't familiar to her, either," Adele said when she returned to the telephone. "And she doesn't know whether Kevin hurt his back or not."

"What about Gerald Egan? Did Kevin ever mention him?"

"Isn't he the man who—?"

"Yes."

"You think Kevin knew him as far back as Boston?"

"I think he might have."

"You really *are* looking into things, aren't you?"

"I'm trying."

"Bless you."

We chatted for a few minutes. Adele asked about Carol. I said that Carol had developed pneumonia and was in very bad shape.

"I can't begin to tell you how sorry I am, Brock."

I quoted Dr. Yarborough. "We mustn't give up hope. Miracles do happen."

"You're a staunch man, my dear. But then, you always were."

"What about Gerald Egan?" I asked again. "Did Kevin ever speak of him?"

"No, not to me. But of course it's hardly likely that he would. This Mr. Egan—is he the one who knew you, do you think?"

"I'm not sure, but I'm grasping at every straw, Adele."

"So some good may come out of this, after all. I'm glad."

On that note, we ended the conversation.

A few minutes later, Helen announced that Mr. Cole was waiting to see me. I told her to send him in.

George had never in his life burst into a room, I guessed, and he didn't quite burst into my office then. But he did reach my desk in record time. "What's up?" he asked.

"That magazine you were reading the other day," I said. *"Advanced Optics,* I think it was called. Where did you get it?"

"There's a magazine and book store a few blocks from here, on Broadway. Why?"

"Do you have a lot of magazines like that, George? High-technology stuff?"

"Sure. A whole drawerful. And more at home. That's one of the ways I keep up. Don't you?"

"No. I buy one every now and then, but that's all."

"What's this about, Brock?"

"I'd like to see your drawerful."

We went into the office George shared with Joe, Brian and Harriet. He opened the drawer. There were at least thirty magazines in it, arranged alphabetically and chronologically.

I took several of them out, looked at the publication data and noted that different publishers were involved. It would be impossible to get the mailing lists of all of them, I realized. And even if it were possible to get the lists, a special computer program would have to be devised to pick out the names of people who subscribed to more than one of the magazines. Besides, the man I was looking for might buy his magazines at a store, as George did.

"*Now* will you tell me what this is all about?" George asked.

We returned to my office and sat down.

"You remember what I said about Bill Arden trusting the wrong stone, George?"

George nodded. "I've been playing with that. I still don't have the answer, but—"

"Well, I'll give you the answer." I told him what had happened at Arden Electronics. Then I summarized my interview with Dr. Yarborough. "Someone is doing what you're doing," I said, in conclusion. "He's keeping up. And at the same time planting traitors in strategic spots. Kevin Rand and Alfred Stone could be two of many."

The hard glint that I'd seen in George's eyes before reappeared. "Where do I fit into this?" he asked in a flat voice. "What would you like me to do?"

"First, check on exactly how Kevin and Stone got their jobs. Who hired them. The complete procedure, with names. Talk to the people at Calthorp and Arden. Do whatever is necessary. Then I want you to arrange to meet this Jerome you've been talking about. I want to know how he got *his* job."

"That's easy, Brock. Jerome got his job through Carris Associates. I know that for a fact. Minton gets a lot of his people through them. He's probably their best customer."

"Well, I want you to question the man."

"What about questioning Carris?"

"I'll do that myself. I know him personally."

George's expression, and voice, softened. He seemed to become more remote. "I really do think, Brock, that in checking with Calthorp and Arden on the hiring I'll be on ground the FBI has already covered. That was probably the first thing they looked into, and the thing they looked into most thoroughly. Don't you agree?"

"They might have missed something, though. Get right on it."

George left my office.

I got up from my desk and began to pace. My mind was racing. I had the feeling that, although I didn't know quite where I was heading, I was on the right track. It was a feeling that sometimes came to me when I was nearing the solution to a research problem that had been worrying me; I didn't know what the solution was, exactly, but I sensed that it was within reach. My associates claimed that at such moments my personality changed. My normal tempo was a fast trot, they said, but at such moments I went into a full gallop. I also became impatient, irritable and intolerant. This was the opposite of the way I'd behaved during the past spring and summer, when I'd been doubting my capacities. Then, I'd been pleasant but vague. Now I had a strong sense of my own competence. I was on top of things. In charge. Unstoppable.

As I paced, I made a mental timetable. Locating Jerome—three hours. Exploring Calthorp's and Arden's executive hiring routines —a day and a half. Consultation with Minton—thirty minutes. Then Boston.

In making the timetable, I considered George. I compared him with myself. His way of responding to challenges was completely different from mine. Vagueness, in him, indicated that he was traveling at his top intellectual speed, which was very high indeed. When he appeared not to know what he was doing, or even where he was—watch out.

Perhaps he would locate Jerome in less than three hours. Perhaps it would take only one day to get the information from

Calthorp and Arden. Perhaps I would be able to leave for Boston tonight.

I thought about what I was going to say to Hattie Sargent: Irving's daughter was particularly interested in music; would she be able to take private piano lessons from a member of the Falmouth faculty? If not, whom would Hattie recommend?

That would get me the appointment. What I would say later . . .

The encounter took shape in my mind. I began to pace faster.

Suddenly my telephone rang. I stopped abruptly, and frowned. I'd told Helen not to put through any call but Quick's.

Helen must have gone to lunch, I thought. But I decided to check.

She was sitting where she always sat. Her face had lost all color, and her mouth was twitching. "You'd better—take this, Mr. Potter," she said in a ragged voice. "It's—important."

I hesitated a moment, then went to my desk and picked up the telephone.

It was Mrs. Fox. She wanted me to know that Carol had just died.

31

"YOU REALLY OUGHT TO EAT SOMETHING," Tom said solicitously. He was sitting in the den with me.

I shook my head. For the past hour I hadn't spoken a word to anyone.

Daisy came in with the whiskey decanter. She'd taken it into the living room a few minutes earlier; Mr. Fox had needed a drink. As she put it on the desk, she gave me an anxious glance and said, "You really ought to eat something, Brock."

Once more I shook my head.

Daisy left. Tom got up and followed her. I heard them talking in the foyer, but couldn't make out what they were saying, and didn't care.

I looked at the decanter. Carol had said I should put it away while I was being televised—people would think I was a lush. That was the last time we'd been together in this room. The last time we ever would be.

The chance for us to make corrections had gone. It was no longer possible to change course, do things differently, try again. The options had been canceled. Our relationship was only a memory, its imperfections unalterable.

It had been getting better, I thought. We'd been making progress. If we'd continued, we might eventually have known a really good sort of love.

But now we couldn't continue. Continuation was out. Our permit had been revoked.

Mark walked into the den. He'd been in the living room with Joyce, Daisy and the Foxes. "Are you all right?" he asked.

I nodded.

"Mr. Fox . . . " He hesitated.

I nodded again. I knew what Mark wanted to say: Mr. Fox was taking it very hard. So was Mrs. Fox, I thought, but in a different way. There was nothing I could do for either of them, though. I couldn't bring their daughter back, or help them get used to the idea that she wasn't coming back. I was still trying to get used to that idea myself.

"A drink?" Mark suggested.

I nodded.

He poured some Scotch into a glass. "I'll get ice cubes," he said.

I shook my head and took the glass from him. I'd had a lot to drink in the past few hours, but it hadn't affected me—I didn't feel the least bit anesthetized.

Mark watched me sip the Scotch. He didn't say anything. I stroked Tiger, who was curled up on my lap. Presently Mark returned to the living room.

Tiger made a restless movement. He wanted to be released, I guessed; I'd been holding him too long. But I couldn't bring myself to let him go.

I tried to remember what time I'd come home. Tom had gone to the hospital with me in a taxi. At the hospital we'd had problems with Mr. Fox, but eventually we'd persuaded him and his wife to come to my house. Then Tom and Mrs. Fox had gone back to the hospital to make what Tom called "the arrangements." After a while, Joyce had arrived at the house, and she'd been followed by Mark, with Daisy. I still couldn't figure out how Mark had got together with Tom's wife instead of his own, or who'd told Joyce that Carol was dead, or at what hour the various comings and goings had occurred, but I had the feeling that the afternoon had been extremely long.

Except for being confused about time, I was all right, it seemed to me. I'd made plane reservations for the Foxes and myself. They were leaving for Minneapolis tomorrow morning, with the body. I was leaving tomorrow night, to be there for the funeral on Saturday. I'd also placed an order with the deli, because Louise couldn't handle dinner for six extra people on the spur of the moment.

I was all right, really. I just didn't want to talk.

It was past Louise's quitting time, I thought. Nice of her to stay. And I was glad she'd brought Tiger; I needed him.

Joyce appeared in the doorway. "Brock . . . "

I acknowledged her presence with a nod.

She didn't really have anything to say. After standing in the doorway for a few moments, with a troubled expression, she went away.

Carol had said, "This may not be the real thing, but I think it's as close to the real thing as either of us will ever come."

A dismal forecast, and not entirely accurate. We'd been coming closer to the real thing. We definitely had been. Given another few months, another few years, we might have made it.

But the clock had run out. The game was over. The score was final. We'd done the best we could.

A man in a ski mask. A man who claimed to know me.

I pondered for a long while. Alone in the den, with my dog on my lap.

Finally Tom reappeared. "Are you O.K.?"

I gazed at him, then said, "No. I'm angry."

"You really ought to have something to eat," he urged.

"Yes," I agreed, "I suppose I should." I deposited Tiger on the floor, got up from the chair and went in to the dining room.

The strangeness of Thursday lasted into Friday. I wandered about the house in slacks and a sport shirt, not knowing what to do with myself. At times I thought I should go to the office, but when I pictured myself there, I changed my mind. I wouldn't be effective, and I didn't want to listen to all the expressions of sympathy. Eventually I would have to cope with them, but I didn't think I was ready yet.

Tom called, Mark called, Irving called. So did their wives. I assured everyone I was fine. It might take me a little while to get back to normal, but I expected to be at work on Monday morning.

At noon I gave Louise my key to Carol's apartment and told her to drop Carol's things off there; I didn't want them around as reminders. Then I went out for a walk, circling the block in order to avoid the spot where the murders had occurred. Murders, now; plural; no longer one dead and one wounded.

New York hadn't changed, I noted. Sixth Avenue was still Sixth Avenue, a good-bad street where people earned and spent their livelihoods and ran the many little errands that were so much a part of everyone's week. The bakery where Carol and I had sometimes shopped was operating as usual. The dry-cleaning establishment had customers. The restaurant where I'd taken Carol on the night I'd told her about the call from Adele Rand wasn't open yet, but it would be at five o'clock, and meanwhile someone was vacuuming the carpet.

Eventually Sixth Avenue would get better or worse, like everything else. But the improvement or deterioration would be gradual.

Gradual is better than sudden, I thought. Sudden is hard to take.

I paused outside a shop near Eighth Street. There was a sweater I liked in the window. I didn't buy it, however. I had enough sweaters.

Gradual, sudden. Carol had lived for a week after being shot. Deep down, I'd expected her to pull through somehow. But I'd been wrong. Whoever or whatever made the big decisions had decided otherwise. He, She, It had given Carol a week. A week and no more.

The empty feeling would take some getting used to, I supposed. I stopped at a bar I'd never been to before and ordered a margarita, something I seldom drank, simply because it *was* something I seldom drank. After lingering over it for a half hour, I left. This would be the pattern for a while, I guessed: new places, new faces. A sort of aimlessness, at least on weekends. But then, some weekends I would be out of town. No need to fly back to New York every Friday night; Sunday would be soon enough.

Raincoat, hat, ski mask. Why shoot Carol?

A thought came to me. It was one I'd had before, but now I played with it at length.

On the way home, I forced myself to pass the spot where the murders had occurred. Forced myself to stand there for a few minutes, imagining someone else's thoughts.

Finally I continued the rest of the way to my house, to change clothes and pack my bag—my flight was due to leave in two hours.

I really didn't want to go to Minneapolis, I admitted. I wanted to stay in New York and get on with what I had to do. But the trip was obligatory. One has to say good-bye to one's friends.

So I placed a call to George Cole and gave him additional instructions. Then I took a cab to the airport, flew to Minneapolis and spent the night there.

And when Carol was buried, at one o'clock on Saturday afternoon, I was part of the crowd at the graveside.

32

I BEGAN THE STAFF MEETING with a short speech that probably wasn't necessary. "I guess you all know what happened," I said, "and I know how all of you feel. You knew Carol and liked her, and she liked you. Well, she isn't here anymore, and I'd just as soon leave it at that. Simply—she isn't here anymore. But I still am, and Price, Potter and Petacque still is, and as far as I'm concerned the job still has to be done and I'll continue to do it."

After that, we got down to work. I wasn't able to contribute much, because I'd been out of touch. And it took all the power of concentration I could muster to stay with what the others were contributing. But I did preside, and I did keep my thoughts focused, and I did manage to act as arbitrator of conflicting opinions.

At the end of the meeting, I told Irving that I expected to be tied up with personal matters for a few more days, and that I might need some help from George.

"Anything you want, Brock," Irving replied.

Later, I invited George to have lunch with me.

"All right, now," I said, as soon as we were seated in the restaurant, "what did you accomplish?"

He unfolded his napkin with delicacy and placed it on his lap. "First, Konklin University Press. Saturday I talked to a man I know who's in publishing. The press doesn't make any money. In fact, it loses money. The university would be glad to shed it, if it could. So far it hasn't been able to, because of Cordelia Konklin Fisher, Abner Konklin's granddaughter. She wants it kept going, because it publishes two religious books a year, and she has a say about them. But she's near ninety.

"Years ago, the press did publish some good stuff; but that was then, and this is now, and it's been a downhill slide for quite a while. The man I talked to has never heard of Hattie Sargent and doubts that she's known outside of academic circles, or even has much of a reputation within them. He guesses that Konklin breaks even on her books, though, and she writes with enough of a religious slant to satisfy Mrs. Fisher. And from the other side, as you said, the books give Hattie Sargent the feeling that she is somebody, and at the same time they make Falmouth College look good.

"More to the point, in my own opinion, is the fact that Konklin itself isn't doing well. The university, I mean. None of those small private universities is having an easy time, and Konklin is no exception. I suspect that it could be persuaded to part with the press, despite Mrs. Fisher, if the price was right."

"And the right price would be . . . ?"

"Roughly a million and a half." George opened his menu, studied it and said, "Liver and onions, I think."

I wasn't hungry. A grilled cheese sandwich would have suited me fine, but this wasn't the sort of place that served grilled cheese sandwiches, so I picked something else. "Cold roast beef for me," I said.

The waiter took our orders, pouted when we said we didn't want wine, and left.

"So who's the man I should talk to?" I asked George.

"Roger Merriman is head of the press. He's where you'd begin." George smoothed out a wrinkle in the tablecloth. "It's none of my business, of course, but do you really intend to buy the press, Brock?"

"You're right," I said. "It is none of your business." Then I apologized. "Forgive me. I'm on a peculiar frequency right now."

He nodded.

"What about Jerome?" I asked.

George folded his hands in his lap, gazed over my head and went into a state resembling a trance. "I met with Sid Jerome yesterday from a quarter past three until ten after four. Dr. Jerome, he likes to be called. He lives here in New York, although he's getting ready to move to Maryland a week from Tuesday—the Seaboard Experimental Center is where he's going to work. But this is where he's lived for the past four and a half years, and, oddly enough, he's your neighbor. He has a one-bedroom apartment on East Thirteenth Street, less than four blocks from you."

I raised my eyebrows, but George didn't notice—he was still gazing over my head. He seemed to be talking to what he saw there—telling it, in extraordinary detail, what he'd observed and thought during the fifty-five minutes he'd spent with Herb Minton's most recently acquired expert. I was accustomed to George's precision, but he was making a special effort now, describing everything about the man from his pencil-line moustache to his rubber-soled shoes, which, George said, were the color of Georgia clay.

The picture he painted was of a thirty-three-year-old introvert who had a head so filled with mathematical abstractions that it was difficult for him to communicate on a normal level. A man of modest physical needs, with little interest in his surroundings—the sort of man who would have to be reminded that it was time to eat and wouldn't notice that he was wearing a blue sock on his right foot and a brown one on his left. And yet a man who knew what he wanted. He'd been persuaded to leave his present job and join Seaboard not because of the salary he'd been offered but because at Seaboard he would have his very own computer—he didn't like having to wait for computer time. And

George ventured the opinion that the exclusive use of a computer served the same purpose for Jerome that being published did for Hattie Sargent: It enhanced his sense of himself.

The waiter brought our food and again suggested wine.

"Not today," I told him.

George attacked the liver and onions with gusto, and went on talking about Jerome.

Finally, however, he came to the end of his mental notes, and I was able to ask, "Did you detect any signs of bitterness? Would you say he's resentful about anything?"

Putting down his fork, George considered the question. "Perhaps," he said cautiously. "A little. About not having free use of the computer where he is now, mainly. But as for his being the type to work for the East Germans—that's what you're getting at, isn't it?—I don't know. I doubt it. That kind of bitterness I didn't sense."

"That kind of bitterness often doesn't show, George."

George drank some water. He said nothing.

"Kevin," I prodded. "Stone. How they got their jobs."

"Kevin Rand applied for the job and got it. Simple as that. Nothing unusual at all. He submitted his résumé, there was an opening, he was hired."

"He was screened, I believe."

"Definitely. Background check, verbal interview with the personnel director and the vice-president in charge of engineering. The personnel director has since been fired, as you might guess, and the director of engineering came close to getting fired, but actually neither of them really did anything wrong."

"No employment agency?"

George shook his head.

"And Stone?"

"I've talked to a contact I have at the Charlton Corporation, where you said he used to work. Stone was a wonder there. They loved him. But, as you said, he was mentioned in an article, and apparently Bill Arden saw the article and made it his business to hire the guy. The lady I talked to didn't know the details, but she believes Arden made the overture himself. Arden was a great salesman—I don't have to tell you that. Probably took him all of twenty minutes to persuade Stone to drop everything and move right out to California." George paused. "I haven't verified any of this, and I can't unless I go to California, but, based on what the lady told me, Arden didn't use a middleman either. He picked out his own stone, you might say." George smiled at his own choice of words. Then he sobered and asked, "You want me to go out to California?"

"I don't think so," I replied. "Dessert?"

"I wouldn't mind some melon."

George had his melon, and we walked back to the office.

Herbert Minton had called twice, Helen informed me. "Shall I get him back?" she asked.

"Not just yet, Helen. First I'd like to talk to a Mr. Roger Merriman at the Konklin University Press, and then I'd like to talk to a Mr. Ronald Carris—Carris Associates, here in New York."

"And, ah, Mr. Bakersfield called." Helen lowered her voice to almost a whisper. "The FBI."

"Oh? Well, he can wait, too. Right now get me Merriman."

I sat down at my desk and waited.

Merriman was in. So was Carris.

"All right," I told Helen after making my date with Carris, "now I'm ready for Mr. Bakersfield and Mr. Minton."

Both men wanted to see me at their offices. Both men were angry, but didn't want to explain why over the telephone. Minton was the angrier of the two.

"There's something I'd like to discuss with you," he said in an icy voice. "I'd like you at my office at four, if that's convenient."

"What's on your mind, Herb?"

"We'll discuss it when I see you."

"O.K., but I don't think I can make it at four. I'll be tied up until at least seven."

There was a long and very hostile silence.

"I'll wait," Minton said, at last.

Of course you will, I thought. Then I placed my final call. To Perry, the man who had been Carol's boss.

He agreed to cooperate.

33

THE OUTER OFFICE was pure Mies Van der Rohe—clean lines, functional materials, and nothing sexy.

The receptionist was a man. He was rather Mies Van der Rohe, too. The same air of trim, cool, neat efficiency. A slender, good-looking fellow with high cheekbones, pale skin and gray eyes, he rose as I approached the glass table behind which he sat. I judged him to be between thirty-five and forty, and athletic.

He gave me an impersonal smile. "Mr. Potter?"

"Yes."

"I'm Frank Roche, Mr. Carris's assistant. Mr. Carris will be with you shortly. He's on a long-distance call at the moment. Please sit down." He didn't offer to shake hands, and neither did I.

I sat, and noted the magazines on the table beside my chair—*Fortune, Forbes* and *Business Week.* I also noted the room's one concession to nature: a rubber plant.

Roche went back to his station and folded his hands on the table. He seemed to have nothing to do. There was a typewriter on a stand near one wall and some books and supplies on a single shelf above it, but no other evidence of incoming or outgoing mail. And the only suggestion that Roche ever did anything besides sit with his hands folded was offered by a telephone and an executive appointment book that were positioned just off his left elbow.

"Busy day?" I asked.

"Normal," he replied.

"People are always changing jobs, I guess."

"It's like anything else."

I gave up and spent the next few minutes watching the rubber plant grow. It grew very slowly.

Presently there was a buzz from an undisclosed source.

Roche got up. "Mr. Carris will see you now."

He crossed the room and opened the door to the inner office. I followed him.

Carris came forward to greet me. His handshake was almost an embrace. "Sorry to keep you waiting," he said. "Dallas."

Roche withdrew and closed the door noiselessly.

"Come and sit down," Carris said, taking me by the arm and leading me over to a pair of facing Mies Van der Rohe chairs. "It's a pleasure to see you. Really."

"As I explained over the phone, this is sort of a nuisance mission," I said. "I hope you'll forgive me."

"Someone like you is never a nuisance," he said, dropping into one of the chairs and waving me toward the other. "You represent wealth and power, both of which I love with a passion and fawn over."

I laughed. "You? Fawn? Never!"

"Oh, but I do! How else do you think I got where I am? Me, a lean, hungry kid from Brooklyn, mingling with corporation presidents and CEOs! I fawn and fawn and fawn. Surprising how well it works."

"I can't see you as lean and hungry, ever."

"Good. I'd hate to think my origins showed. Tell me more about your mission."

I looked around. This was where all the work got done, apparently. There were two tall stacks of manila folders on the desk, and they were surrounded by the sort of clutter I was familiar with. But there were only two doors in the entire suite: the one between the inner and outer offices, and the one that connected the outer office with the public corridor. "Where are the Associates?" I asked.

"There aren't any," Carris replied. "Unless you want to call Frank an associate, which he isn't—he's simply a damn good assistant. No, it ought to be called Ronald Carris, period; but when I was just starting out, I didn't think that sounded impressive enough. I debated between 'Associates' and 'Limited' and decided on 'Associates'—somehow, it sounded bigger to me." He paused. "I've had plenty of chances to take in partners and expand, but I've never wanted to. I don't want all the clients in America; I merely want the best."

The telephone rang. Carris excused himself and went to answer it.

I couldn't help overhearing his end of the conversation. Evidently the person he was talking to was upset, for Carris kept saying things like "Calm down" and "You're taking it too seriously." Twice he glanced at me and extended his hand, palm up, in a gesture that seemed to mean: What can a guy do? But toward the person who was calling he was patient and reassuring.

Finally, he said, "Look, you're making much too much of the whole incident. Why don't you and I get together for dinner and talk it all out? I'll switch you over to Frank, and he'll set up a date." He pushed a button on the telephone and said, "Take this." Then he put the telephone down and came back to me.

"Egos," he said. "Always egos."

"You're an ego specialist," I suggested.

"What else?" he replied. "It got me from Brooklyn to Park Avenue." He sat down again. "Soothing egos and fawning. They go together. But tell me about your mission. You said it was for a friend."

"Yes. He's looking for a sales manager and hasn't been able to find one. I said I'd see what I could do. I thought maybe you could help."

"It's possible. Tell me more."

I described Perry's company. Essentially, I said, it was a buying service for women's ready-to-wear stores around the country that weren't large enough to maintain offices in New York. When the owners and their buyers came to town, Perry introduced them to manufacturers, made recommendations, consolidated orders. At other times he did the buying for them. His sales manager visited the customers periodically, studied their needs and kept them up to date. The company's volume was roughly four million, I added, and the sales manager got thirty-five thousand, plus expenses.

Carris nodded encouragingly while I was speaking, but when I finished he said, "I don't know that I'm the best person for something like that, Brock. I don't have contacts in the soft-goods business. It's never been my thing."

"I didn't know you specialized."

"I don't really 'specialize,' but there are certain things I've always stayed away from. Soft goods, advertising agencies, the entertainment field—anything volatile, where there's an unusually high rate of personnel turnover. Unlike some I could name, I'm not after the fast buck. Once I get an individual placed, I like him to stay placed. I don't think people in my profession do themselves any favors when they place the same individual too often. I believe in lasting relationships."

"Isn't that rather difficult with someone like Herb Minton?"

Carris smiled. "Herb does try my patience, at times."

"Requires a lot of fawning, does he?"

A twinkle appeared in Carris's eyes. It made me a fellow conspirator. "Strictly between you and me, yes. He has an ego the size of Texas. Or so it appears to most people. Actually, within himself, he's very shaky. You have to understand that when you're dealing with him. I've known him a long time and I do understand it. I find him easy to get along with."

I looked around the room again. A couple of filing cabinets, an electric calculator, a nice bar. The place was beginning to make sense to me. Carris didn't do a lot of office work; what he did was mix martinis, buy meals and supply tickets to major sporting events. He was telling the truth when he said he fawned. He didn't need a big staff; all he really needed was a telephone and plenty of credit cards. "How long have you known him?" I asked.

"Years. . . . You seem to like my office."

I nodded and said, "Actually, I think, you're your office. Wherever you happen to be—that's the office. It's all contacts."

"Contacts are a large part of it."

"Does Herb like girls?"

There was a barely perceptible tightening around Carris's mouth.

"Oops," I said, "I've gone too far."

"Not you," said Carris. "Me. Normally I don't let my hair down the way I have with you. Do you have that effect on everyone?"

"Not as often as I'd like. But about Perry—"

"I'll keep it in mind. If I run across anything, I'll let you know. Anything's possible."

"I'd appreciate it." I got up. "Sorry I made a nuisance of myself, but as I said over the telephone, it's a nuisance mission."

"Not at all." He got to his feet and walked me to the door. "I wish I could have been more helpful."

We shook hands, and I proceeded into Frank Roche's domain. Carris closed the door behind me.

I went over to the glass table. Roche looked up. "How do you stay so slim?" I asked.

"I jog," he said, startled.

"I thought so," I said. "Great for the legs. Have a nice day." And with that, I left.

34

THERE WERE ONLY TWO of them this time—Bakersfield and Dillon—
and even that was one too many. Bakersfield could have handled
me by himself. The only purpose Dillon served, I concluded after
a while, was to give Bakersfield someone with whom to exchange
significant glances.

"Mr. Potter, we've had a disturbing communication from our
San Francisco office," he began, his expression that of a poker
player who's holding four aces but is determined not to let you
know. "It concerns you. The substance of it is, you've been harassing the wife of a man who figures in an inquiry we're conducting."

His language intrigued me. We'd referred to Stone by name the
last time I'd been here. Why had he suddenly become simply "a
man who figures in an inquiry"? The only reason I could think of
was that Bakersfield was more afraid of sharing the secrets than
he'd been before.

"Could you be more specific?" I said.

Bakersfield looked at Dillon. Dillon looked at Bakersfield. Then
both of them looked at me.

"What you did is liable to be construed as interference with an
ongoing investigation," Bakersfield said.

I met his gaze. "It depends on who's doing the construing, I
suppose, and what you mean by 'harassing.' If you're talking

about Clarice Stone, I didn't harass her, I called her a liar. Which I believe she is. But if she's unhappy about that, she's even more unhappy about the attention you guys have been paying her. She complained bitterly. She feels you're picking on her."

He wasn't deterred. "What we'd like to know, Mr. Potter, is why you went to see her and why you questioned her about her husband. She says she'd never met you before—she consented to meet you only because she'd been asked to by a mutual friend, a Martin Zweifert. What stake in the matter do you think you have?"

"I hope you'll forgive my saying this," I replied, "but you knock me out, Mr. Bakersfield. Here you're asking me the very thing I spent over an hour trying to tell you a week ago last Saturday. If you have notes of that interview, take a look at them."

The two FBI men exchanged another glance. The exchange was meant to intimidate me, I guessed. And it almost worked. But I continued anyway.

"Furthermore," I said, "Mr. Zweifert is a stockbroker, as I am. He has, or did have, a substantial position in Arden Electronics, which as of last week had already caused him to lose three-quarters of a million dollars. And Arden is a stock I've recommended, and unrecommended, to my own customers. Since the value of the stock is being affected by the inquiry you people are conducting, Mr. Zweifert and I have a professional interest in the situation out there. Clarice Stone, I thought, might be worth a few questions. And I called her a liar because I think she is a liar. I think she knew exactly what her husband was up to. She might even have encouraged him. I can't prove it, and you may not be able to prove it either, but that's my opinion."

"That's a serious allegation. Do you have anything to support it?"

"Unfortunately, no. It's just a gut feeling."

"I see. Just a gut feeling."

I studied the picture on the wall behind him. It was a touched-up photograph of the Director of the Bureau. The photograph made him look like rather a nice man. A bit solemn, perhaps, but decent. Justice, tempered with mercy. I thought of the time I'd come close to meeting him. A mutual friend had invited both of us to a fund-raising dinner. The Director hadn't been the Director then, but he'd been a prospect for the job. I'd had to skip the affair at the last minute because of an unexpected trip to Detroit, but I wished now that I'd gone. It would have been nice to be able to tell Bakersfield I knew his boss.

Studying the picture, I felt sorry for the Director. He had his hands full. Drug enforcement. Organized crime. Subversive activities. Fraud. Kidnapping. Sabotage. And above all, budget cutbacks and Congressmen who were on his back one week for not being aggressive enough and the next week for being too aggressive.

Yes, the Director had his problems. So did Bakersfield, who had to deal with matters like getting court orders from judges who had their own ideas of right and wrong, and witnesses who refused to testify, and evidence that was liable to be thrown out on technicalities.

I was glad I was a free agent.

"I tried to tell you before," I said. "I have certain ideas about what happened."

"You did tell us before, Mr. Potter. You gave us your ideas. Unfortunately, you didn't give us the one thing that would have helped us: an accurate description of the man who shot Bill Arden and his girlfriend."

"Not his girlfriend. My girlfriend. And she's dead now."

"You didn't give us anything we can go with."

"I've learned more. I'm convinced the East Germans have infiltrated quite a few companies and one man is making it possible. I don't have any proof yet, but—"

"Mr. Potter, we know about the East Germans. We watch the same television documentaries you do."

"Then how come you blew the Kevin Rand case?"

Bakersfield and Dillon didn't bother to look at each other first; they stared straight at me.

"You let Gerald Egan and Leslie Michaels slip through your fingers."

There were a few tense moments.

"You seem to want to get yourself into trouble, Mr. Potter." Bakersfield's voice was ominous. "If necessary, we'll take steps to prevent it."

"I hope that won't be necessary," I said. "But there's no law on the books that keeps me from going around asking questions and talking to people." I glanced at my watch. "I'll be glad to stay, if you'd like, but I do have another appointment."

There were some more tense moments.

I gazed thoughtfully at the picture of the Director. "Your boss looks like a nice man," I observed. "We almost met once, but I had to go out of town. Too bad."

Bakersfield and Dillon continued to eye me coldly. At last, however, Bakersfield got up. "That's all for now, Mr. Potter, but we'll be in touch."

"Good," I said. "Let's not lose contact."

He didn't walk me to the door, as he'd done the last time, but I managed to get out of the office anyway.

With three hours to kill before meeting Minton, I went shopping. I bought a knife, an ice pick and, for good measure, a screwdriver.

35

THE GUARD IN THE LOBBY was two hundred and fifty pounds of hostility tightly wrapped in a blue uniform. "The building's closed," he growled. He seemed on the verge of drawing his gun.

"I have an appointment with Mr. Minton," I explained. "Seaboard Optics."

"Closed, I said." His hand actually moved toward his gunbelt.

"Before you shoot, I suggest you check with Mr. Minton."

He glowered at me. I smiled back. He waddled over to the marble pedestal that supported the directory of tenants. He had some trouble finding Seaboard, but eventually located it and picked up a telephone.

I waited, off to one side.

Finally he put down the telephone and said to me, "Seventeenth floor. Sign the register."

I smiled, and he pointed to the register. I signed.

"Middle elevators," he said gruffly.

I rode up to the seventeenth floor and, before entering the Seaboard offices, checked the door to the fire stairs. Once you were in the stairwell, I noted, you couldn't get out unless you walked all the way down to the ground floor.

The thick glass double doors were unlocked, and a lamp was lit in the reception room, but the receptionist had gone home.

Another pair of glass doors connected the reception room with the thickly carpeted corridor on both sides of which Seaboard's top executives had their offices. The corridor was dimly illuminated, but the offices were dark. Evidently Minton was the only one working this evening. His office was at the end of the corridor, I remembered.

The door was closed. I didn't knock. I just turned the knob, walked in and said, "Hi, Herb."

He'd been standing at the far end of the room, his back to the door, gazing through a window at Third Avenue. He turned around, but didn't come toward me.

"Sorry I'm late," I said. "It took me longer than I'd expected."

He didn't answer right away. He stood there looking at me for a while, letting me see the anger on his face and wonder what it was all about. At last, however, he took a few steps in my direction and said, "Potter, you're a disgrace to your profession."

"Well, now," I said, "it's always refreshing to hear dissent. What have I done to offend you?"

Again he didn't answer right away. It was an effective device, but I wasn't affected.

"I intend to take the matter up with the New York Society of Security Analysts and with the Securities and Exchange Commission."

Neither of which would do him one damn bit of good, and he knew it. "Good grief!" I exclaimed. "What have I done?"

"Yesterday one of your people—George Cole—took the extraordinary step of contacting one of my people at home and questioning him about his job."

"No!" I hoped I sounded sufficiently aghast.

"He did it with your full knowledge, I'm sure, because no one in his position would dare to do such a thing on his own."

"I can't believe it!"

"What your motive was and is, I have no idea and I scarcely care. I simply want you to know that no one from your company will ever be allowed to set foot in this office or any other Seaboard facility again. Ever. Furthermore, I intend to take the matter up with—"

"You've already said that, Herb."

"You're a disgrace to your profession, and I'm going to spread the word to everyone I have contact with."

"The best thing for you to do, I think, would be to write a letter for the Op Ed pages of the *Wall Street Journal.* Maybe one for the *New York Times,* too—there may be a few *Times* readers who don't subscribe to the *Journal.* After that—"

"Don't get smart with me, and don't smirk like that. I'm deadly serious about what I say."

I heaved a deep sigh. "It worked once, Herb, but it won't work a second time. I'm not as nice now as I was in those days."

The expression on Minton's face made the guard in the lobby seem like a friendly puppy, and his voice rose. "You're devious and disreputable!"

"You're spitting," I said. "That spreads germs." Actually, he hadn't spit.

"I—I—" He began to sputter.

"Calm down," I said. "You'll give yourself high blood pressure."

"I—I—"

"You really have a terrible temper, Herb. You ought to learn to control it. . . . I tend to admire what you've done with Seaboard, but not the way you've done it, and I can't help wondering whether somebody else wouldn't have done as well. Thanks to Ron Carris, you happened to be in the right place at the right time, and you've made some pretty good decisions. But somebody else might have made those same decisions without driving so many people into sanatoriums.

"The New York Society of Security Analysts has never taken a vote on the matter," I went on, "but if it did, you'd be chosen the least liked chief executive of any major corporation in the United States. You're a bully and a sadist, and everyone knows it. . . . I let you push me around once and I've hated myself for it ever since. Others you've pushed around undoubtedly feel the same way. There's a small army of Herbert Minton victims out there who'd just love to see you excommunicated by your board of directors—which could happen, Herb. So far the board has backed you, no matter what you've done, but if the company ever began to slip, that would change.

"Price, Potter and Petacque doesn't have many customers, Herb, but those that it does have pack a lot of weight. A few words from me in the right ears could change your future. So don't threaten me with spreading rumors. In a war of rumors, you'd lose."

Minton came at me with upraised fists and lowered head. He looked like a charging bull.

I sidestepped, and his own momentum carried him forward until he bumped into a chair.

"You're a sicko," I said. "A weirdo and a sicko."

He turned around, uttered a bull-like snort and came at me again.

This time, as I sidestepped, I stuck one foot out and, when he went by, gave him a push. He fell on his face.

I hurried out of his office, entered the corridor and tried the first door on my right. It was unlocked. I darted into the room and got my bearings. I was in a large office with a desk in the middle.

Leaving the door open a crack, I flattened myself against the wall beside it and waited.

For what seemed a very long time, nothing happened. There was no sound and no change in the amount of light coming through the opening between the door and the doorframe. The palms of my hands began to tingle from anxiety.

I tried not to think about the arrival of the cleaning crew. Or to speculate on how long it would be before Minton decided to go home. If I'd made him sufficiently angry, he might go home very soon. On the other hand, he might sit in his office, brooding, for hours. I'd been too hasty. I should have spent more time reconnoitering, looking for places to hide.

Had he hurt himself? I wondered. No, he couldn't have; the carpeting was thick, and he'd broken his fall with his hands.

Did he really believe I'd left, or would he start searching?

A door slammed. The sound came from the direction of Minton's office. My heart began to slam, too. I pressed my back against the wall.

I heard no footsteps, but I detected a momentary change in the light. Minton passing? I held my breath.

Nothing more happened.

I forced myself to count to twenty, slowly. Then I opened the door another inch and peered into the corridor. I saw no one. Opening the door still wider, I stuck my head out.

Minton was at the far end of the corridor, going into the reception room. He was moving purposefully. I stepped back and counted to a hundred.

When I emerged the second time, Minton wasn't in sight. I went to the reception room and looked out. There was no one in the public hallway. I guessed that he'd left the building.

Had he stopped to check the register? Had he questioned the guard?

I hurried back to his office and turned on the light. I gave myself ten minutes.

Taking the tools from my pocket, I sat down at the desk and prepared to use them. I'd gone to a lot of trouble for nothing, however; the desk was unlocked.

Working with intense concentration, I went through the drawers systematically, starting at the top. I didn't know specifically what I was looking for, but I had a general idea. An address book, a letter, a canceled check—anything that mentioned at least one of the people in the Calthorp or Arden cases: Kevin Rand, Donald Calthorp, Bill Arden, Alfred Stone or someone whose surname was Kincaid.

In the second drawer on the right, I located an address book, but none of the names I'd hoped to find were in it. Continuing my search, I came upon a checkbook. The stubs were explicit, and not one of them linked Minton with any of the people I had in mind.

Could I be wrong? Was I picking on an innocent man?

I glanced at my watch. Eight of the ten minutes were up.

Give yourself more time, something said. Think more carefully. I closed my eyes and pictured my own office. Where did I keep my most private papers? I groaned aloud when the answer came to me. I didn't keep them in my office at all; I kept them in my safe-deposit box at the bank.

A wild-goose chase, that's what this was. An irrational, ill-conceived, crazy-man approach based on nothing more than rash assumptions.

Give yourself more time. Another five minutes, another ten minutes. So said the voice.

But I won't find anything, I argued mentally. Not in ten minutes, not in ten hours.

I opened my eyes and glanced at my watch again. I'd already been in Arden's office twelve minutes. It was seven fifty-five. I closed the desk drawers and started to get up.

And that was when I saw it.

It had been right there in front of me the whole time I'd been at the desk, but I'd been so preoccupied with looking for something hidden that I hadn't seen what was exposed. In a silver frame beside a clock was a small photograph of Flora Dexter's son.

36

IT WASN'T THE WORK of a professional photographer; it was an ordinary snapshot. The boy was squinting into the sun, his head cocked to one side, and he wasn't wearing a sweater or jacket. The trunk of a tree was visible in the background.

I examined the picture closely. I had no doubt as to who the boy was, but I wanted to determine, if I could, how recently the photograph had been taken. It was no more than six months old, I decided at last; the weather must have been warm, and the boy was about the same height and weight I remembered him as being.

He'd called Flora "mom," I recalled.

I resisted the temptation to put the photograph in my pocket and returned it to its place beside the clock. Then I straightened the contents of the drawers, got up from the desk and left Minton's office.

I walked quickly down the corridor, crossed the reception room and noted through the glass doors that the public hallway was clear. But at that point my luck ran out. The one thing I hadn't even considered had happened: When he'd left, Minton had locked the doors. They wouldn't budge.

The tools, I thought, and took them from my pocket. They were useless, however. This was a sophisticated lock that required a professional locksmith.

For some moments I stood there, looking through the glass at the bank of elevators, fighting panic. I'd been stupid. I was trapped.

But when I thought of the cleaning crew, my panic subsided. The crew would have a passkey.

I went into one of the offices, turned on the light and sat down at the desk. In my mind's eye, I kept seeing the photograph. The boy didn't resemble Minton very closely, but there were certain features . . .

I dredged from my memory bits and pieces of what Flora had said.

The minutes crept by. Finally, shortly before nine o'clock, I heard the front doors being unlocked, and voices. I stepped into the corridor. Two women and a man were in the reception room with their equipment. I rehearsed my story and said a brief prayer.

The prayer was answered, and I didn't need the story. All I needed were a smile and a nod and a brisk pace. One of the women looked up at me and said, "Goodnight," and immediately returned to her chores. Her two co-workers didn't even look up.

I rang for an elevator and descended to the lobby.

The guard was eating a doughnut. I picked an appropriate hour and signed myself out, swung through the revolving doors and emerged into Third Avenue, aware that I'd been more fortunate than anyone deserved to be.

But then the accumulated tension of the afternoon caught up with me. Suddenly I began to tremble, and within seconds I was shaking uncontrollably. The spasms were so severe that I couldn't walk. All I could do was stand there, convulsed, hugging myself.

After a while, the shaking let up enough for me to cross the street and turn the corner, but the letup was only temporary. Before I'd gone a block, the trembling began again, and the next thing I knew, I was huddled in the doorway of a building, with my head against the wall, thinking: This can't be happening, it isn't real.

Yet it was happening. The spasms were genuine. So was the feeling that I'd fallen into a deep black hole.

Be still, I instructed my nerves. Don't do this to me.

But for what seemed an incredibly long time, my nerves wouldn't obey, and when at last they did, they didn't obey fully. The shaking abated, but I was too tired to leave the shelter of the doorway.

"I need a drink," I said aloud.

The prospect of a large cognac provided motivation, but not immediately. It was several minutes before I could bring myself to venture out to the sidewalk.

Slowly I made my way toward Lexington Avenue. When I got there I hesitated, uncertain whether to turn left or right. Then I saw the Waldorf a few blocks away, and that decided me. At the Waldorf I would be able to get some cognac and a comfortable chair.

And at the Waldorf, as I began to recover, I realized what had gone wrong with my nervous system. I'd taken on too many people and assumed too many threatening poses for one day. I'd been effective, I thought, but I'd used up an awful lot of myself in the process. That wasn't smart. I still had a distance to go.

Furthermore, all I'd had to eat since morning was half a slice of cold roast beef and three-quarters of a roll. That wasn't smart, either.

When the cognac was gone, I ordered another and some hors d'oeuvres to go with it.

Was it only yesterday, I wondered, that I'd come back from Minneapolis? It seemed so much longer.

Minneapolis—that was another cause of the problem. The past four days were the worst I'd ever lived through. And the week preceding them hadn't been much better. As for the future . . .

I shook my head. Dismal.

Plans had to be made, though. Events were in motion. I called for the check, paid it and rode the escalator down to the ground floor, where I went into the coffee shop. Hungry or not, I had to stoke the furnace.

A steak sandwich, French fried potatoes and a side order of

coleslaw did even more for me than I'd expected. My energy returned. The future took shape in my mind.

There were three taxis lined up at the Waldorf's Lexington Avenue entrance. I climbed into the first of them and gave the driver the address of my house. Then I settled back in a corner of the back seat and thought about the photograph on Minton's desk.

Ten minutes later, we turned the corner from Fifth Avenue and moved slowly along West Eleventh Street.

"Trouble," the driver remarked.

I looked out the window. A police car was double-parked directly opposite my front steps, its revolving light flashing. Two patrolmen were standing on the sidewalk, and a small crowd had collected around them.

The taxi stopped. I paid the driver and jumped out.

"Here he is now!" cried Evelyn Natwick, one of my next-door neighbors.

"What's going on?" I asked.

Evelyn came over to me. "There was a suspicious-looking man," she said excitedly. "I called the police."

I had an icy sensation at the back of my neck.

"You the tenant?" one of the policemen asked.

"Yes."

"The lady here called us."

"The man was right in front of your steps," Evelyn broke in, pointing to a space between two parked cars. "He was watching your house, Brock. I saw him through the window. After what happened week before last, I didn't think I should take any chances. I dialed nine eleven."

"Thank you," I said in a low voice.

"When the police car came down the street," she added, "the man took off."

"How long ago did this happen?" I asked her.

"No more than ten minutes."

"We answered the call at ten forty-five," said the policeman. "Shall we come into the house?"

"If you wouldn't mind."

The two policemen accompanied me up the steps and into the house. Evelyn decided to come, too, and hurried after us.

Nothing on the ground floor had been disturbed. Nothing upstairs, either.

"Thank you very much," I said to the policemen when we returned to the foyer.

"They were very prompt," Evelyn added, with a smile. She knew when to smile at policemen and when not to. She was a lawyer.

The policemen left, and the little crowd dispersed. Evelyn stayed.

"You saved my life," I said.

"Well, after what happened before . . . "

"Did you see what the man looked like?"

"Not really. He was wearing a coat and hat. But he was up to no good, Brock, I'm sure of that."

I was sure of it, too.

"Aren't you at least going to offer me a drink, after all I've done?"

"No. I'm going to ask you to invite me up to your place, instead. Then I'm going to call a taxi and wait there until it comes. If that's all right with you."

Evelyn eyed me thoughtfully for a moment and then said, "Certainly."

We went next door to her apartment, where I telephoned for a taxi. Evelyn didn't ask me why I wanted to wait in her apartment or where I was going, and I didn't explain. I merely stood at the window, watching the street until the taxi came.

"La Guardia," I told the driver.

Thirty minutes later, we arrived at the airport.

"Which airline?" the driver asked.

"Any airline," I replied.

He turned around and gave me a look.

"TWA."

He let me off at the entrance to TWA, and I went in search of a car-rental agency.

By midnight I was crossing the Throgs Neck Bridge, and shortly after that I reached the New England Thruway.

I spent the night at a motel near Greenwich, Connecticut, where I felt temporarily safe.

37

FINALLY, AT FOUR-THIRTY, I spotted her coming down Commonwealth Avenue. I'd been waiting across the street for almost two hours.

I intercepted her just as she reached the entrance to her building. "Hattie! What a coincidence!"

She'd been preoccupied, and was startled. Her mouth opened and closed, and she blinked a couple of times, like someone coming out of a trance. "Brock Potter?" It was more a question than a statement.

"I was just on my way to pay you an unannounced visit."

"I—" she shifted her tote bag from one hand to the other— "I—"

"The damnedest thing has happened. I can't wait to tell you. I'm buying the Konklin University Press."

I'd anticipated a reaction, but not as much of a reaction as I got. Her eyes seemed to grow twice as large, and one of the handles of the tote bag slipped out of her grasp. The bag tipped sideways. The contents almost spilled.

"It's a fact. I talked with Roger Merriman yesterday. Everything's in the works. I need your advice."

"I—the apartment—I—"

"Shall we go somewhere else?" I took her arm, and the contents of the tote bag tumbled onto the sidewalk. Notebooks and papers were strewn about, and the papers began to blow away.

Hattie uttered a cry and went chasing after stray pages, stuffing them into her bag. I helped her.

"A near-disaster," I said as I handed her what I'd picked up. Then I took her arm again. "Come. A drink."

"No." She was breathing hard. "My apartment."

We entered the building, and I waited while she collected her mail. It appeared to consist mostly of advertisements. Then we climbed the steps, and she preceded me into her quarters, apologizing for the way they looked.

The living room was no messier than it had been the last time, but I noticed a man's jacket on one of the chairs. Hattie noticed it, too.

"A friend of mine—" she began, and picked up the jacket, taking it into the bedroom.

I followed her. She tossed the jacket onto the unmade bed and threw her own coat on top of it.

"A friend of mine has been staying here for a few days," she explained. "I guess he's gone out."

"Friends come and go," I said with an understanding smile.

We went back to the living room. "You're buying the press?" she said. "I can't believe it! You? The Konklin University Press?" She cleared some space for us to sit down.

"It's a long story. The whole thing came up rather suddenly. For years my accountant has been urging me to buy something like that—taxes, you understand. Even if the press doesn't make any money—I mean, from my point of view it would be better if it didn't make any money. But, yes, I've had people out looking for an investment of that sort, and the other day I heard about the Konklin University Press. I mean, it would be kind of fun, I think. I'd change it around, of course. Drop the religious books and the academic stuff. Who knows? I might even end up defeating my own purpose and making a profit."

"Drop the religious, the academic . . . ?"

"Well, after all, not many people read it. If it weren't for old what's her name—Cordelia Konklin Fisher—most of it would never have got published anyway."

"But you can't! You shouldn't! You'd be doing a great injustice!"

"To whom?"

She couldn't bring herself to say it.

"To you?"

She laced her fingers together. Her face had turned a shade paler. I glanced at the desk. "The abbess of what? Saint-Esprit *de* something or other? Well, really, I don't think she's well enough known. Probably didn't have much of a following even in her own time. The press would be much better off with books about how to make money, in my opinion. I have a lot of friends who could write on that subject. Times have changed. The abbess of whatever—how did you come to choose her, anyway?"

"I—"

"Well, I suppose I can understand, in a way. All the really important people have already been written about. You had to find somebody new. And the abbess probably was kind of an interesting old bird. Wanted to change things, I expect. After all, there was a lot that needed changing. Still is, for that matter. Yes, I can understand. But when I own the press, I don't think I'll have any use for *that.*" I waved my arm dismissively toward the desk, with all its books and pages of manuscript.

"I must be dreaming this," Hattie said.

"Dreaming? No, you're not dreaming. I'm here, I'm real, and I'm a businessman, with all a businessman's hang-ups. I mean, to me things have to add up. It's the bottom line that counts. I've always believed in the bottom line. Figures don't lie, is what I say, and liars don't figure, and, Hattie, the last time I was here I don't think you figured."

She opened her mouth but said nothing. She just looked at me.

"Incidentally, I mentioned your name to Roger Merriman. I hope you don't mind. If you'd care to check with him . . . "

"Later," she said. "Go on. I'm fascinated."

"Yes, do check with him. But all right, I will go on. You should have done more figuring, Hattie. Like when we were talking about Kevin and his friends and you mentioned a man by the name of Peter Cottly, who, you said, belonged to the same health club. You should have figured that half the truth is worse than no truth at all."

"You're insane!"

"No. Just angry."

She jumped up. "I refuse to listen to any more."

"Sit down, Hattie. I haven't finished."

"I've heard enough. You and your philistine—"

"Sit down, I said!" My tone surprised both of us. I hadn't known I could sound like that.

Reluctantly, she sat down.

"Half-truths are a form of arrogance, Hattie. I prefer whole truths, so I'm going to supply some of the missing halves. Kevin did get acquainted with a man up here, some months before he decided to change jobs. You met the man, too. I don't know how the acquaintance began, but I suspect the man simply called Kevin up and said he'd read about him and wanted to meet him. They met, and a friendship developed. It had nothing to do with Jackson's Health Club, but they did jog together. As you said, Kevin jogged regularly—he allowed nothing to interfere with it—and Kevin's sister-in-law Rosalie said the same thing. Because he was trying to develop a relationship with Kevin, the man spent a lot of time up here. His name might have been Cottly, or it might have been Egan, or it might have been something else—right now he's calling himself Frank Roche. He has nothing to do with surgical instruments or any other kind of instruments; he works for an executive-personnel consultant. He introduced Kevin to his boss, and the two of them sized Kevin up—they're good at that sort of thing. They realized that Kevin wasn't completely happy with his job—or with you. More important, they recognized in him certain traits they could exploit. So they suggested he change jobs. They knew there were openings at the Calthorp Research Center—it's their business to keep up with who needs what where—and they persuaded him to send Calthorp a résumé. My guess is that by then he'd already agreed to feed them information. Also that if for some reason Calthorp hadn't hired him, they would eventually have placed him somewhere else.

"Those are the missing halves, as far as Kevin is concerned. As for you, there are a couple of other missing halves: one, you met Kevin's jogging partner and could identify him; and, two, the man got in touch with you after Kevin was arrested, warned you that you'd be questioned by the FBI, and told you that the only way to avoid being implicated was to say you knew nothing about anything." I paused, then added, "He didn't prepare you for me, however. You handled me on your own—and made a mess of it."

For a while Hattie said nothing. She just stared at me as if I were a scorpion. It was so quiet in the apartment that I could almost hear the air circulating.

Finally she spoke. "You've got it all wrong," she said. "You've got me all wrong. You're trying to blackmail me."

I shook my head. "You were dealing with East German intelligence agents, Hattie. If you didn't know it at the time, you've had plenty of opportunity since to figure it out. You withheld information from the FBI, and you're still withholding it."

"I'm not. I—God, you're a terrible person."

"You're in trouble, Hattie."

Her mouth gave a couple of twitches. "He was a very nice man," she said presently. "His name wasn't Cottly—I don't know what made me think it was Cottly. It was Egan. Gerald Egan. I've never heard of Frank Roche. Gerald was very nice. He came for dinner several times. We didn't talk politics, we just talked. About everything. Kevin and I weren't getting along so well then—that's true enough. But I didn't know Gerald was a spy, I swear I didn't. I didn't know anything of the sort. He was just a nice man and he had a furnished apartment that he used when he was in Boston, and he and Kevin jogged. All the rest of what you said—you're making that up."

I shook my head again.

"You are. You must be. You're a terrible human being and you're threatening me. You're trying to blackmail me. I don't believe you've bought the Konklin Press. I don't believe anything you've said."

"Describe the man, Hattie. Tell me what he looks like. And no more half-truths—they're dangerous."

"I can't. I won't. I don't remember."

"You're in trouble, Hattie."

She began to beat her fists against her knees. "Stop saying that!" It was almost a shriek.

"Describe him."

"I don't remember . . . everything. He was about your height, I think. He had sort of light-colored skin. Blondish hair. He was nice-looking. Slim. I don't remember everything."

"Go on. You're doing fine."

She gave me a few other details. There was no doubt that she was describing the man I knew as Frank Roche. Or that, if she ever had to, she could identify him.

"What about the other man?" I asked.

"I didn't meet any other man. I don't know any other man. God, you're awful! Am I really in trouble?"

"Tell me the truth, Hattie. The whole truth. What about the other man?"

"I *am* telling you the truth. I didn't meet any other man. I swear. Just the one who jogged."

I believed her. "All right. Now what happened after Kevin was arrested? How did this Egan get in touch with you? Because I'm sure he did get in touch with you. He told you what to say."

She opened her mouth to speak, but then clamped it shut.

"Did he call you on the telephone? Did he come to see you?"

"I'm going to phone my lawyer."

I tapped the face of my watch. She got the point. It was after five o'clock. No telling where the lawyer was.

"He called me on the telephone," Hattie said.

"And what did he say?"

"More or less what you said he said. Look, I've told you! I didn't know! When I heard about Kevin, I was shocked! Believe me. I didn't *know!*" She appeared to be on the brink of tears.

Enough was enough, I decided, and got up. "Thanks for your help," I said. "And don't stop working on your book. Who knows —the deal may fall through."

"God!" she exclaimed, and then she did burst into tears.

I felt genuinely sorry for her. She'd had a rotten afternoon. "Drink some Chianti," I said. "It'll make you feel better."

At the door I almost collided with a man who was about to come in. The friend, I supposed. He was a pudgy fellow with protruding eyes and he reminded me of a fish.

"Be kind," I said. "She's upset."

He entered the apartment, and I hurried along the hall to the stairwell.

At Logan Airport I turned in my car and checked on flights. I learned that it was too late for me to make a connection with any flight to Raleigh-Durham, so I bought a ticket to Washington, D.C. That was as good a place as any to spend the night, I figured, since no one would know I was there.

38

THE INDUSTRIALS had been down for most of the day, Irving reported, but had staged a recovery by closing time. The transportation stocks had followed a similar pattern. The utilities hadn't done much of anything. It was rumored that the Russians were planning to step up their sales of gold—their wheat harvest was disappointing.

"What about the letter?" I asked.

The Tuesday letter had gone out on time, Irving said, and at my request he read it to me. "Now what about you?" he asked. "Will you be in tomorrow?"

"No."

"Where will you be, in case we need you?"

"That's hard to say. Right now I'm at the Statler-Hilton in Washington, but I plan to leave in the morning."

"For where?"

"I'd rather keep that to myself, Irv."

"Brock!" Irving sounded unhappy and disapproving. I'd made it a cardinal rule that each of us should know where the other was at all times. Now here I was, mysteriously flitting in and out of the office, calling from cities I hadn't said I was going to, and refusing to disclose my future whereabouts.

"I'm sorry," I said, "but it's better this way."

"Are you all right?" he asked uneasily.

"Yes."

"Are you alone?"

"Yes."

"I don't think you should be alone, Brock. You're not yourself."

"Oh?"

"Your voice, your—"

"I've covered a lot of ground in the past two days, Irv. I'm tired. This is a tough period."

"That's what I mean."

"Forget it. I'll be back in New York in a day or so. Meanwhile, I don't need mothering."

"It's not just me that's worried, Brock. Tom has been coming in every hour on the hour to ask if I've heard from you, and Mark has been wandering in and out of your office with that strange frown of his. Honestly, Brock—"

"I'm sorry to be causing so much anxiety, but I can't help it. I have to do this particular thing my way."

Irving changed the subject. He told me that George had been sitting around the office, waiting for my instructions, which hadn't come; that Jonathan Dickson, the television director, had been driving Helen crazy, trying to get an appointment with me; and that Arden Electronics had stabilized temporarily, after a wild day yesterday—Martin Zweifert had dumped a hundred thousand shares, people were saying.

After hanging up, I gave some thought to my personal needs. They were relatively simple. I'd bought toilet articles in Greenwich, but I hadn't bothered about clothes. Now I had to do something about shirt, socks and underwear. It was too late to go shopping now, but first thing in the morning I would replenish the wardrobe.

I turned on the television set to watch the late news. I wasn't exactly shocked to learn that the world was still dealing with the same old problems, but I was a bit startled; I'd become so involved in my own pushing and shoving that I'd forgotten larger events.

It was refreshing to be reminded that turmoil was a universal condition. Also that, despite the turmoil, the World Series was approaching, the football season was already under way, and tennis matches were still drawing crowds.

The weather forecast for the Washington area was hot and humid, with only a thirty percent chance of precipitation, while elsewhere in the nation . . .

I fell asleep while the weatherman was talking. And dreamed that Carol was still alive. She and I were in Boston, on our way to Hattie Sargent's apartment for dinner. When we arrived, Kevin wouldn't let us in. He stood there, with his arms outstretched, blocking the door. And over his shoulder I saw Frank Roche.

It wasn't a particularly frightening dream, but something about it must have disturbed me, for I woke in the middle of the night and remained awake for several minutes. But then I fell asleep again and slept soundly until the telephone rang.

I picked up the telephone thinking that this was my wake-up call. However, the voice at the other end of the line wasn't that of a switchboard operator.

"Brock?" it said. "This is George Cole."

Suddenly I was bolt upright. "George? What's the matter? What's happened?"

"Nothing's the matter," George replied. "Irving said I should come down here. I'm in the lobby. What's your room number?"

39

AFRAID OF MISSING ME if he waited until morning, George explained, he'd left home at midnight and driven through the night. And the trip had been an education; judging by the number of trucks on the highway, economic conditions were better than anyone claimed.

"Irving shouldn't have sent you," I said. "This is my personal problem."

"It wasn't his decision alone," George replied. "Tom and Mark had a say in it, too. Why Washington, Brock?"

So, sitting on the bed in my underwear, I told him what I'd been up to since I'd last seen him, and where I planned to go later in the day.

His only comment was "I'm glad I'm here."

"You're probably tired," I said. "You should get some sleep."

But George insisted that he wasn't the least bit tired. He'd found the drive stimulating. He was rather hungry, though. His wife had served fish for dinner, and he wasn't much of a fish eater.

I shaved and dressed, and we went down to the coffee shop for breakfast. He hadn't been kidding about being hungry. He put away a large glass of orange juice, two eggs, four strips of bacon, two slices of toast, an almond Danish and three cups of coffee.

"Looks rather skimpy," he observed of my single poached egg.

"It's all I can handle," I said.

"Some of the running around you had me do," he remarked presently, "was it necessary? I mean, the Konklin University Press—"

"Hattie will check, George. And she could have done so while I was there."

"Jerome . . . "

"I thought he might be another Kevin Rand or Alfred Stone. And I believed he'd tell Minton about your visit. Apparently I was wrong about his being a potential spy, but right about his running to Minton—thank God. He's new at Seaboard, and your thoroughness worried him. He isn't used to dealing with people like us."

George nodded thoughtfully.

"What bothers me," I went on, "is that I have no proof. None whatsoever. The FBI men I told you about—they were right. I have theories but no evidence, and evidence is something the FBI really understands. It doesn't like to lose cases, and the lack of evidence is the surest way of losing them. I'm positive my theories are right, but without tapes, without documents of any sort, there's nothing to back them up. And I don't even know how to *get* the evidence. Carris is too smart to keep anything incriminating in his office or home. Hell, there may not even *be* anything incriminating."

"And you're hoping that Flora Dexter—?"

"Yes, I'm hoping."

"Well, I have a couple of suggestions."

George outlined his suggestions, and shortly thereafter I checked out of the hotel. It would take us at least five hours to reach Durham by car, we estimated. But, as George pointed out, it was better to drive than to fly and rent a car when we got there; in order to rent a car, one of us would have to show identification.

At a shopping center outside of Richmond we stopped to buy me some haberdashery and change places. I took the wheel.

We'd done little talking during the first part of the trip, and we did none at all during the second. George slid down on his side of the front seat, and I couldn't tell whether he was asleep or not. When I pulled into a gas station south of Petersburg to fill the tank, he didn't stir.

The Virginia countryside was all shades of green and where the trees had started to turn it was dappled with gold. This was an area I'd never had occasion to visit before, and I found it very pretty. At times I was almost able to forget where I was going and why. But every few minutes an anxiety would begin to nibble. What was Minton doing? What would have happened if Evelyn hadn't called the police, or if I'd come home ten minutes earlier?

Time was running out, I knew. I'd advertised myself as a threat. The people I'd threatened had to act.

Thoughts of Bill Arden nagged at me. Bill must have realized that the hiring of Alfred Stone hadn't been quite as much his own doing as he'd thought. He'd seen an article about a promising young executive, had made a point of meeting the man, and on the spot had talked him into going to work for Arden Electronics—and for seven years he'd been congratulating himself on his accomplishment. Typical example of the Bill Arden initiative, he'd thought; he'd made up his mind quickly, acted boldly and gone home with the prize. He'd done it all himself. But then the prize had exploded in his face, and he'd begun to think back. Eventually he'd remembered that the article about Stone had been called to his attention by someone else. And that the person who'd called it to his attention lived in New York. And when he'd learned that Stone had fled to New York, he'd jumped to the right conclusion.

A few miles north of Williamsboro, we crossed the state line and continued southwest across North Carolina. As if he had his own internal directional system, George roused himself ten miles outside of Durham.

"You know where the Calthorp Research Center is?" he asked.

"Yes," I replied.

He slid down on the seat again and didn't move until we got to Research Triangle Park.

* * *

I waited in the car while George went inside. He was gone for forty-five minutes.

When he returned to the car, his expression was as bland as usual, but I noticed a bulge in the pocket of his coat.

"Any trouble?" I asked.

"No," he said, "but everyone was surprised to see me."

I could imagine. George was acquainted at the Calthorp Research Center, but he'd never dropped in unannounced.

"Would you believe it?" he said. "A place like that, where some of the most sophisticated sound equipment in the world is developed, doesn't have one of its own tape recorders around anywhere." He took a small recorder from his pocket and showed it to me. "This damn thing is made in Japan."

"What did you tell them?"

"The truth. That I was on my way to an important meeting and had left my tape recorder at home."

"And they lent you one?"

"Why not? It's the sort of thing you can buy anywhere." He paused. "I'm disappointed. I'd hoped for something more sensitive. This should serve the purpose, though."

I started the engine and guided the car out of the parking lot.

"Incidentally," George said, "I asked about the antenna for the CSX-1. No one would confirm or deny anything, but I got the distinct feeling that the wiring is being modified."

"So the East Germans didn't gain anything, after all."

"Yes and no, Brock. They can now duplicate the antenna, provided they have all the technology, which I don't think they do. But they won't be able to jam our transmissions."

"That's good. But if they don't have all the technology yet, they're well on the way to getting it. There's no telling how many companies they've penetrated. If we could only find out. . . . " I glanced at the little Japanese-made recorder George was holding. Could it do the job? I wondered.

I steered the car onto the highway that led to Durham, and this time I didn't get lost. We pulled up in front of Flora's house at exactly four o'clock.

George gave me the recorder. I put it in my pocket and walked across the front yard.

The boy opened the door. He was eating a cookie.

"Hi, Dick," I said. "I'm Brock Potter. We met a week ago last Sunday—remember?"

He nodded. "My mother's not home," he said. "She won't be home till after work."

"Can I come in and wait for her?"

He didn't answer until he'd finished the cookie. "I guess so," he said.

I walked into the house and closed the door behind me. "You have the telephone number of your mother's office?" I asked.

Dick said he did.

"Why don't you call her and tell her I'm here?" I suggested. "Maybe she'll want to come home a little early."

He thought about that. "I'm not supposed to call unless it's something important."

"She may think it *is* something important. Why don't we let her decide?"

He thought about it some more. I was struck by how the photograph on Minton's desk had captured the boy's solemnity and shyness. And now that I was seeing him in person, I noted more of a resemblance between him and Minton.

"O.K.," he said at last, and went down the hall to the telephone.

I moved quickly into the living room and looked around for a place to hide the recorder. The fresh flowers were gone, but the vase was still there. It was too far from the chairs, though. So was the étagère. But there was a small bowl on the table beside the couch. I put the recorder behind the bowl and stepped back to see if it was visible. It was, but very slightly; you would have to know it was there in order to spot it.

"Mom wants to talk to you," Dick said.

He showed me where the telephone was, and I picked it up.

"I said I'd be back," I said, "and here I am."

"You know of a job opening for me?"

"Not exactly. We have to talk, though. I spent some time with Herb Minton."

There was a brief silence.

"Shall I wait here?" I asked.

"Yes," she said, after a moment. "I'll leave early. Let me talk to Dick again."

I called the boy, and he took over. I went to the front of the house and signaled to George. He got out of the car and walked down the street. Then I entered the living room.

The boy joined me. "Want a cookie?"

"I wouldn't mind," I said.

He strolled into the kitchen and returned with a package of cookies. I took one, and so did he. Then he put the package on the table where I'd placed the tape recorder. "What's that?" he inquired.

My heart sank. "It's a recorder," I said. "Want to see how it works?"

40

DICK SPOKE, and I spoke, and I played back our exchange.

"Doesn't sound like us," he said.

"It is, though," I replied. "An expert could prove it."

I gave him the tape recorder, and he examined it. Then he lost interest.

"You want to watch TV?" he asked.

"O.K." I put the recorder in my pocket.

He turned on the television set and selected a program. I looked at the screen, with no idea what I was seeing, until a cat food commercial came on and Dick said, "I wish I had a cat. The man who was here before was going to buy me one."

"Kevin?"

His face lit up. "You know him?"

"I used to."

The light went out of his face. "He's dead."

"Do you miss him?"

He nodded.

Like Alfred Stone's sons, I thought. And felt a swell of anger. The list of casualties was very long indeed.

The cat food commercial was followed by one for a chain of drive-in restaurants and some scenes from the next day's film, which had to do with a man who could turn himself into a wolf. After that, the program we'd been watching resumed. We only saw a few minutes of it, though, before Flora arrived.

She seemed to materialize from nowhere. I hadn't heard the car pull up, or the door to the house being opened, but suddenly I was aware of a presence, and when I looked away from the screen, there she was.

She smiled, but her smile was strained. "This is somewhat unexpected," she said to me, and turned off the television set. "Why don't you go over to Jimmy's?" she suggested to Dick.

"Can't I stay?"

"No. I'll call you when it's time to come home."

He made no move to get off the couch. "Mr. Potter has a—"

"Do as I say!"

He scampered to his feet. "Mr. Potter has—"

"I'll call you when it's time to come home."

The boy shrugged and left the room. A moment later I saw him crossing the backyard.

"You should have told me Herb Minton is Dick's father," I said.

The smile remained in place.

"I've known him for years," I added. "You have my sympathy."

The smile became a little less strained.

"Do you happen to have any Scotch? This has been a God-awful day. If you don't have Scotch, anything will do. No water. Just ice."

She hesitated for a moment, then went into the kitchen. I put the tape recorder behind the bowl and turned it on. When Flora came back with the drinks, I was sitting near the recorder with what I hoped was a composed expression on my face.

"I don't know what you're after," she said as she handed me one of the glasses, "but I know you're after something." She seated herself on the other side of the coffee table.

I estimated that she was six feet away. Close enough, I believed. "I'm after the man who helped Kevin and others like him become spies," I said, "and I need your help. It would be to your advantage to give it to me."

"It would?"

I drank some Scotch and set the glass on the coffee table. "Definitely." No outright threats, I cautioned myself, just hints. "You're in an unenviable position, Flora. Not only were you Kevin's lover, but you're the mother of Herb Minton's son."

"I fail to see—"

"Were you and Herb married?"

"Of course. But what does—?"

"Bear with me. Kevin was associated with Ron Carris. So, in a way, is Herb. And Ron Carris is an East German agent."

"I don't believe you!"

"Yes, you do. You didn't know it originally, but after Kevin was arrested you put two and two together. In a sense, Flora, you're Carris's accomplice."

"That's not true!"

I took another sip of Scotch. "Then suppose you tell me what *is* true."

She said nothing.

"Who'd look after Dick if something happened to you? The court would give custody to his father, wouldn't it? That would be unfortunate, in my opinion. In yours, too, probably. He's a nice youngster, and Herb isn't the best person to raise him. Yet that's how it would be. You must have nightmares about it."

"On what grounds—?"

"On the grounds that you're in jail."

"But I've done nothing wrong!" The hand holding the glass trembled slightly, and she put the glass down.

"Being associated with one spy could be seen as bad luck—and in your case it has been. But being associated with two . . . "

"Herb isn't a spy! He's some other things I hate to mention, but he's not a spy."

"How long were you married to him?"

She hesitated for a moment and looked away. "Would it surprise you to know I'm still married to him?"

"Yes."

"Well, I am. He won't give me a divorce. We're separated, but not legally, and he doesn't support me. He sends me money for Dick, but otherwise I'm on my own."

"But your name . . . "

"It's my maiden name. I use it for work, but legally I'm still Flora Minton. And legally is the only way I feel I *am* Flora Minton."

"Did he have anything to do with the fact that you didn't testify at Kevin's trial? I've read the transcript. Your name wasn't mentioned."

"I didn't testify because no one asked me to. The prosecution didn't want me as a witness because I didn't know anything that made Kevin look guilty, and the defense didn't want me because I didn't know anything that made him look innocent. After all, he didn't *live* with me, he simply spent time here. For some reason, you're trying to frighten me."

"What's the relationship between your husband and Ron Carris?"

Flora looked away again. Finally she said, "Business. Business and pleasure. I don't understand your questions about Ron. I don't know why you say he's a foreign agent. You *must* be trying to frighten me."

"Then let me give you the scenario," I said. "Ron Carris is a headhunter, specializing in middle- to upper-echelon people. He doesn't have many clients, but he does have some very important ones and he does place a certain number of good people in good jobs. But every now and then he places a bad person in a good job. A person who's willing to steal company secrets for him. Furthermore, he has excellent contacts; he's friendly with a lot of top management people who aren't clients but whom he sees socially. He's in a position to know which companies need what kind of talent at a particular time; to offer helpful suggestions for which he doesn't get paid; to work people into jobs with companies he has nothing to do with. Seemingly he plays no active role in the people's getting the jobs, as in Kevin's case, but actually he has a lot to do with it. He himself told me the other day that contacts are an important part of his success, and he was telling the truth.

I believe he does have an extremely wide range of contacts, among employees as well as employers. And at the employer level, your husband is one of his most reliable. Carris uses names freely—he even used mine when it suited his purpose, and I scarcely knew him. At any rate, I'm sure your husband's name is one of the ones he makes use of most often—with your husband's permission. He refers to Seaboard Optics as a company he does business with, and your husband recommends him highly. He even brought him to a party I was at a couple of weeks ago where some of the most important businessmen in the country were among the guests. I don't think there was anything unplanned about their coming together."

Flora leaned forward in her chair. "You mean Herb is Ron's . . . sponsor?"

"In a manner of speaking, yes. Not his only sponsor—there are probably others—but certainly one of the most cooperative. And the only one *I* know of at the moment."

She reached for her glass and took a large swallow. "But that doesn't mean Herb's working for the East Germans, even if Ron is."

"No, it doesn't. All it means is, he's allowing himself to be used by one of their key agents. He's liable to have a hard time proving his innocence, though, when his bosom buddy goes on trial. At the very least, he's going to be damned embarrassed." I smiled. "And it couldn't happen to a nicer guy."

She got up and began pacing the floor, her hands clasped in front of her.

Don't let her notice the recorder, I prayed. Please.

"Ron Carris arranged to have Kevin killed," I said.

My words had the desired effect. Flora dropped her hands and sat down, her gaze fixed on me.

"I don't know whether he accomplished it through bribery or threats, but I'm convinced he did arrange it. There's a constant flow of information into and out of prisons. Information, drugs, you name it—there's an awful lot that prison walls don't stop.

According to Adele Rand, the man who stabbed Kevin has a wife and child. She believes that someone got at him through them, and she's probably a hundred percent right. Kincaid must have felt that he himself had little to lose—he had no hope of being paroled, anyway. All the facts about how Kevin's murder was arranged will never come out, I suspect, and it really doesn't matter—Kevin's dead. What matters is finding out who else is doing what Kevin did, and where. That's my scenario. What's yours?"

"My . . . scenario?"

"Herb, Ron, Kevin, Flora—that's the cast. What part do you play?"

She sighed. "The victim, apparently. Herb Minton's victim, Kevin Rand's victim."

"Ron Carris's victim?"

"So it would seem. If what you say is true. Ron was Herb's friend. He and Herb . . . Herb's sexual tastes, at times, are . . . unconventional. I've never known for sure, but I've occasionally wondered whether Ron gets women for Herb. Women who'll submit to things I wouldn't."

I nodded.

"As for Kevin, Ron introduced us—or at least he tried to. I'd left Herb and gotten myself a job. The job happened to be here. I kept in touch with Herb; I still do. I mean, he sends a check every month for Dick, and I have to let Dick go up to New York every now and then to visit him—that's part of our understanding. Anyhow, I'd been here about a year when Kevin came. He called me—he was new in the Triangle, and Ron had given him my name as someone to look up. It was perfectly harmless, I suppose, but I didn't think so at the time. Ron was a friend of Herb's, and I was still recuperating from Herb. Anyone who was a friend of his was no friend of mine. When Kevin mentioned Ron's name, I said thank you very much but no thanks—I'm busy. So we didn't meet until maybe nine months later, at a party. And in the course of a single evening, I fell in love with him."

I felt a surge of triumph. Here it was, at last. The thing I'd been looking for, but had begun to doubt I'd ever find: a link between Kevin Rand and Ron Carris. Evidence that the two men knew each other. And I had it on tape. I could turn the tape over to the FBI. My theory was no longer unsupported. The FBI would now have something to go on.

Mentally I thanked George for his suggestion that I bring a recorder with me. Two heads were better than one. Always had been, always would be. Especially when one of the heads was George Cole's.

"Why are you looking at me like that?" Flora asked.

"I'm thinking about the irony of things. How strangely they sometimes work out." With the tape in mind, I phrased my next question carefully. "What you're saying is, Kevin Rand and Ron Carris were acquainted."

"Yes. They must have been."

"When you were questioned by the FBI after Kevin's arrest, did you mention this?"

"I'm not sure. I don't think so."

"Why not?"

"You'd have to have been through what I went through, to understand. They questioned me for hours and hours and hours. They kept asking all sorts of things, including how Kevin and I met. We'd met at a party, I said. They wanted to know who gave the party and who else was there, and I told them all that, and they questioned those people, too. And actually I was telling the truth —Kevin and I *did* meet at a party. I was so upset when I was being questioned, so positively ragged, that it never occurred to me to tell them we might have met months earlier if I'd been less on my guard. As far as I was concerned, the party *was* the beginning. I felt something that night . . . well, you've probably experienced it yourself. I don't think that either of us even talked about the fact that he'd tried to meet me before. Not that night, and not afterward either, as I recall. If you hadn't started telling me about Ron, I probably wouldn't have remembered now."

I wondered whether this was the truth, but decided that it didn't matter. The two essential facts were on tape: Kevin and Carris had known each other, and Flora hadn't mentioned this to the FBI.

Carris's one mistake, I thought with satisfaction. He'd wanted Kevin to feel at home in the Triangle, to become part of the community, and he'd figured that Flora might pave the way. Well, no one was infallible, not even Ronald Carris; he'd made one introduction too many.

Would my tape be sufficient evidence? I wondered. By itself it wouldn't be. But it would give the FBI grounds to question Carris, perhaps even to take him into custody. What happened after that was up to them. The FBI was good at putting together a case, however.

I finished my drink, held out my glass and said, with a smile, "If you'd be so kind . . . "

Flora took the glass into the kitchen.

I turned off the recorder and put it in my pocket.

"This conversation," she said when she returned, "it's frightened me." She looked quite worried.

"Don't let it," I said. "I'm on your side. I like your son and I don't like Herb Minton."

"That's not what I mean. I mean I'm frightened of Ron. I didn't know . . . I never dreamed he's a dangerous man."

"He won't bother you. He's going to be busy with the FBI."

"If I'd thought . . . if I'd known . . . I never would have told him you're here."

I felt my jaw drop and my mouth open, but I didn't hear myself saying anything. Something inside me started to jump. "You . . . what?" finally got past my lips.

Flora's expression became one of genuine alarm. "I didn't know. . . . I thought . . . He's in town. He phoned me this morning. He said you'd come. He said you'd make trouble. He said I should let him know if I heard from you."

"Where is he?"

"At a motel. Then when Dick called and said you were here, I realized Ron had been right. I didn't know what to do."

"You *trusted* him?"

"I didn't know. I—yes, I did. I called him. He thanked me. Now I'm frightened. What's going to happen?"

"I've got to get out of here," I said unevenly. "You'd better come too." I got up and looked about, breathing heavily. Then I grabbed her hand and pulled her out of the chair.

She didn't resist. She merely said, "But where . . . ?"

Carris had had enough time to reach the house from anywhere in the Triangle, I thought, pulling her toward the kitchen. "We'd better go out the back door," I said. "We'll cut across the yard to your neighbor's and call the police."

We reached the kitchen. I asked Flora to give me a knife, just in case. She opened a drawer and handed me one.

I opened the back door and preceded her into the yard.

"Drop the knife," said a voice at my right.

I turned.

Frank Roche was standing less than three feet away, pointing a revolver at me.

41

"Drop it," he said.

I dropped the knife.

He came a step closer. His face was expressionless. I looked at the gun. It was aimed at my head and seemed very large.

"Move," he said. "Around to the front of the house. You, too, Mrs. Minton."

Flora uttered a sound—part sob, part whimper.

I began to walk. I was aware of Flora in back of me, but couldn't see her. Roche adjusted his pace to mine. His gaze shifted back and forth between Flora and me, but I was the one at whom he kept the gun leveled.

When we reached the end of the house, we turned, following its outside wall toward the front yard. Roche gave a low whistle. Carris appeared. Evidently he'd been waiting at the other door. He, too, had a gun. He came toward us.

"The car's in the driveway," he said grimly.

As we approached the front yard, I saw the car he was talking about. It was a pale gray sedan and was parked halfway between the street and the carport. I also saw George's brown Oldsmobile at the curb. George wasn't in it. I cursed myself for having told him to stay out of sight.

Roche closed the distance between himself and me, pressing the

muzzle of the gun against my right temple. Carris stepped behind
me, and a moment later Flora exclaimed, "You're hurting me!"

We crossed the front yard. I looked around desperately for
George—or anyone else. No one was visible. The yard of the house
next door was deserted. So was the one across the street. It was
as if the neighborhood had been evacuated.

Silently I shouted to the entire world: Do something! Don't let
this happen!

No one came to our rescue. Or even showed his face.

This isn't possible, I thought. Two people can't be kidnapped
from a populated area in broad daylight without someone's noticing and calling the police.

It was happening, though. Flora and I were being taken away at
gunpoint, and not a soul was around to witness the event.

Roche opened the rear door of the gray sedan with his free hand.
"Get in!"

I hesitated, but he pressed the muzzle of the gun harder against
my temple, and I climbed into the car. Flora climbed in after me.
Roche kept the gun aimed at us while Carris slid into the front seat
on the passenger side. Then Carris covered us with his own gun,
and Roche slammed the door. Seconds later, we were backing out
of the driveway, with Roche at the wheel.

Jump, I thought. Jump before it's too late.

I glanced at the door handle.

"Don't," said Carris, and moved the gun closer to my head.

I stayed where I was.

"Where are we going?" Flora asked.

Neither man answered.

She began to cry, her fingers laced together under her chin like
those of a supplicant.

Roche backed the car into the street and swung it around. Then
he shifted the gear lever and put more weight on the gas pedal. The
car accelerated with a lurch, passing the Olds, leaving Flora's
house behind.

Carris spoke sharply in German, and Roche slowed our speed.

The sound of German came as a shock to me. I'd believed Carris when he'd said he was from Brooklyn. Another of my stupidities, I realized now. I'd been right about the big things, but wrong about the little ones, and it was the little ones that had beaten me. I hadn't expected Hattie to tell them of my visit, but she'd done so, and they'd anticipated that sooner or later I would get around to Flora. All they'd had to do was fly down to Durham and wait for me to turn up. I'd been too preoccupied with my own moves; I hadn't given enough thought to theirs.

Staying within the speed limit, Roche guided the car along the winding street. Presently we came to Hope Valley Road, on which George and I had traveled in the opposite direction earlier in the afternoon. The sun had been bright then, but now it was setting, turning the clouds pink.

Unless I did something in the next few minutes, I knew, this would be the last sunset I would ever see.

Once more I glanced at the door handle.

"Don't," Carris said again. Then he looked at Flora, whose sobs were a soft and irregular rhythm without much tune. There was no compassion in his eyes, and his mouth was set in a thin, tight line. The charming Ronald Carris, man of the world and pimp to the powerful, had become someone else altogether. It was easier to hate what he now was, but hating was futile—the gun was in his hand, not mine.

"You didn't have to kill Carol," I said. "She couldn't have identified you."

"My eyes," he said.

His face had been covered, the street had been dimly lit—she couldn't possibly have recognized him by his eyes. Not through the narrow slits of a ski mask. No, he'd killed her simply because he'd recognized her as the woman who'd commented on his hair, and because he was, at heart, a man who didn't value life.

"Who recommended Kincaid?" I asked.

"A lawyer I know."

"Kevin's lawyer?"

"Halt den Mund!" Roche snapped.

Of course it was Kevin's lawyer, I thought. Carris had probably been the one who hired him.

"The man with a thousand contacts," I said.

Carris didn't reply.

I glanced at the back of Roche's head. He wasn't the assistant, I decided, he was the boss. The man with all the identities—and one of East Germany's top agents in the United States. That fact wasn't on the tape, and it should have been. But then, the tape would probably never be found. If the two men in the front seat were as thorough as I believed they were, they would clean out my pockets before they left. And that would be the end of the trail. Two bodies, and no evidence of any sort.

We were passing through the southern part of Hope Valley now, and the houses were farther apart. Soon we would be coming to Route 54, the east-west highway that George and I had taken when we'd driven from Research Triangle Park. There were populated areas along that highway, I recalled, but there were also unpaved side roads leading into the woods. Was that where we were headed—into one of the wooded spots? Probably. And if we were, I didn't have much time. Ten minutes, at the most. A very limited future.

Death—I'd sometimes wondered when and where it would catch up with me. Now I knew. It was going to catch up with me in a clump of pine trees beside a North Carolina highway, in a late September twilight. I'd never expected that the experience would be so ignominious. I'd always imagined I would be in a position to resist, if only for a little while. Instead, I was going to be marched into the underbrush and shot like a diseased animal. And I was going to die not feeling good about myself, for I'd gone hunting and been caught by the prey.

Studying Carris's face, I could detect no gleam of triumph in his eyes. His expression was merely one of wariness. I was a threat that had to be eliminated, and he was determined that nothing go wrong. For a man whose special talent lay in guessing other people's thoughts and motives, he showed no interest whatsoever in mine. I was just something that had to be handled with caution until it could be disposed of. Flora, too, apparently.

Rattle him, I thought. Shake his composure. Then, when his hand moves . . .

"Everything I know about you is on record in a safe place," I said wildly. "Everything about both of you, and about Herb Minton and Hattie Sargent." I forced myself to keep my eyes on his face, not on the hand that was holding the gun. And I tried not to think about the other gun, which Roche had tucked into the waistband of his slacks when he'd got into the car. "It's all on record. How Carol and I saw you at the party Jonie Stiles gave, and how Herb Minton heard me mention Bill Arden, and how Herb must have told you."

Carris showed no sign of losing his composure. He simply made a contemptuous sound through his nose and kept the gun pointed at my forehead.

But a moment later he glanced over my shoulder.

Were we being followed? I started to turn in my seat, to peer through the rear window.

Carris's gaze came back to me. "Don't move," he said. "Not even an inch."

He didn't sound alarmed, or look it. I surmised that, from his point of view, everything was proceeding satisfactorily. A number of cars had passed us going in the opposite direction and no one had paid the slightest attention to us. Anyone should have been able to see the gun Carris was holding and should have realized that we weren't an ordinary foursome, but evidently no one did.

I resumed my former position, facing the front of the car. In the distance I could see the light that controlled the flow of traffic at the intersection of Hope Valley Road and Route 54.

Carris spoke a few words in German, and Roche gave an affirmative grunt. The exchange had to do with our destination, I guessed, and the two of them were in agreement.

Flora's sobbing subsided. "Dick will be worried," she said in a strangled voice. "I told him I'd call."

I nodded, and the loathing I felt for the two men in the front seat intensified. The boy's prospects were very bleak.

As we neared it, the light at the intersection changed from green to red, and Roche slowed the car. There were two other cars ahead of us, and both of them stopped. Roche pulled up some thirty feet behind the second one.

Carris advanced the gun toward my head. "Sit very still," he ordered.

I willed the people in the car in front to turn around and look at us, but they didn't get my message. The only ones doing any close observing were Carris and I. His gaze was fixed on my face, and mine on his.

But suddenly his eyes widened, and his expression became one of horror. Roche glanced over his left shoulder and uttered a shout.

I swung around just in time to see a car coming at us from the rear and from the left. In a split second the information traveled from my eyes to my brain: brown Oldsmobile, George driving, crash imminent. I braced myself.

Carris shifted the direction of the gun, but he didn't have time to fire it. George's car plowed into our left front door at a thirty-degree angle. Metal crunched, glass shattered. Our car rocked, tipped, then righted itself.

Pinned between seat and steering wheel, Roche fell sideways and forward, and his head struck the dashboard. Carris's head and right shoulder slammed against the window frame. Flora slid toward me, but put her hand out and braced herself against the front seat.

Carris recovered. So did I. I reached forward, slid my left arm under his chin, grabbed my left wrist with my right hand and jerked it backward as hard as I could, pressing my knees against the front seat for leverage.

He probably died quickly, but I couldn't be sure. I continued to hang on to my left wrist long after I felt his body go limp and saw the gun slide from his hand.

George jumped from his mangled car and ran toward us with a large metal object in his hand. I saw him appear at the window on Roche's side of the car, smash the remaining glass from the window frame, reach into the car and slam the metal object twice across the base of Roche's skull, but I wasn't fully aware of what was going on until he opened the door beside me, tapped me on the shoulder and said, gently, "You can let go now. They're both dead."

42

It was two days before George and I were released from jail.

"American jurisprudence leaves something to be desired," he observed as we walked out of Durham's Public Safety Building, where we'd been held.

"Well, anyway," Jonie Stiles said consolingly. "You aren't going to be tried for murder."

"Or for anything else," Fred Tillman added.

Jonie had been in Durham for the past twenty-four hours, and Tillman was the local lawyer he'd hired to represent us.

"Even so," George said unhappily. "They *wanted* to. They *threatened.*"

"You can't exactly blame them," said Tillman. "You'd brutally killed two men, in front of witnesses. Two men who had no criminal record."

"Killed them unnecessarily, some might say," Jonie put in.

"You weren't there," I reminded him acidly. My feelings, just then, coincided with George's. I hadn't enjoyed my stay in jail. In my opinion, our detention had been unfair.

"No," said Jonie, "but I kind of wish I had been."

I looked at him. He seemed serious. "You wouldn't have liked it," I said. "It was—" I groped for his sort of word—"upsetting."

George gave me a startled glance. "Is that what it was?"

Under my breath, I said, "Stiles, Levin and Sullivan is a world apart."

He turned to Jonie. "The means you used . . ." He didn't finish. The expression on his face was one of dissatisfaction.

I knew what he meant, though. Things were turning out well, but for the wrong reasons. The method by which the lawyers had got us off the hook left George and me under a slight cloud. Despite the guns with Carris's and Roche's fingerprints on them, despite the tape recording, despite Flora's earnest testimony—despite everything that supported what George and I said, the law-enforcement officers of Durham County weren't fully convinced that the two dead men had been what we claimed they'd been, or that we'd been justified in killing them. The lawmen's attitude had been: Prove it. Our release had been obtained not on the strength of evidence but through influence. Jonie had applied pressure in high places—specifically, on the Attorney General of the United States and the Governor of North Carolina.

Two television reporters and their cameramen suddenly appeared in front of us. One of them shoved a microphone in front of me and said, "Is it true—?"

Tillman grabbed the microphone and pulled it toward himself. "Mr. Potter and Mr. Cole have been completely cleared," he said. "No charges will be filed."

The reporters and cameramen preceded us, walking sideways, for half a block, but all they got for their trouble was a string of "No comment"s from Tillman and tight-lipped silence from the rest of us.

The silence lasted until we reached the garage where Tillman had parked his car.

"I'd like to call my wife," George said as we waited at the foot of the ramp for Tillman to pick us up. "To let her know I'll be home tomorrow."

"She already knows," Jonie said. "I spoke to Tom Petacque a couple of hours ago, and he relayed the message. But you can call her yourself when we get to Fred's office." He turned to me. "Tom's quite a worrier, isn't he? It was all I could do to keep him from flying down here with me. The poor, misguided man genuinely likes you, I gather."

I smiled.

"And he's all fertutzed about your being back in New York to do a telecast for a bank in San Francisco," Jonie added. "My personal reputation, as far as Tom's concerned, hinges on my delivering you to some television director in time for you to go on camera."

"Jonathan Dickson," I said. "I'm speaking on investment policy for the decade ahead. I promised, weeks ago." Life and obligations, I thought. They're inseparable.

Tillman's car appeared, with Tillman at the wheel. George got into the front seat, Jonie and I into the back. Tillman explained, as we turned onto Main Street, that his office wasn't located downtown; it was in a complex adjacent to one of the highways that led to Chapel Hill.

"Do me a favor," I said. "Avoid Hope Valley Road."

He laughed. "No problem." Then, sobering, he said to George, "Please don't take this the wrong way, but I still can't get over the fact that you did what you did. You seem so, ah, nonviolent."

"I *am* nonviolent," George replied righteously.

A miasma of doubt descended upon the front seat.

I could understand Tillman's problem. Even the deputy sheriffs had been misled by George's mild manner. They'd found it hard to believe that someone who seemed so inoffensive had trailed two armed men for miles, rammed their car with his own, and beaten one of them to death with the base of an automobile jack.

The deputies and Tillman didn't know George as I did.

What surprised me was not his courage but his recklessness. He'd hidden in the shrubbery that separated Flora's yard from the one to the north of it. He'd seen Carris and Roche arrive, but had taken no action, because he wasn't sure who they were, and because I was inside the house. Not until he'd seen Flora and me being escorted across the yard at gunpoint had he realized what was happening, and by then it was too late to do anything other than what he did—grab the jack from the trunk of his car and set out in pursuit.

The one sensible precaution he'd taken—allowing other cars to get between his and ours—had been mostly a matter of circumstance; the other cars had been there, and he hadn't been able to get around them. As a result, Carris and Roche hadn't realized they were being followed until it was too late.

He hadn't intended the collision to occur where it did, but the traffic light had caused us to stop, and he'd seized the opportunity.

As for crushing Roche's skull with the jack, all he'd said was "Brock was being kidnapped. Emotion got the better of me."

Insane recklessness, I thought, but thank God for it.

And actually, according to George, I hadn't behaved with complete sanity myself. "It wasn't pretty," he'd said to me in jail. "Carris's head against the headrest at an odd angle, and you with your arm locked around his throat, squeezing and squeezing. You had a look in your eye I hope I never see again."

Both of us had plenty of material for future nightmares. No question about that.

Meanwhile, we had one more ordeal to face: an interview with the FBI. "Debriefing," Jonie had called it, adding that it was unavoidable. Two top-level agents from the Bureau's counterespionage division had flown down from Washington and were waiting for us in Tillman's office.

"But we've already told everything we know," I'd protested. "No one seems to believe us."

"These men will believe you," Jonie had said. "They've already ordered an investigation into the activities of the lawyer who defended Kevin Rand."

"So soon?" I'd been surprised, and very pleased. "What about Herb Minton?"

For the first time since I'd known him, Jonie had looked discomfited. "Er, yes, I expect . . . eventually. You've given us a problem there, all right."

"Us?"

"Stiles, Levin and Sullivan represents him."

Thinking about the situation as we drove through the city, I came to the conclusion that, while nothing lasts forever, Stiles, Levin and Sullivan would probably endure longer than any firm of its sort ever had.

The debriefing took place in Fred Tillman's private office, a splashy, unlawyerlike room that was all cubes and primary colors. Neither of the attorneys was present. George and I simply talked with the two FBI men, Edgarton and Stevens, about the events leading up to the deaths of Carris and Roche. It was the sort of rambling conversation I'd hoped to have, but hadn't had, with Bakersfield after the shooting of Bill Arden and Carol. Different agents, different styles. With Edgarton and Stevens, I could communicate. They weren't afraid to reveal what they knew, and they didn't seem to think it strange that I had hunches and acted on them. When I expressed the opinion that evidence often marks the end of the trail rather than the beginning, they nodded.

I learned that what Flora had reported as rumor was true, although she still didn't know this. The information that the Calthorp Research Center had been penetrated by East German intelligence had indeed come from a defector, and Michaels had been inadvertently tipped off by his landlady. Edgarton admitted that the Calthorp investigation had led to failure as well as success; the American had been caught, but the two East Germans had got away.

The whereabouts of Alfred Stone were still a mystery, Stevens said, but it was believed that he'd managed to escape to Europe by way of Canada. Michaels, on the other hand, had already been spotted in East Berlin.

To my surprise, Edgarton said that in his opinion Stone had received no early morning telephone call warning him of the arrest of the courier. The arrest had been reported on television the night before, and Stone had probably fled hours before his wife claimed he had. The FBI placed no more credence in the statements of Clarice Stone than I did.

Both Edgarton and Stevens agreed with me that Bill Arden had probably turned up at Carris's office in an overwrought state and made accusations, after which he'd been killed at the first opportunity. The investigation into past security leaks at Arden Electronics was ongoing, they said, but it would be a long time before the extent of the damage was known.

I made a conscientious effort to describe the indescribable—to put thought processes into words. I didn't know exactly when I'd begun to suspect that Bill and Carol had been shot by someone who knew both of them, I said, but the fact that the two of them had been shot, while a noisy bystander, Sylvia May, hadn't been, had had something to do with it. Until then, I'd believed that Adele Rand had told the truth—that Kevin had been recruited by someone who knew me—but I hadn't concentrated on the matter. Afterward, I did. Someone who knew me, someone who knew Bill, someone who knew Carol at least by sight. I remembered introducing Carol to Carris the week before at a party given by Stiles, Levin and Sullivan. I remembered what had occurred to me at the time—that Carris and I had met previously, at Herb Minton's office. And I remembered that Carol had commented on Carris's hair, which, to someone as perceptive as Carris, would have marked her as a person who noticed physical details.

"When did you know for certain?" Edgarton asked.

"I can't pinpoint the moment," I replied. "It was a gradual process. After Carol was shot, something happened to me, I think. I wasn't myself. Normally I go according to plan, but as I look back now it seems to me that the only plan I had was to crowd as many people as possible. It worked, but it wasn't really like me."

"And when did you decide that the man we called Egan was actually Ronald Carris?"

"Hold on a minute," I said. "I'm still not sure about that. It was a possibility, and still is. On the other hand, there may actually have been a fourth member of the team—the man you call Egan. If so, either he escaped to East Germany with Michaels or else he's still at large somewhere in the United States."

The two FBI men stared at me.

"The thing I did come to believe, after talking with Hattie Sargent and meeting Frank Roche, is that Kevin wasn't recruited by one man but by two working together. Roche was the sort of man Kevin would have responded to, but he wasn't a skilled personnel man—and he hadn't met me before." I took a deep breath and prepared to go on at length about how I thought Carris and Roche operated, but Edgarton didn't give me a chance.

"What you're saying is, the Bureau might have been right about Egan," he said, leaning forward and eyeing me narrowly.

"What I'm saying is, I don't know," I replied. "Egan may exist or he may not. My guess is that there are any number of Egans—couriers, like you caught with the Arden chips. And any number of people like Alfred Stone and Kevin Rand supplying them with classified material. Carris and Roche were the brains of the network, the planners, but the people who worked for them are still out there."

It was a long while before anyone spoke.

"If Carris and Roche were alive now," Stevens said reproachfully, "we'd be able to question them, to get names."

"You'd be able to question them," George said, "but I doubt that you'd get any names."

I thought about mixed blessings, but felt no regret. I simply said, "If Carris and Roche were alive now, George and I wouldn't be. And you'd know no more about Carris Associates than you did before."

There were no further reproaches. The debriefing continued for another hour, after which George and I rejoined the two lawyers, who drove us to a motel for drinks, dinner and a good night's sleep.

The next morning Jonie, George and I flew to New York. There was still one weapon left in the arsenal, and I intended to use it.

43

JONATHAN DICKSON, standing midway between the two cameras, made a slashing gesture with his hand.

The red light on the camera near the door went off, and the two cameramen began to disconnect the arc lights. The room grew darker.

I unclipped the microphone and removed it from my necktie.

Louise applauded. "You was real good, Mr. Potter," she said. She, together with Dickson and the cameramen, had been my only visible audience. "Now I best let Tiger out."

Tiger had been banished to the basement, lest he bark during the telecast.

I glanced at Dickson, hoping for a reaction.

He gave me one. "A lot of shit is going to hit a lot of fans," he said, bemused.

"I hope so," I replied, and went into the dining room to retrieve the whiskey decanter. Remembering Carol's admonition, I'd removed it from the den.

"Drink?" I said to Dickson when I returned.

He shook his head. He still looked bemused.

I poured some Scotch into a glass and drank it neat. The cameramen were disassembling their equipment. Tiger bounded into the room, ran joyfully around in a circle, then planted his forepaws on my leg and barked twice. I picked him up and scratched him behind the ears.

Dickson frowned. "Those two men you talked about—Carris and Roche. If they did the things you claim, a lot of companies are in trouble."

"That was my point," I said. "And now some of those companies will begin investigating themselves."

I thought of my unseen audience, a few hundred movers and shakers seated in an auditorium in San Francisco. Some of them, perhaps, had had dealings with Carris Associates. And others would spread the word. From coast to coast, corporations would quietly examine their personnel records and security procedures. A few might even contact the FBI.

"Aren't you afraid that some innocent people will be hurt, though?" Dickson asked.

"Yes," I admitted. "But that's the lesser danger, in my opinion. The greater danger would be to do nothing. And in the end, most likely, the innocent will be able to establish their innocence." I watched the cameramen carry their equipment out of the room. That equipment had given me access to people I would never have been able to reach otherwise, I realized, and had lent me the sort of credibility that only television could provide. "My point, really, was vigilance," I went on. "You can't make long-term investments without considering the moral climate of a company or an industry, or even a country. The best company in the world can be destroyed by a few corrupt employees."

The telephone rang. I answered it.

"What have you done?" Bob Gerard demanded excitedly. "Everybody's rumbling and muttering. Nobody wants to listen to the next speaker."

"I'm sorry," I apologized. "I had to say what was on my mind."

"Don't be sorry. You've made the seminar an event. Everyone was getting bored. Thanks." He paused for breath. "When are you coming back to San Francisco? Two people have already collared me. They want to meet you."

"Soon," I said. "Real soon."

"Good. Let me know. I'll set up some appointments. I've got to go now. Thanks again." Gerard put down the telephone with a clatter.

I glanced at Dickson, who was helping the cameramen with the last of their equipment. "I was effective, it seems," I told him.

He looked up. "I expect you were." He ambled over to shake hands. "Nice meeting you. My girlfriend's waiting. I'm taking her to dinner. 'Bye."

I accompanied him to the front door and watched him climb into the van with the cameramen. A moment later, the van pulled away from the curb and headed toward Sixth Avenue.

Louise, wearing her hat and coat, came into the hall. " 'Less you wants somethin', I be goin'. Tonight's Bible class, and I's late. A meat loaf's in the oven."

She, too, departed.

I returned to the den and poured myself another drink. The house suddenly seemed very quiet and empty. A feeling of loneliness set in. I thought of Dickson and his girlfriend, and of other men and other girlfriends.

At the office, I was already back in the swing of things. The past two days had gone by quickly. But the past two nights hadn't.

Adjustments take time, I reminded myself. Meanwhile, be glad you have so much work to catch up on.

The telephone rang again.

A man named Charles Logan asked if I would be willing to appear on "Inside the News." The network had just received a call from its affiliate in San Francisco and was considering a program on industrial espionage.

No thanks, I replied, I'd already said all I ever hoped to say on that subject.

I finished my drink and went into the kitchen. Louise had outdone herself. The meat loaf was a work of art. So was the salad she'd left in the refrigerator. And there was a pan of cornbread on the countertop. I assembled dinner and began to eat it. Unseen presences kept me company.

They came one and two at a time, left, reappeared with different companions. Carol, Bill Arden, Adele and Sean Rand, George Cole, Jonie Stiles, Hattie Sargent and Flora Dexter—all the people who had been so important in my life since my return from Switzerland. Each of them had something to say, and some demanded explanations. The explanations were difficult. I still didn't know why I'd done certain things. The only answer I could offer was that I was my own particular self, with my own unique set of responses, and, given the circumstances I'd been in, I'd done the best I could.

Above all, I felt the presence of Kevin Rand. He wasn't responsible for everything that had happened in the past month, I told him, but he was responsible for much of it. And I added that I wished I'd understood him better. I'd made the mistake of assuming he was what he appeared to be—a mistake Ronald Carris and Frank Roche hadn't made.

An invisible Kevin remained with me while I stacked the dishes and settled down in the den to study the quarterly reports I'd brought home from the office. He said that he, too, had been his own particular self, with his own unique set of responses; that he'd merely obeyed his impulses; and that he'd paid a high price for doing so.

I conceded him that, but no more. The price he'd paid was fair, in my opinion. He hadn't been overcharged.

Gradually, as I became absorbed in profit-and-loss statements and the remarks of chief executive officers, the presences went away. I began to make notes in the margins of the reports, to jot down questions for members of my staff and for some of the corporate executives I intended to interview during the next few weeks. It was the sort of work I enjoyed and knew I was good at, and it made the future seem reasonably bright.

I was still working at nine-thirty, when the doorbell rang. Startled, I went into the hall and called out, "Who is it?"

"Evelyn Natwick," was the muffled reply.

I opened the door.

"I was passing and saw your lights on," Evelyn said, with an uncertain smile, "and I thought I'd be neighborly."

"Come in and have a drink," I said.

She entered the hall and was enthusiastically greeted by Tiger, who'd always been fond of her. The three of us went into the den.

I gave Evelyn a martini, and she drank part of it, and I thanked her properly for calling the police when she'd spotted the stranger watching my house.

"It seemed the sensible thing to do," she replied. "You haven't had any further trouble, have you?"

"Not around here," I said, and changed the subject.

We talked for a few minutes, and then Evelyn got up, explaining that she had to go home in order to prepare for a trial that was scheduled to begin the next morning.

"Oh, and by the way," she said casually as I walked her to the door, "I'm having a few friends over for dinner Saturday. Would you like to come?"

I hesitated. She was an attractive woman, and I liked her, but we'd never been on dinner-party terms. "Thank you very much," I said.

With the same sort of uncertain smile she'd given me on the doorstep, she asked, "Does that mean yes or no?"

I hesitated again, thinking of a past that couldn't be relived and a present that needed bolstering. "It means yes," I said, at last.